A Christmas Rose by Paula Marshall

This was Chri... when everything was... ...ould she not pretend... ...t her and not the virt... ...it not be a splendid joke if Rose took him at his word and then tried to have her revenge on Sir Miles Heyward by making him fall in love with her?

The Unexpected Guest by Deborah Simmons

He was lonely. Joy looked about her at the vast hall and wondered how the man could want for anything. Yet he did. And the knowledge made him not so omnipotent, but oddly human. That tiny peek had whetted her appetite for the true Campion. She let herself meet his gaze and wished that she could see behind those enigmatic eyes to the man who dwelled within.

Christmas at Bitter Creek by Ruth Langan

"If I'm going to share this cabin with you—" his voice lowered seductively "—I'm going to need a lot of things to keep me busy." Matthew's gaze roamed her face before coming to rest on her lips. "Or I might do something we'll both regret."

Laura felt a rush of heat and knew that the stain on her cheeks would give her away. She would have to keep fighting. Fighting him. Fighting herself. And fighting her reaction to his simplest touch.

SAFE HAVEN
FOR CHRISTMAS

Paula Marshall
Deborah Simmons
Ruth Langan

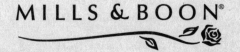

MILLS & BOON®

MILLS & BOON and MILLS & BOON with the Rose Device are registered trademarks of the publisher.

First published in Great Britain 2002
Harlequin Mills & Boon Limited,
Eton House, 18-24 Paradise Road, Richmond, Surrey TW9 1SR

Safe Haven for Christmas
© Harlequin Books S.A. 2002

The publisher acknowledges the copyright holders
of the individual works as follows:
A Christmas Rose © Paula Marshall 2002
The Unexpected Guest © Deborah Siegenthal 1999
Christmas at Bitter Creek © Ruth Langan 1990

ISBN 0 263 83148 5

Set in Times Roman 10¼ on 11¼ pt.
04-1202-91389

Printed and bound in Spain
by Litografia Rosés S.A., Barcelona

CONTENTS

Author Note

When I wrote *A Christmas Rose* my aim was to try and recapture the magic of a season which I have always enjoyed since I was a very little girl. I remember vividly how we, as a family, longed for the beginning of the Twelve Days of Christmas so that we could decorate the tree—brought in from the garden—with the bright baubles which were fetched out each year from the box in which they were saved. Next we hung around the house the paper chains which we had spent the previous weeks making. Finally our Christmas cards were lined up along the mantelpiece. Nearer to the day there was the joy of carol singing while my mother played the piano. Christmas Day brought a chicken, rarely a turkey then.

At the time of my story, however, Christmas was celebrated quite differently—no tree, no baubles, no Christmas cards and the decorations were usually branches of holly and some mistletoe. Two things remained constant, though: the abundant food and drink and the singing of carols. I spent many happy hours checking which carols would have been sung at that time.

I hope you enjoy my story—and this Christmas, too.

Joy to the World

Paula Marshall

A CHRISTMAS ROSE

Paula Marshall

Chapter One

No! It wasn't possible, she must be mistaken, she couldn't really have come all the way to Yorkshire to spend her Christmas in happy anonymity only to see her *bête noire*, Sir Miles Heyward, walking into her cousin Isabel's drawing room at Morton Castle in north Yorkshire.

Miss Rose Charlton, noted for her air of calm, very nearly lost her self-control at this unexpected and unwelcome sight. To make matters worse he was looking, as usual, totally in command of himself and was gazing straight at her, his eyebrows raised a little.

If it shocked her to see him, could it be that he was equally astonished to find her there, waiting for him, as it were? More to the point, what might he have to say about her that would shatter the fragile peace which she had hoped to find in Isabel Morton's home, so far from London society and its malicious gossip? Rose remembered only too well her encounter with Isabel shortly before she had gone down to dinner, and Isabel's unhappy face while she had been speaking to her…

"My dear Rose," she had murmured, as gently as she could, "while I personally was very happy to invite you to stay with us this Christmas, I needed to defy my husband in order to do so. As you know, he never visits town these days and so has little knowledge of the *ton* and its scandal. Unfortunately, just after I had written to you, he received a letter from his friend, Lord Sheffield, informing him, among other gossip, that the latest *on-dit* circulating society concerned you and that wretched business with Lord Attercliffe. I was under the impression that it had been hushed up and forgotten, many years ago. Indeed, I know no details of it, seeing that your father and mine succeeded at the time in preventing it from becoming common knowledge.

"Anthony immediately ordered me to withdraw my invitation to you, but I refused, for once, to obey him. After all, you are *my* cousin, you were very young at the time, and were my best friend before your father died and you retired to the country. I was aware that you were in London for the season this year—which I suppose was why the scandal was revived. I assured Anthony of your innocence and he reluctantly agreed to receive you.

"On the other hand, I trust that you will behave yourself while you are here so that he may not have occasion to—well, I need not go on."

Isabel was uncomfortably aware that, despite her very real determination not to distress Rose overmuch, she had not been completely successful. Rose was trying hard not to lose the cool composure which had become her most notable characteristic in the years since she and Isabel had last met.

Her answer was as measured as she could make it. "That being so," she said, "I trust that you will not take it amiss if I choose to leave for home as early tomorrow morning as possible."

Isabel was aghast. "Oh, you must not put me in the way of being the subject of yet another of Anthony's moans of 'I told you so'. Between ourselves he has become a positive bear these days. You *must* stay, and by your impeccable conduct prove him to be wrong for once."

Rose had had no notion that Isabel's marriage had become an unhappy one. The infrequent letters which she had re-

ceived from her had always suggested the exact opposite—
that she and her husband were a youthful Darby and Joan,
in fact.

"If you insist," she said slowly. "I had much rather leave,
though, for I would not wish to come between you and your
husband. Nor would I wish to embarrass any of your guests
who might have heard of the rumours."

"Oh, you won't do that. They are all local gentry and none
of them are acquainted with the *haut ton*. No, rest assured
that all will be well and that you will enjoy a happy Christmas far from the back-biting of the London gossips. Anthony
will soon come round and you can join in all the wassailing
with a light heart."

If Rose thought that she would never have a light heart
again, she did not say so. Instead she tried to stifle her misgivings. After all, Isabel probably had the right of it.
Yorkshire and London were miles apart in more than distance
and it would be a pity to throw Isabel's kindness back in her
face. She would try to enjoy Christmas as it ought to be
enjoyed and forget the unhappy past.

Earlier that same day Sir Miles Heyward had been eating
a rather poor nuncheon at a post-house on the London to
York road. He was making for Morton Castle, just outside
York, and was wondering why he had agreed to spend Christmas at the home of a friend, Anthony Morton, whom he had
not met since shortly after they had left the Versity—as Ox-
ford and Cambridge were always known. They had come on
the town together and for a brief time had enjoyed themselves
right royally.

Anthony's father had died young, however, and as a consequence he had gone north to run the family estates. He had
never visited London, or the south, again. He had married
early, had once talked of entering Parliament, but was now
content to be a country squire. He had written to Miles earlier

in the year, asking for news of another old friend and reminding him of those earlier, more light-hearted, days.

"I understand that your mother married again," he wrote,
"and is settled near Selby. If you are not visiting her this
Christmas, I wonder if you would care to come to Morton
Castle instead, so that we might talk of old times together—
I am beginning to miss them."

At first, Miles had thrown the letter on one side, meaning
to decline the invitation when he had time. He had arranged
to marry the Honourable Emily Sansome shortly before
Christmas and would be celebrating it on his honeymoon in
Brighton.

Alas, the wedding never took place. His Emily had met a
richer and greater prospect than he was and she had handed
him his ring back after quarrelling with him over nothing,
with the excuse that they were not well suited. He generously
took the public blame for the breach between them, absolving
her of all wrongdoing. Her marriage to her Marquis was soon
announced in the *Morning Post* and was arranged to take
place two days after the date on which he had been due to
marry her.

On mature reflection he thought that it was a blessing that
she had jilted him—for that was the real truth of the matter—
since it appeared that she had been meeting her new fiancé
in secret even before the quarrel which had ended their engagement. Yet Miles still felt demeaned by her cavalier rejection of him.

Women were lightskirts all, had been his grim conclusion—after the main chance, all of them, and when that
chance came along, why, to the devil with everything and
everyone else. To visit Anthony Morton in the far north of
England suddenly seemed attractive. Away from London he
would be able to avoid the pitying stares with which he had
recently been favoured.

Besides, he was beginning to be bored with town life, and
to regret the fact that he had no country estate, only a vast

amount of inherited wealth and a grand town house. As a very young man he had joined the Army and had served under Wellington in the Peninsular War. After being seriously injured at Salamanca he had recovered just in time to take part in the battle of Waterloo.

Waterloo had seen the end of his army service and the beginning of his lack of occupation, which was beginning to trouble him more and more since his occupation had been his life—particularly after he had become a member of Wellington's staff.

Lately he had been thinking of buying a country estate and settling down to manage it. He had decided to emulate old Coke of Norfolk and the Duke of Bedford, both of whom had run their own lands rather than hiring others to do it for them. An old friend who worked for the Board of Agriculture had compiled for him a list of books and papers on farming and the management of country properties. As a result of his reading he had become particularly interested in the breeding of better animals and plants and had recently hired an agent to look for a suitable place for him, preferably in the Midlands or the South.

On thinking matters over he had suddenly realised that Emily's desertion of him had almost certainly been sparked off by his telling her of his dream of living in the country. She was a town girl, not a country one, and she had pouted at him all the way through his recital of the delights of rural living and experimental breeding.

He also admitted to himself for the first time that, although he had found her a pretty and lively companion, she was not quite the sort of woman whom he had once thought to take for a wife. His mother had been reproaching him for his unmarried state and perhaps that had made him offer for Emily without taking the time to discover the truth of her.

Miles put down his knife and fork with a sigh. Now that he was on the way to York, though, the prospect of Christmas spent among people whom he did not know was beginning to seem less attractive than it originally had. He rose and sent for his valet, Blagg. It was time for him to be on the road again if he wished to reach Morton Castle before dark. He would be travelling through wild country where Luddites and penniless soldiers, demobbed after the wars, roved the moors, deeming lonely travellers to be their lawful prey. It would be a mistake to let the night overtake him.

It was always possible that among the guests at the castle there might be an attractive young woman present who wouldn't resent a man whose ambition was to be a grand sort of farmer. He laughed quietly to himself for entertaining such an unlikely idea and muttered, ''Lightskirts all,'' again under his breath. He spent the time before the Castle came into view in reading through the papers which his agent had sent him regarding his progress in finding a suitable estate.

At least by the time he arrived there he would not have to wait long for his dinner.

After her unhappy conversation with Isabel, Rose had found herself in Morton Castle's drawing room among a group of people whom she did not know and who did not, by their expressions, appear to know of her. Well that, at least, was a relief: that the name Rose Charlton meant nothing to them. They were all engaged in lively gossip about various members of the county families who lived around York and Harrogate with whom they were all acquainted— and to most of whom they were related in some way.

They were, however, perfectly polite to her after she had been introduced to them as Isabel's cousin, which caused at least two of the older women to put up their lorgnettes to inspect her a little more closely.

''I collect that this is your first visit to Yorkshire, Miss Charlton,'' one of them commented.

''Indeed, I must confess that this is the first time that I have ventured beyond Nottingham—I had not thought to find the countryside here so wild and beautiful.''

This piece of quite truthful flattery appeared to please her hearers and started a lively discussion about the various kinds of beauty which one might find in different landscapes. Rose sat back after catching a glance of smiling approval from Isabel who had been looking rather apprehensively at her during Anthony's welcoming speech.

So, she was anonymous, and sitting there, quiet, letting the warmth of the beautiful room envelop her, Rose felt happier than she had done for months. Alas, this was not to last long. One of the women, tiring of erudite discussion about Capability Brown, landscaping and the proper placing of trees, drawled, "Well, I think that Nature ought to be left to arrange where trees should stand. Tell me, do any of you know whether it is true that Lord Attercliffe is back in Yorkshire and intends to settle at Cliffe House?"

The sound of Attercliffe's name was the first thing to disturb Rose's feeling of well-being. It was also enough to set the whole party talking vigorously about him and the many scandals in which he had been involved as a very young man, although little had been heard of him lately.

One large and assertive fellow, standing near the fireplace, who had been talking confidentially to Anthony Morton, offered with a sardonic laugh, "They say that he is looking for a wife, preferably one with a handsome fortune."

"He may look," observed a dark beauty who had been eyeing Rose with interest ever since she had entered the room, "but I doubt whether he will find one. He has nothing to offer a bride but a bad reputation, a broken-down estate and near-bankruptcy."

"He has a title, which could count for a lot with an ambitious cit who might choose to buy him in order to ennoble his plain daughter," said the sardonic man whose name had escaped Rose during Anthony's hurried introduction. He turned his attention to her. "I believe, Miss Charlton, that Anthony told me that you had recently been in town. What is his reputation there?".

All the company gave her their full attention for the first time, something which Rose could have dispensed with. Nevertheless she managed a rueful smile. "Bad, I must admit, although of course I know no details."

"Of course," quipped the sardonic gentleman. "Not fit for ladies' ears. I wonder if anyone here will receive him, and whether he will choose to receive anyone, for that matter."

"I believe, Major Scriven," offered Anthony to him, "that Cliffe House is in bad repair. None of the Attercliffes have lived there for years."

Several heads nodded wisely at this; then Isabel said, perhaps to spare her pain, Rose thought, "I have been hearing hushed whispers about Attercliffe's misdoings all my life, and I suggest that we wait until we discover whether the rumours about him coming to live among us are true." She looked around the room. "Dinner should be announced any moment. I believe that everyone is present, Anthony—except your old friend."

"Who has arrived rather late after a long and difficult journey. He should be down any minute. I would rather not start without him, if you would be so good, my dear—he has had a tiring day."

Anthony had scarcely finished speaking when the door opened and the butler announced, "Sir Miles Heyward, if it pleases you, sir, and dinner is almost ready."

Everyone in the room, except Rose whose heart sank at the very sight of him, looked expectantly at the newcomer. Any strange man or woman arriving in a society as closed as that around Morton Castle was always sure to arouse a great deal of interest since they were likely to bring with them news of the great world outside it.

Rose, however, wished that she were anywhere on earth other than the Mortons' drawing room with Sir Miles Heyward gazing coldly at her.

She shuddered as she remembered her one and only encounter with him. How, once they had been left alone after being introduced, he had reproached her bitterly for her treatment of his friend, and after giving her the strangest look had stalked away, saying that he never wished to encounter or speak to her again. Hence her very real, if concealed, distress at the sight of him.

Any hope which she might have had that the scandal that had recently surrounded her would remain unknown was now a vain one. For of all the people whom she had met in London society Miles Heyward would be the most likely to reveal her blown-upon reputation to his hosts.

And what might happen then?

Of a certainty she would have to go on her travels once more in the hope that she might yet reach a place where Miss Rose Charlton's supposedly disreputable past would remain unknown.

Chapter Two

Miles was equally surprised—as Rose had already guessed. The last person whom *he* might have wished to encounter at Morton Castle was the elegantly composed mermaid who was seated on a sofa exactly opposite to the door by which he had entered.

No one could possibly guess from the face and figure which she showed to the world what a fraud and sham she was, he thought savagely. Exquisitely turned out after a fashion which seemed to proclaim her innocence, she was wearing a simple pale blue and white muslin gown with a silk spray of lilies of the valley at her throat and waist, and, as was her habit, no jewellery other than a single pearl on a slender chain around her swan-like neck.

Again, as usual, her clothes were chosen to emphasise the classic beauty of her face rather than distract attention from it. Her hair, golden in colour, cut short and curling gently, served only to enhance blue eyes, a porcelain complexion and a sweetly curving and tender mouth. In short, she resembled an angel rather than the houri she really was.

The devil of it was that every time he saw her Miles's hot-blooded body took over from his cold mind and told him that what he really wanted was to have Miss Rose Charlton in his arms or—better than that—beneath him. Once she was there he might be able to drive away the superior expression that she always wore, and compel her to reveal her true nature by having her writhing with pleasure at his lightest touch! The very thought was sufficient to rouse him immediately.

Did his old friend have no notion of the reputation of his guest that she should be sitting here so quietly among his family and friends? That the cool and serene gaze with which she fixed him on his entrance was as big a sham as the rest of her?

He knew not only of the rumours about her which were circling around London, but also of what his friend, Oliver Fenton, had told him of his disastrous encounter with her. Of how she had led him on, and then dropped him after refusing his honest proposal of marriage, and of how he had then learned of her blown-upon reputation. "She broke my heart," he had said, "after trampling upon it. Damn all women!" he had finished, a sentiment with which Miles had sadly agreed after his own unhappy relationship with Emily.

No matter, for the moment he would say nothing. He allowed Anthony to introduce him to the assembled company, bowing and smiling at them until he reached Rose. At this point he put his hand on his friend's arm and said, as cool as she and with a perfunctory bow, "No need to introduce us, Morton. Miss Charlton and I have met before, have we not?"

Rose inclined her head graciously, and said, still calm, so that no one could guess at the fear which burned within her, "Indeed, Sir Miles, but only briefly—as I remember it."

"True—my stay at Morton Castle, however, might enable us to know one another better—if that were possible. Our last meeting left certain matters unexplored—as doubtless you would agree."

His smile for her was an ambiguous one. Rose seethed inwardly. How dare he speak to her as though they were bosom bows, at least, and then look at her with those mock-

ing eyes and that dubious smile? At least, however, he was
apparently not prepared to betray her immediately—which in
one sense was a boon, but in another meant that she was
living in a kind of limbo where he might unmask her at any
moment.

Yes, he might merely be waiting to inform Anthony
Morton privately of exactly whom he was entertaining in his
home rather than immediately creating a public scene which
would cause embarrassment to his hosts and their guests.

Whatever further might have been said was cut short by
the sounding of a gong and the arrival of the butler to announce that dinner was served. Worse was to come, however,
for Rose was led in by the sardonic Major Scriven and arrived at the table to discover that she had him on one side
of her and Miles Heyward on the other.

"So, Miss Charlton, you are already acquainted with Sir
Miles," was the Major's opening speech.

"A little," she replied in as low a voice as possible.

In vain, for Miles heard her and said, "Come, come, Miss
Charlton, we know one another very well, do we not?"

Rose had to make some sort of answer to him in the hope
that Major Scriven had not picked up the derision in Miles's
voice. She said in her coolest manner, "I had not thought so,
since our previous meeting was very short."

"But enlightening, would you not say?"

"I would not say so, Sir Miles."

"Then what would you say, Miss Charlton?"

That I would wish you to the devil, Sir Miles Heyward,
would have been Rose's most truthful reply. Instead, a faint
smile on her face, she rallied him with, "That I am delighted
to be in Yorkshire and staying in such an interesting family
home. My cousin Isabel has informed me that every gener-
ation of Mortons has added new buildings to the Castle since
it was first erected in 1272 on the ruins of a previous, more
primitive, one. The Great Hall in which we are dining dates
back to some time in the fifteenth century."

There, that display of erudition should silence him—which it did for a moment, before he answered her. Miles had begun to regret his harassing of her by the use of two-edged comments full of double meanings known only to his victim. Instead, this time he gave her an unambiguous answer. "I like it because it is so very different from my own home, which is a relatively new one—a simple Palladian villa built by my grandfather in the outskirts of London. I find the Great Hall here most impressive."

Now, was that plain statement meant to be a flag of truce—or had Miles Heyward tired of trying to unsettle her since he was plainly failing to do so? Rose simply smiled graciously back at him, only to be assailed by Major Scriven, who asked her whether she had ever spent Christmas in Yorkshire before—apparently having forgotten that she had told the company that this was her first visit to the county.

"I have spent my recent Christmases alone," she told him, "so that I am looking forward to celebrating a family one. I collect that you are a cousin of the Mortons."

"Indeed, and as you are Isabel's cousin. I am surprised—and also regret—that we have not met before."

The look he gave her was full of admiration. This did not flatter Rose; rather it made her uneasy, since she had learned that the dark beauty, who had earlier been eyeing her a trifle balefully, was Mrs Major Scriven. Had she been scenting a rival? If so, she need have no fear that Rose would show any interest in her husband. Rose had taken him in some dislike from the first time he had spoken to her. She knew his kind only too well—he was obviously a man who thought that he was God's gift to the ladies.

In fact, after enduring his flattery for several minutes, Rose decided that she probably preferred Miles Heyward's straightforward dislike of her to the Major's greasy unctuousness, which was so obviously designed to please. He wasn't as handsome as Miles, either.

Not that Miles's good looks were those of the statues of

the Greek gods that filled some of the alcoves in Morton Castle. Instead he took after the dark warriors who appeared in the late Renaissance paintings that filled the long gallery through which Rose had walked from her bedroom. He had the same hawk-like appearance of being ever ready for anything. His dark hair was severely cut, his cold grey eyes were as penetrating as theirs and his figure was as athletic. He also possessed something which the Major lacked: an appearance of self-control which was so strong that it was formidable. On top of that he was plainly dressed in the dark clothes favoured by Beau Brummell and not the garish, and out of date, outfits of the earlier years of the century which the Major was sporting.

Goodness! What in the world was she doing? How could she be sitting here mooning about a man who was convinced, on what Rose considered to be little evidence, that she was a lightskirt of the direst kind?

She stole a sideways look at Miles to check whether her imagination was running riot. His face was turned a little away from her, giving her a perfect view of his stern profile. No, it wasn't her imagination. Miles Heyward really was what she thought he was, and that was enough to cause Rose to ask herself how in the world could she be so drawn to him as to contrast him favourably with other men!

After all, were there not enough other young fellows in the room who it would be more sensible for her to admire, some of them single and none of them ready to insult her, either directly or indirectly, as Miles constantly did?

Rose shivered. She could not, must not, feel that she was attracted to him. The mere thought made her shiver again, and this time Miles must have heard her or seen her, for he looked in her direction and asked, ''Are you feeling the cold, Miss Charlton? The room is large and we are seated well away from the fire. Ought you not to order a footman to ask your maid to bring you a shawl?''

''No, no,'' she said distractedly. The last thing which she

had wanted was to have drawn his attention back to her and for him to unsettle her by being kind where always before he had been cruel. "I am not cold. Truly, I am not."

She was not lying, but the heat she was feeling was inward, not outward. Her body was telling her one thing and her mind another. Miles, however, thought that her pale face and yet another shiver told a different story. He put his large brown hand gently on her small white one.

"You *are* very cold, Miss Charlton. We must remedy that. Allow me…"

He turned in his chair and summoned the footman who was standing to attention at the door behind them. "Young man, pray find Miss Charlton's maid and ask her to fetch her mistress a shawl and give it to you to bring here. She is feeling the cold."

"Immediately, sir."

"You need not have done that," Rose said faintly.

She could see Mrs Major Scriven sneering at her and could only imagine what it was that she was whispering to her neighbour. She glared at her husband when he leaned over towards Rose to say confidentially, "You should have informed me earlier that you were feeling the cold. I thought that you looked a trifle pale."

"I'm not really feeling cold," said Rose, a trifle desperately, since she feared that the whole table was now inspecting her with avid interest, "and I had not wished to cause such a commotion."

Miles found himself wanting to comfort the woman whom earlier he had wanted to discomfort! "Then you should not have looked as white as a Christmas rose. Look, here comes the footman with your shawl. I hope that your maid has sent you a warm one."

Rose tired of feeling sorry for herself, took the shawl from the footman and draped it around her shoulders. "Delightfully warm," she murmured, in an effort to end this whole unfortunate scene. "I'm sure that with it on I shall turn a delicate pink. Are Christmas roses ever pink, Sir Miles?"

"Not to my knowledge. I believe that they are not roses at all, but something called a hellebore."

Again he was surprised to grasp how pleased it made him to see Rose look a little happier now that the table had lost interest in her.

"You looked charming before," the Major told her, "but now you look even more delightful. I wish that I had spoken earlier so that I might have had the pleasure of being your cavalier."

Rose's sense of humour, dormant since she had first seen that Miles Heyward was of the party, was quite revived by this absurd speech.

"Oh, I don't think that Sir Miles was in any danger when he so kindly arranged for my shawl to be sent for. My cousin Isabel tells me that there is a ghost which haunts the castle, usually at Christmas time, but I hardly think it likely that it would appear in the Great Hall while we are all at dinner."

Miles said robustly, "All truly ancient castles are supposed to harbour a ghost that appears at inconvenient times. And, no, I am not a cavalier. A true cavalier would be on horseback and that, too, would be an inconvenience in the Great Hall."

He had not meant to be so pleasant to Miss Rose Charlton and decided that he must try to avoid her as much as possible in future lest he, too, should fall into her toils. Had she shivered to attract him? He thought not, but even a mermaid of the first water might shiver genuinely, and he was still too much of a gentleman, even where she was concerned, to let her suffer the cold unduly.

Like Rose he was beginning to feel an unwanted attraction for someone whom he thought of as, to put it bluntly, an enemy, but it had still given him pleasure when he saw her small smile at his reference to the cavalier on horseback and the Great Hall. He was beginning to find the Major tiresome, with his greasy compliments to Rose and his feeble attempts at being a wit.

The dinner ended without any further distractions for either of them. Isabel led the ladies out and the Major made a point of moving nearer to Miles whom he thought of as your usual ignorant civilian and, as such, ready to be instructed by someone who was in the know militarily.

He got his chance to display his expertise when one of his fellow guests made a passing reference to the Battle of Waterloo, criticising the Duke of Wellington for not having defeated Napoleon before Blücher and the Prussians arrived.

"Very true," the Major said, taking another swig of Anthony Morton's good wine, "one wonders whether Wellington was as good a general against Napoleon as he was in Spain when he didn't have to face him."

Miles leaned forward and said politely, "I take it that you were present at Waterloo, then?"

The Major coughed and said importantly, "Not exactly at the battle, no, but I was engaged in important work behind the scenes—in Brussels, you understand."

"Oh, I do understand," said Miles sweetly, he having been one of the Duke's aides and therefore at the centre of the battle. He had been fortunate enough not to be wounded or killed, unlike many of his fellow officers. "I am most grateful for your analysis, distant though you were from the action. One might also ask the question whether, if the Duke's lines had not held, the Prussians might have arrived to find themselves fighting the battle on their own against a general who had beaten them several times before. Perhaps, seeing that you were behind the lines, you might find the course and meaning of the battle hard to fathom."

His smile was sweeter than ever.

"Oh, but," spluttered the Major, not to be outdone, "I was in a much better position to understand what happened than a civilian back in England, like yourself, sir, was—if I may so say."

''Oh, you may, Major, indeed you may, and while you're saying it, it might be a good idea to pass the port. It seems to have got stuck at your end of the table.''

Anthony Morton, who knew of Miles's splendid war record and his rank of Lieutenant-Colonel that he never used in civilian life, guffawed at this and was about to tell the Major of them when he saw Miles's baleful eye on him. He knew that look of old and consequently said nothing other than, ''Yes, do pass the port, Major, there's a good fellow.''

Miles, having succeeded in roasting the Major without the poseur knowing it, was consequently in a good mood when he and the rest of the men, all very mellow, joined the ladies. To her surprise Rose welcomed their arrival, even Miles's. The small talk in which the women were engaged did not interest her overmuch, since it was mainly local in nature.

Unfortunately for her peace of mind the Major, who had been rather more mellow than most, and had reached the point where mellowness had disappeared and oafishness had taken over, made a beeline for her. He pulled up an armchair, plumped himself opposite to her and immediately began to tell her a long and involved story of how he had personally tried to advise the Great Duke on the eve of Waterloo as to how the battle should be fought.

''Of course, he took no notice of me,'' he concluded mournfully, ''and so the battle was nearly lost. What do you think of that, hey?''

Not much, was Rose's instinctive reaction, but it wasn't one which she could offer him.

''Nothing to say, my pretty dear? Just think of it, if he'd listened to me we shouldn't have needed the Prussians to save us. Worth an answer, wouldn't you say?''

Not really, Rose thought wildly. She didn't know much about warfare but she knew enough to be aware that the Major, deep in his cups, was telling a very tall story indeed. She was saved from having to think something up which might not offend him when Miles Heyward, of all people, intervened on her behalf.

"Still fighting Waterloo, Major?" he drawled. "Not a pretty subject for a drawing room, I would have thought. Nor for the ladies, either."

"All very well for you civilians," began the Major belligerently. "You've no notion of what sacrifices we soldiers had to make in the late wars."

Rose could not stop herself. "Well, Major Scriven," she replied, "you can't have made too many seeing that you are still here to tell us all about it—and unharmed, so far as I can see."

Several of the guests who had heard the interchange, and had become tired of the Major's patronage of them, could not prevent themselves from laughing at this riposte. Miles was one of them. Miss Rose Charlton was a saucy madam and no mistake. One could not help admiring her.

The Major was not so far gone that he realised that he dare not reply to a lady as he might have done to a man. He was saved by his wife, who had been an unwilling witness of his latest piece of folly. She rose and walked over to him, oozing treacle. "My dear, I do believe that you ought to consider retiring for the night. Your labours in the late wars have left you prey to the megrims after a hard day such as you have had, travelling from Selby."

Perforce he rose, mumbling something to the effect that his wife, at least, understood the trials and tribulations which he had endured. Miles promptly sequestrated his armchair and moved it back a little.

"Well, Miss Rose Charlton, I perceive that you have a pretty wit. Would that the Major's resembled it."

Her recent seeing off of the Major had freed Rose of the anxiety which had ridden on her shoulders since Miles's arrival at Morton Castle.

"Pray do not tease me, Sir Miles, I have had quite enough of the Major's clumsy attempts at flattery without having to endure yours—which our past history tells me must be false.''

''Better and better,'' said Miles beginning to enjoy himself. ''I see that there is more to you than I had thought when we first met. You must allow me a compliment where one is due.''

Rose could scarcely believe her ears. He was smiling at her and the smile transformed his harsh face. She was smitten by a sudden realisation of the true nature and profession of the man before her.

''Correct me if I am mistaken, but you were a soldier, were you not? And at Waterloo? There was something particular in the way in which you spoke of the battle. Like the Major, you have doubtless had your conquests!''

''Now that would be telling, Miss Charlton. Suffice it to say that you are in the right quarter of town—or rather the battlefield.''

''Really, Sir Miles—I had thought that I could never be in the right quarter of anywhere for you.''

Better and better indeed! She had a most lively mind, no doubt of that, and could pick a man's words up and murder him with them—or use them to seduce him. Which line of business was she now engaged in with him? He would try to find out.

''You know, Miss Charlton, that I was of half a mind to tell my friend Anthony Morton the details of the scandal about you that burst upon the town this season—and my own particular reason for wishing to sink you because of it. Instead, I now have a better notion. The company here is not of the liveliest, as you will agree, so to joust with you, knowing what I do of you, will give me more pleasure than having you turned out of doors in disgrace. And if, at the end, you should choose to oblige me as you have obliged others—why, that would be the crown of the work, would it not? What say you?''

As with Major Scriven, Rose would have dearly liked to

give him a piece of her mind, as her old nurse used to say—
but she could not do that, here, publicly, in her Cousin Isabel's drawing room. Instead she thought furiously for a moment, her eyes fixed on his mocking face.

This was Christmas, the time of Misrule when everything
was turned upside down. The King became a peasant and the
peasant a king. Why should she not pretend to be the cour-
tesan he thought her and not the virtuous maiden that she
was?

Would it not be a splendid joke if she took him at his word
and then tried to have her revenge on him by making him
fall in love with her? The joke would be that, whatever he
thought, she would never oblige him. What a horrid word
oblige was, for he had used it to suggest that she might,
ultimately, become his mistress.

She had never been Attercliffe's mistress, whatever the *on-
dits* said, nor would she ever be any man's—no, not even
Sir Miles Heyward's, however much he attracted her, and
attract her he did. She would live and die a spinster, defying
the whole male sex and their wanton ways, but not before
she had had her fun with him.

So she smiled a slow smile and said softly, "What a superb notion, Sir Miles. By behaving thus we shall save our
hosts as well as ourselves embarrassment, and no one will
be hurt. We may celebrate Yuletide in peace—and part afterwards."

If he were surprised by her immediate capitulation, he did
not show it. Doubtless he thought that it was merely one of
her wiles, designed to seduce him. If he did, why, so much
the better.

Miles was thinking exactly that, but it wasn't going to
deter him from enjoying himself with her over Christmas—
and after that…well, afterwards they would part, as she had
said, never to meet again, leaving her to deceive other fools,
and him to try to find an honest woman. And if he managed

to bed her, that would be a bonus, too, as the money-men would have it.

"Excellent," he said, smiling at her. "I can see that you are a woman of great common sense."

Rose nodded at him over her fan. She had seen Isabel coming towards them and did not wish to say anything that might upset her.

"You will excuse me breaking up your little tête-à-tête," sighed Isabel, who had come over especially to do that since Anthony had asked her to keep a sharp eye on Rose, "but I know that Rose is not only an excellent pianist, she also has a good voice; I wondered if she would care to favour us with a few songs."

"If you wish," Rose replied, although she had never felt less like performing in public.

"Excellent!" exclaimed Isabel—which was the second time Rose had been thus praised in the last few minutes, and she wondered whether either of the pair who had been complimenting her really meant what they said.

"The piano is one of Broadwood's best," Isabel told Rose, while leading her over to it. "It was a wedding present from Anthony's rich cousin. We have just had it tuned. Oh, I never thought to ask—do you have any of your music with you?"

"No," said Rose, giving her cousin a smile as false as the ones which Isabel had been gifting her with, "but I don't need any for those I shall play to you. They are old folk songs and popular airs. Sheet music would be a distraction for me."

"I always knew you were clever," gushed Isabel. "Now, let me leave you in peace."

The piano was in excellent condition and Rose played a few scales on it to loosen her fingers. What should she offer the company? Should she distract Miles Heyward by playing the provocative folk-song "Oh, no, John," or would it be better to behave herself by playing something more seasonal, and then something sentimental? Yes, that would be better.

Very gently at first and then gaining strength she began to sing "The Holly and the Ivy", sure that in the next few days the Great Hall would be decked with both of them, and the church, too, for which they were bound on the morrow. She had the pleasure of realising that some of the guests were sufficiently impressed to stop talking and to start listening, and that by the end the whole company were giving her their full attention.

This was not surprising. Her voice was a true one and her singing master had told her grandfather that if she were not a young gentlewoman he would recommend that she ought to have it trained so that she might sing professionally. As it was, her performance revealed its uncommon quality, and when she had ended Anthony Morton clapped his hands and said, "That was splendid, cousin Rose. Will you entertain us for a little while longer?"

It was the first time since she had arrived that he had spoken more than a few words to her. Gratified, Rose agreed, and treated the company to Tom Moore's touching song "The Last Rose of Summer", which she performed with all the pathos the lyrics required.

The room fell silent at the end in tribute to her, and Rose was just beginning to think that she might be allowed to retire into obscurity again when Miles Heyward called out, "Very splendid, Miss Charlton, but do you have anything a little more lively in your repertoire?"

That did it, that absolutely did it! The unregenerate girl who still lived inside Rose's demure exterior suddenly asserted herself.

She raised her head and smiled at him. "Indeed, I have. Will this do?" And she began to sing "Oh, no, John" in a mocking voice quite different from the pathetic one which she had earlier used.

The verses of the song told of a young man courting a pretty girl and the chorus at the end of each of them had the girl rebuffing him by singing vigorously, "Oh, no, John, no, John, no!"

Oh, yes, it was a bravura performance, and if Rose had thought beforehand to design her little programme in order to show off her voice and her skill on the piano she could not have chosen better. What was more, the company, after the first verse, sang each chorus with her and when the song ended started to clap.

Miles Heyward was leading the men in shouting, "Bravo!" The ladies, however, clapped their hands together sedately, and only forgave the men for their rowdiness on the grounds that, as usual, they had been drinking hard after dinner. Whatever else Rose had done she had succeeded in destroying the rather decorous and dull atmosphere which had reigned at Morton Castle during and after dinner.

One plump, red-faced fellow howled, "More, more," at her, but Rose stood up, bowed to the company and when there was a break in the noise said, sedate once again,

"Oh, pray excuse me, I think that was quite enough for tonight."

Isabel, her smile a true one this time, walked over to her cousin and led her back to Miles, saying, "I had no notion that you could sing and play so well, Rose—and without music, too. Wherever did you learn to do that?"

"I had an Italian singing master who made me perform without music as well as with." Rose kept her voice low, but Miles, whose hearing was acute, caught what she said. His smile for her this time was a true one, no mockery in it.

"My dear Miss Charlton," he told her, aware that others were now watching her curiously, and that he must not embarrass her after their recent truce, "you are full of strange talents, are you not? I would never have guessed that you were able to give a performance that a professional songstress might envy."

"Now that, sir, is flattery," Rose said. "I am competent, no more."

Miles shook his head. "I can't agree, but I shall not argue with you. Was the last song for me?"

Fortunately by the time that he posed that question Isabel had moved away and the company's attention was now on other things. Tables had been set up for whist after Rose had finished playing, so Rose was able to say frankly to him, "Of course, Sir Miles, did you not ask for something lively?"

"Indeed, I did, and you promptly obliged me. Which was a good start to our truce, was it not?"

"A start and a finish, too," quipped Rose. She pulled her pocket watch from the small reticule she carried with her and examined it. "If you will forgive me, I think that it is time that I retired. I have had a long and hard couple of days."

Miles rose. "Of course, I will excuse you. You will be going to church in the morning? If so, may I claim the privilege of escorting you there?"

Rose was not sure that she wished him to behave towards her in such a particular manner, but felt it best that she should agree to accept his offer. "Of course. I will see you at breakfast." She made her adieux to her cousins and left.

All the way up the wide staircase to her bed she was asking herself whether she had been a fool to allow Miles Heyward to talk her into some kind of ridiculous agreement of which she was sure he would take advantage.

Chapter Three

Rose looked out of her bedroom window to find that, outside, Sunday was bright, clear and cold. Isabel had told her guests on the previous evening that the elderly wise-acres in Morton village had been forecasting snow for Christmas Day. This morning, however, the sun was shining, the pathways were dry and it would be possible for those who wished to walk to church to do so, rather than to ride there.

She arrived in the breakfast room to discover that the only person present was Miles, who was busily heaping his plate with food while the attendant butler poured his coffee for him.

He smiled across at her when she joined him. She looked around the room before saying, ''Are we the only persons up?''

''I collect that the Mortons are breakfasting in their room. Mrs Major Scriven left just as I arrived, but not before informing me that the Major was a little under the weather and would not be going to church with her—which left me offering to accompany her.''

Rose did not know whether she was glad or sorry at this news. ''Did she accept?''

''Only too readily, even when I assured her that I would be walking there, since the church is quite close to the Castle.

I gather that it was part of the original building which was torn down in the early Middle Ages." He smiled at her a trifle ruefully. "You must understand that, since she was obviously expecting me to ask her to be her escort instead of her husband, I had to play the part of the gentleman and oblige her."

"Oblige her—as, last night, you said that you wished me to oblige you?" Rose could not help remarking.

If she had thought to overset him she was mistaken. Miles shook his head reprovingly at her before carrying his plate to the table. "Now, now, Miss Rose Charlton, you know perfectly well what I was saying to Mrs Major Scriven. It was most improper of you to suggest otherwise just before going to church."

She might have guessed that it would be difficult to quiz or roast Miles Heyward successfully—he was obviously shameless. Nevertheless Rose found herself murmuring, "Dear, dear, Sir Miles, I fear that you have misunderstood me quite," when she took her place at the breakfast table opposite to him.

"Oh, I think not, Miss Charlton. By the by, don't you think that we could unbend a little and address one another as Miles and Rose? We have surely gone beyond Sir and Miss."

"You may have gone beyond, as you put it, Sir Miles, but I have not. Our acquaintance is not yet sufficiently long for formality to be abandoned."

Miles forked up a large kidney, but before putting it into his mouth, he asked, his expression as innocently enquiring as he could make it and with his black eyebrows raised, "Pray, what is the tariff relating to the relaxation of the rules of intercourse between us, Rose—I mean, Miss Charlton? Will a fortnight's acquaintance at Morton Castle allow us to use our Christian names, and how long do you think would be proper before we pass on to more intimate terms?"

After which he began to eat his kidney with relish.

What to say to that? Nothing might be best, but for some reason Rose was reluctant to allow him the last word. She was sure that Sir Miles Heyward was always the one who had the last word with either man or woman, but she was not going to allow that with her.

"I really have no notion, Sir Miles. So far as I am aware there is no book of etiquette which deals with such questions."

"Then I propose that we write one, together, how say you, Miss Charlton?"

He was beginning to enjoy himself. Teasing Rose Charlton was more entertaining than he had supposed that it might be since she was resolutely refusing to be set down.

What a charming minx she was! The pity of it was that she was not virtuous. To be both virtuous and witty, too, might have had him changing his mind about the inconstancy of women, whereas his knowledge of her true nature was making him regret that his mind must stay fixed.

As for what his body wanted, that was quite another matter. Nevertheless it was a long time since any woman had roused him so much at breakfast time! He put that down to his recent continence, but he knew quite well that it was not the true reason. Her very demureness was exciting, allied as it was to a lively mind.

Oh, yes, he was going to enjoy himself at Morton Castle after all, no doubt of it, and if he could conjure the witch into his bed before the end of it, well, that would be a Christmas present beyond compare!

In the meantime there was church to attend, carols to sing and possibly punch at the end of it when nuncheon was served.

He was looking so happy that Rose could not help but wonder what it was that was pleasing him so much. But, of course, she knew, mistaking what she was, he hoped to conquer her. Well, he was wrong and she ate buttered rolls and jam, smiled at him, and looked forward to him escorting her to church.

In spite of everything he fascinated her, and knowing that, she would take advantage of him, if she could—and not let him take advantage of her. Which was not the sort of thing that she ought to be thinking of on Sunday morning.

She told her imagination to behave itself, avoided looking him in the eye, looked at her plate instead, and decided rue-fully to allow him to have the last word after all, before she stood up to leave.

"At what hour do you propose to set out?" she asked.

A question which certainly left Miles with the last word in their recent short but lively exchange!

"At ten of the clock," he informed her, pulling out his watch. "It will also allow us plenty of time to walk to church and settle ourselves when we get there."

Rose nodded and retired to her room, passing several of the Mortons' guests who were on their way to breakfast. Most of the men looked rather the worse for wear, but all the ladies looked uncommonly cheerful. She felt rather cheer-ful herself.

All things considered, quite a reasonably-sized party was assembled in the entrance hall when Rose arrived there. Is-abel and Anthony were both present as well as Mrs Major Scriven, who had attached herself to Miles. She glared bale-fully at Rose when she came in as though defying her to detach him. Well, she was welcome to him, was Rose's first thought, but her second was rather different.

In any case, Miles, either wittingly, or unwittingly, rapidly stalemated Mrs Major Scriven by offering her his right arm and Rose his left, which made them, Rose thought, resemble a parody of the sentimental drawings in one of the *Book of Beauty* entitled "A Rose between Two Thorns". Except, of course, that in this picture the thorn was in the middle and the rose was on the left.

Fortunately, perhaps, neither she nor Miles had any opportunity to converse, since Mrs Major Scriven talked non-stop all the way to St Helen's church, saying how much she missed her two dear little children whom she had left at home in the care of her maiden aunt.

''Of course, Hannibal was determined to come, and since he was sure that the children would find the occasion tedious, I was compelled to leave them behind, alas.''

Hannibal! Rose stifled a laugh and sternly told herself not to ask Mrs Major when her husband was due to start his march on Rome. All the same, her mouth twitched, so much so that Miles, turning his head to ask her a question when Mrs Major's relentless and boring flow had ceased for a moment, wondered what she found so amusing in it. He determined to ask her when next they were alone together—or as alone as two members of such a house-party as the Mortons could ever be. For the moment he would say nothing, it would not be fitting.

The church proved to be as small and pretty as Morton Castle was large and rugged. It was full of the stately tombs of dead-and-gone Mortons, and of brass plaques remembering bygone vicars. It was already decorated with holly and ivy, ready for Christmas, and a small crib stood in one corner with a doll inside it representing the baby Jesus. The beautiful medieval stained glass windows had survived the ravages of Henry VIII's Commissioners and Cromwell's Puritans, as had the brass lectern in the shape of an eagle about to fly.

Rose found that its hushed atmosphere, together with the multi-coloured glory of the sunlight shining through the windows, settled her own troubled soul a little. She sat on Miles's left, but for the first time his nearness did not disturb her. She scarcely knew he was there. Mrs Major Scriven, perforce now silent, sat on his right, but they might as well have been in another country so far as Rose was concerned.

Her almost holy stillness intrigued Miles by contrast with Mrs Major's fidgeting and constant resettling of herself in the rather uncomfortable pew. He looked again at Rose's perfect profile. He found no amusement in her face this time, only an intense concentration. Unaware of his interest, she had picked up the hymn book from the ledge in the back of the pew before her and was obviously engaged in identifying which of the hymns, listed on the board against the pulpit, they were about to sing.

Of course, that was a quite natural reaction from her. She was a musician, almost a professional one, but he thought that her response to the church was more than that—and that it sat at odds with the kind of woman he thought her to be. Unless she was a consummate hypocrite, which was always a possibility—and that would make her a superb actress as well.

He sighed, only gently, but this must have disturbed Rose's concentration, for she turned to look at him.

''You are impatient for the service to begin?''

''No,'' he said, truthfully, but he could not tell her what the sigh really meant for that would be to betray to her the paradox she presented him with. He was saved from further explanation by the organ beginning to play, by the small choir leading the singing, and the priest entering to conduct the service.

After that the ritual of Sunday worship claimed the full attention of both of them. The vicar, a youngish man, proved to have an excellent voice, and his sermon on Christian charity was a touching one. Later, when the congregation left, he stood at the church door to bid them all goodbye—except that they would be meeting him again, Isabel had told Rose earlier, because he had been invited to nuncheon at the Castle.

''He is a man of good family,'' she had said, ''a Penrose, Doctor Philip Penrose, and he is to marry one of the Yorkshire Savilles in the spring.''

Which, thought Rose satirically, accounted for the invitation to nuncheon—since country vicars of no birth were un-

likely to be invited to eat at the Castle. She shocked herself
a little with this uncharitable thought, coming as it did in the
light of her decision in church not to use her wit to pass
judgement on others or make fun of them.

I will be better in future, she decided, but she was well
aware that she had made this resolution before and had sel-
dom lived up to it—particularly when provoked by such as
Sir Miles Heyward and Major Scriven. Fortunately, Anthony
Morton had chosen to escort her home, leaving Isabel to
Miles and Mrs Major Scriven to whoever felt like offering
her an arm.

Something of which she complained to her husband when
he surfaced in time to eat nuncheon, which at Morton Castle
was served from half-past noon.

"I really expected you to escort me to church today," she
complained to him when the guests were queuing to collect
their food from the loaded sideboard and the equally loaded
table.

"Now, now, you are well aware that all that parsonical
sermonising bores me, particularly when I have a head on
me like thunderstorm in full cry. You know that I always
leave you to do the pretty in such circumstances," he moaned
back at her.

Now this was unfortunate, seeing that Parson Penrose was
standing by him and could hear every unkind word. His wife
nudged him frantically, but, as usual, he took no notice of
her. Philip Penrose, unruffled, smiled after them. He had few
illusions about his fellow men—or women either—even if he
did hope to bring some of them into a state of grace.

One woman who intrigued him was Miss Rose Charlton,
although he had not yet learned her name, only recognised
her from having seen her in church. Then, as now, she
seemed to be outwardly very calm and composed, but something—he didn't know what—told him that beneath her carefully controlled exterior she was deeply troubled. If he was

right, and he believed that he was, then it would be his Christian duty to help her if he could.

He picked up his plate and wandered over to where she sat. She was seated on her own, a little way away from the rest of the company. Miles, having earlier been cornered by the Mortons, was now being expected to entertain them.

"I hope," Philip said, bowing to her, "that, although we have not been formally introduced, you would not think it forward of me to ask to sit by you."

"Not at all," said Rose. "But, after a fashion, we have been introduced—in church, as it were. Except that I know your name, but you do not know mine. Let me introduce myself. I am Miss Rose Charlton, Mrs Morton's cousin."

Troubled she might be, but his quarry was fully in command of herself.

"Is this your first visit to Yorkshire, Miss Charlton?"

"Yes. I have a home in London and another in Nottingham from which I have never before ventured into the north."

"May one ask your verdict on our county?"

"From the little I have seen of it, it is both wild and beautiful—but then, I have not visited the mill towns which I am told are quite otherwise."

"Indeed they are. My first ministry was in Leeds. It may sound odd to you, but I miss it. There were so many souls to be saved, you see."

"But there must also be souls to be saved in the country."

"True."

His voice was kind, and Rose had been impressed by his leading of the service in church. She leaned forward and said impulsively. "Tell me, Dr Penrose, how far, in order to protect oneself, is it permissible to deceive others? As a Christian, I mean."

So she *was* troubled. How to answer her? "My first response would be to say never, but not knowing the circumstances, and how important that protection might be, I have difficulty in saying other than that I would try to avoid deceit at all times, whatever the cost.''

"Whatever the cost," Rose repeated. She might have known that that would be his answer. "It might be difficult sometimes.''

"I understand that," he said, "but allow me to say that one's conscience must always be one's guide.''

He had not expected to carry on such a conversation during nuncheon at Morton Castle, but a priest was compelled to do his duty anywhere. Rose nodded thoughtfully at him and let the subject drop. She had only learned from him what she already knew.

After that they talked of idle things, but in the middle of it Rose became suddenly aware that Miles Heyward's eyes were fixed on her—and Philip Penrose. More than that, he did not look best pleased.

What in the world could be the matter with him? She was soon to find out. The vicar was called across by Anthony Morton to discuss some problem connected with the collection of Church tithes and Miles took the opportunity to walk over and sit by her instead.

"What the devil did that parson fellow mean by talking to you in such a particular fashion?" he demanded of her.

Miles had not meant to be so rude or peremptory but, to his astonishment, jealousy had him in its thrall. Philip Penrose was a handsome man with a good presence and he had been looking raptly at Rose Charlton after a fashion which Miles disliked.

Rose said, as sharply as she could, "Pray, what business is it of yours, Sir Miles Heyward, whether Dr Penrose is particular with me or not? Your speech to me was not that of a gentleman, I would have you know.''

"Nor am I a gentleman," he retorted, "so to Hades with their manners. My grandfather was a jumped-up clerk who made his fortune in the City of London at the time of the South Sea Bubble and bought up a large part of the City in consequence. He received a baronetcy in return for bribing the politicians then in power. I have no landed estate—yet— and when I eventually buy one I might try to pretend that I am a gentleman by birth, for the sake of my children if nothing else.''

He had never made such a speech before, nor had he ever thought that he might make it to someone like Rose Charlton. He had always behaved as though he were the gentleman his father had claimed to be, but something about Rose had made him half-bellow the truth at her—and why should that be, for did he not despise her?

Rose stared at him. Whatever else she might have expected from him, it was not this odd confession—and offered so brusquely, too.

''Oh, pooh to that,'' she retorted. ''We are all descendants of Adam and Eve and ought to behave and speak decently to one another, whether we are gentle persons or not—except that those who call themselves gentlemen have a particular duty to do so.''

''Now I see what the parson was at. He was teaching you how to sermonise, was he not? Well, you are a fine one to prose at me, Miss Rose Charlton, and no mistake!''

They were both asking themselves why was he so cross with her. Rose thought, however, that what Miles had just told her explained a great deal about him.

''Miles,'' she said urgently, forgetting herself and using his Christian name for the first time. Perhaps, she told herself later, because it was Sunday, she had been to church and Christianity was on her mind. ''Miles, who was your mother?''

''My mother!'' he exclaimed. ''What has that to do with anything?''

''You just told me that you weren't a gentleman because of your grandfather, even if he was later made a baronet, so it might be interesting to know to what family your mother belonged.''

"She was a Wyndham." Miles had adopted the baffled expression of a man who would never understand the female mind.

"One of the Petworth Wyndhams?"

"Yes…" What in the world was Rose rattling on about?

"Well, that explains you, doesn't it? Not only were your ancestors successful and remarkable self-made men, but your mama comes from a family noted for its eccentricity."

"I still don't understand why we're talking about my mother."

"Because, as my grandfather, who was a working farmer and a gentleman, once told me, if you want to understand what an animal is really like then you ought to look at its pedigree, particularly its immediate one. He also said that you could tell a great deal about human beings, too, by learning about their ancestors."

Miles stared at her. He had spent the last few months reading of the new ideas on the breeding of animals and now he was receiving further such instruction from a demure young miss who ought not to know about such things. Well, he might be eccentric, and he had to admit that his mother certainly was, but then so was Miss Rose Charlton with her forthright view of the world.

What more was there to learn about her? She was smiling kindly at him.

"Are you daring to tell me that I am eccentric?"

"Not exactly," said Rose, who thought that she might have gone too far, but that it was time someone did go too far with Miles Heyward, who really needed putting in his place for once, "but you are somewhat out of the ordinary, are you not? Compared with my cousin Anthony, for instance."

Lieutenant-Colonel Sir Miles Heyward thought of a remark which the great Duke of Wellington had once made to him. "I like you, Heyward. You're slightly mad, but you control it—which makes you the best sort of man and soldier." And now here was this chit of a girl saying something similar to him, although not quite in the Duke's words.

And, yes, he was compelled to admit that he was most unlike his friend Anthony, who was just the sort of stolid, unimaginative fellow who had made England great in his own dogged way.

Miles could not help it. He began to laugh.

"I never thought that I should live to hear such home truths in the dining room of a country house from a young lady who looks as though butter wouldn't melt in her mouth." And having said that, he felt the most extraordinary desire to take Rose in his arms and kiss her senseless.

Her great blue eyes were shining at him, her whole body was alight with interest—as it always was whenever she spoke—and, damn him, he didn't mind whether she were saint or whore, he wanted her in his arms, in his bed... Heaven help him, he was becoming roused, and on Sunday too, in a roomful of strangers and with a parson present.

If he had thought that his stay at Morton Castle was going to be a dull one, then he could not have been more far off the mark. Miss Rose Charlton seemed to be determined to make it lively, and that being so he would respond in kind— and let the best man—or woman—win!

After the verbal fireworks at nuncheon Rose thought it wise to retire to her room for a time to avoid another such encounter. She was having second thoughts about her conversation with Miles Heyward. Had she really said all those dreadful things about his mother to him? Her cheeks flamed at the very thought, but it was always the same when she was with Miles, he seemed to bring out the worst in her. She had always, from their very first meeting onwards, ended up by saying to him all the things that one privately thought but never said aloud.

What a mercy it was that Isabel had come over and taken her away to be introduced to Miss Frances Courtney, who was not a house-guest but had been invited to nuncheon at the Castle after the service was over. Miss Courtney was in her fifties, had once been pretty, but was now handsome after the fashion of some middle-aged ladies.

"I have been telling your cousin that I have asked some of my friends to celebrate Christmas with me tomorrow. It would please me greatly if she could arrange for you all to visit me before nuncheon, eat an early and semi-informal meal with us and join in the dancing afterwards."

"Would that not be too much for you?" asked Isabel a trifle anxiously, looking around at her large party.

"Not at all. I have a new and splendid chef and it would relieve you of the trouble of entertaining your guests for one day at least."

Isabel could not demur further. To some extent Miss Courtney was correct; it would be a day off for her, so to speak. But Miss Courtney's notion of hospitality was always delightfully odd, to say the least, and so she told Rose.

"Do I collect that she's eccentric?" asked Rose. The word seemed to be following her about.

"One might say so—not to the degree that she's light in the attic, of course."

"Of course," agreed Rose.

Well, that would make three eccentrics at Courtney House: herself, Miles and their hostess—and perhaps Major Scriven…which would make four.

The small smile she gave on thinking this set her cousin wondering what was amusing Rose now. She remembered that when they had been girls together, years ago, Rose had possessed a most inventive mind, which had occasionally got them both into trouble—and, more occasionally, out of it.

Rose was still amused some hours later. Several of the party had decided to take a walk in the grounds, others, mostly men, had gone to the billiards room where they were allowed to smoke. After reading in her room for a little time, she gathered her box of pastels and her drawing materials together and decided to take them into the library. It possessed one large bay window where the light was always good.

Finally she picked up from the window sill of the small drawing room in her suite a plant pot containing the Christmas rose of which she and Miles had joked.

It would make a splendid subject for a botanic-style drawing, and she ought to be able to finish it before the light dwindled in the afternoon. Besides, at this hour the library was sure to be deserted: its greatest use was immediately after breakfast when the guests retired there to write their letters, read the newspapers—all of them several days old—and try to find something interesting on the shelves to occupy them later on in the hours before dinner.

As she had hoped only the librarian, Dr Smailes, was present when she walked in and set her work out on the great table in the window, which was provided for those who might need to examine one of the many maps which were kept in an especially large drawer.

''Is there anything I can do for you, Miss Charlton?'' he asked her.

Rose smiled and showed him the plant pot, which she had placed on a lace doily that she had brought with her from her room.

''I haven't come to read,'' she told him, ''but I thought a pastel of a Christmas rose would be a pleasant memento of my Yorkshire visit.''

''Quite so,'' he murmured, ''and particularly apt in view of your name. I will leave you to your work. The light dies very early in deep winter.''

Rose began with a couple of rapid pencil sketches before she determined on the shape which her painting should take. As with her music, her father, and then her grandfather, had provided her with the very best teachers and she had proved so apt a pupil that she was more than a mere lady amateur.

Finally she started out on what she hoped would be her finished picture. She was concentrating so hard on it that she failed to hear the library door open and someone enter, and it was not until the someone crossed to the window where she was working that she looked up to find that the newcomer was Miles Heyward.

He was carrying a large quarto book which he placed on the table so as not to interfere with her work.

"Good afternoon, Rose," he said. "I had not thought to find you here but, now that I have, pray do not stop working—I have no wish to disturb you."

He was being so polite that Rose forgave him for the use of her Christian name. Not that he needed forgiveness—for had not she already used his! She put the pastel she had been painting with back in its box.

"Not at all, I have been working for some time and need a rest."

Miles had picked up one of her sketches and was examining it gravely. "So, you have a talent for art, as well as music. May I see the painting on which you are now working?"

Rose pushed the small frame on which the pastel was propped towards him.

Why was he not surprised by her competence? Did it not fit in with the whole manner in which she conducted her life? The drawing was only half-finished, but it combined accuracy of the subject before her with something more than that.

"Excellent," he said. "The Christmas rose of which we spoke. Is that why you are drawing it?"

"One reason, I suppose," Rose said.

"*The* reason?" he riposted, teasing her again, but before she could reply, he added, "No, don't answer. Tell me, do you paint in water colour, too, and in oils?"

"Both, but I am only an amateur."

"A good one, nevertheless."

Rose shook her head, then asked, "And do you paint, Sir Miles?"

"Miles," he said. "Yes, water colours. Military ones for my battle commanders, so that they might know the nature of the terrain in which we were campaigning. They were very prosaic, I fear. This is more than that."

He waved his hand at her sketchbook. "Might I examine it?"

Of all things Rose had not expected this. There were reasons why she did not want him to, but good manners forbade that she refuse him.

"If you wish—it is very ordinary, I'm afraid. Just a series of sketches done at random."

Miles sat down beside her and began to turn the pages. Ordinary it was not. The pencil drawings varied from rapid sketches to more detailed offerings, and all of them were lively and possessed the hint of power which he had seen in her work with the Christmas rose.

But it was the pages near to the end of the book which betrayed why she had been so reluctant to allow him to inspect it. To his surprise—and amusement—four of them were devoted to Sir Miles Heyward! Rose had not only drawn straightforward and truthful portraits of him, but also a number of caricatures, all obviously done during their stay at Morton Castle. In them he was laughing, he was sneering, he was angry: he was standing and sitting, eating and reading.

He looked wryly up at her. Rose's face was scarlet.

"Forgive me," she stammered.

"No," he told her slowly, "I'm flattered by all this attention. You never expected me to see them, did you?"

"No—only the chance of your arrival here, when you ought to have been inspecting the grounds with the rest of the party, gave you that opportunity. If you give me the book I will destroy them—many are very unkind."

"No," he said sharply. "By no means. If you don't want them, I do. You may give them to me: they are too good to

be destroyed. You have caught my wretched self exactly—
and none of them done directly from the life, but later from
memory in your room, I collect. How in the world are you
able to do that?''

He did not say that one thing which the drawings proved
was that her interest in him was as great as his in her. More
than ever, here in the sacred precincts of the library, with old
Smailes creeping around them, he found himself consumed
with desire again. She would be the death of him yet, or
rather, he hoped, the little death which the ancients called
the act of love.

Rose's face began to resume its delicate porcelain colour.
''I don't know. It's just that I have this rather odd memory.
When I have seen something, I can fix it, as it were. That is
how I can play without music before me. It is there in my
head. I can't explain it.''

She hesitated a moment, ''If you would really like the
drawings,'' she said slowly, ''you may have them.''

''That is very kind of you,'' and then, teasing her again,
''Not that you were very kind to me in all of them. Do I
really look so grimly ruthless in repose?

Rose decided to be truthful. ''Yes, exactly like I imagine
a soldier would—which is not surprising, since you were a
soldier.''

''Yes, I served under Wellington until after Waterloo. It
was perceptive of you to guess that last night.''

It was another trait which Rose possessed—the ability to
see the real selves of the people around her—which was why
she could not abide to be near Major Scriven, or that other
of whom she tried not to think. Miles intrigued her because,
away from him, she knew that she ought to detest him because of his low opinion of her. Except that, when she was
with Miles, not only did he give off an aura of masculine
power, mixed with goodness, and a sense of what she could
only describe as duty, but she was also strongly attracted to
him after a fashion which she could only describe as physical.

No man had ever made her feel like that before…

Miles watched her carefully detach the pages from the sketchbook after he had handed it back to her. Everything that she did was measured, even her speech—except when he provoked her. Not only did she puzzle him for appearing to be so different from the light woman which rumour said she was, but his own feelings for her were beginning to trouble him more and more.

Oh, there was lust in them, he knew, but oddly, considering the selfish overtones which the word usually carried with it, he was beginning to find himself feeling protective towards her. He did not want her to be hurt. He wanted to see her smile at him, to feel that she approved of him.

He was growing maudlin, was he not? Fit only for Bedlam if he forgot to be wary, and forgot what Emily had done to him. Nevertheless, when Rose, her task ended, passed him her drawings and their hands touched, he felt a frisson of sheer passion run through his body, so strong that it nearly overset him. What particularly surprised him about it was not its strength, but that it had happened at all. He had thought himself hardened, that life, and maturity, had deadened his ability to respond to a woman so immediately—and now this occurred. He was almost an eager boy again, finding his first love and the sweetness which it brought with it.

Miles was not alone. The only difference between them was that for Rose the experience was a new one. She had nothing with which to compare it. No man's touch had ever moved her before. She wanted to touch Miles again to find out whether she had been mistaken, whether it had been an accident and—more to the point—to find out whether it would happen again.

Rose shivered at the very thought.

All this, surprisingly, seemed to take no time at all. Miles took the drawings from her and murmured his thanks. He bowed to her and began to leave. He had, in fact, forgotten why he had come to the library at all.

Rose said, "Miles, your book, you have left your book behind." She had picked up the heavy quarto and was holding it towards him.

Miles turned. His brains were obviously addled. He had brought the book, which was the first volume of a description by Sir Joseph Banks of his visit to the Pacific and Australia, to the library in order to exchange it for the second volume. Under Miss Rose Charlton's sorcery, for he could find no other name for what had happened, he had forgotten all about it!

He put down the drawings, took the heavy volume from her, and explained that he had come to exchange it for its fellow.

"You will think me a strange lackwit," he told her, "to forget my true purpose in coming here."

"Not at all," said Rose, who had just discovered that when she had handed Miles his book her second touch from him had had the same extraordinary effect as the first. "Finding me here distracted you."

Well, that was true enough, but not perhaps in the way in which she meant it!

Or did she? Was she a mermaid, or an innocent? Miles still did not know, but was beginning to give her the benefit of the doubt. Perhaps his friend, Oliver Fenton, from whom he had first learned of her perfidy, had been mistaken. Oh, to the devil with everything! If he did not leave, and try to cool himself down by joining Sir Joseph on his Pacific adventures, who knew what act of folly he might yet commit?

Rose was feeling the same. Pull yourself together, she told herself sternly as her old nurse had once done when she had been about to make a cake of herself over something or other. I shall be quite myself again when he has gone.

Except, as Miles told himself glumly, when he finally reached his rooms, he had committed yet another act of folly before he finally left the library. For in his distraction, and there was no other word for it, this time he had forgotten to pick up her drawings of him!

On his return Rose could not help it: she began to laugh. "Sir Miles," she choked at him, "this time you have remembered to pick up your book, but you have left your drawings behind!"

Miles set Sir Joseph down on the nearest table, walked over to where Rose stood, the drawings in her hands again, took them from her, and then put them back on the table. Before he could stop himself, he said hoarsely, "Oh, to the devil with everything," then took her in his arms and began to kiss her, first gently, and then fiercely, until sanity reared its head once again. He stepped back from her, saying huskily, "Oh, I'm so sorry, do forgive me. To attack you like that was unforgivable."

For Rose, reason had been overthrown and only passion ruled. How could she be so moved—as never before—by a man whom she hated and despised for his misjudgement of her, all on the solitary word of another man whom she thought, nay, knew, to be light-minded to a degree where women were concerned. She could not trust any man—especially Sir Miles Heyward.

Above all, she must not let him know how seriously he had affected her. Her whole body seemed to have acquired a strange and unwanted life of its own, since the one thing that it most wanted was that he would kiss her again! She must not let that happen, she *must* not.

Perhaps the best way was to show him how little he had affected her. To answer him so that the tension which had grown up between them would be destroyed. So she simply murmured, amusement in her voice, "Well, that should have cleared your head and no mistake—or fuddled it completely!"

At which they both began to laugh, Miles because he, too, was shocked by his response to Rose, so that high passion turned rapidly into abandoned mirth, until Dr Smailes came out of his cubby hole and stared at them, at Sir Joseph deserted on the table, at Rose's drawings likewise, and at the pair of them lost in their own world.

"Is there anything wrong?" he asked in his quiet pedantic voice, the very incongruity of which brought them both back to the everyday world again.

"Not at all," they said together.

This time Miles picked up both Sir Joseph and Rose's sketches, saying to the bewildered doctor when he passed him, "Miss Charlton was showing me her caricatures. She has a real gift, quite the female Gillray, I assure you."

If Dr Smailes wondered why this should have set the pair of them laughing so heartily he did not say so. Instead he walked over to look at Rose's drawing and compliment her on it, wondering where the business about Gillray and caricature had come from when all the poor young lady had been doing was paint a dear little pastel of a winter flower!

Misrule was certainly the word to describe what happened whenever she and Miles met, Rose thought, before she went down to dinner. She must try to control herself and, whenever she was with him, try to conduct herself like the perfect lady which Isabel and Anthony were trusting her to be.

Of course, she was put next to him again at dinner. Consequently she tried to confine herself during the inevitable conversation which ran on throughout the meal to saying "Yes," "No," "Exactly," and "Really?" to every topic which was raised.

The trouble was, though, that when the men came into the drawing room after their port, Miles found her seated on her own, leafing through an album dedicated to drawings and descriptions of the great houses of England. After that, when she refused to join in the fun and games which the men brought in with them, Miles, a worried look on his face, came over to sit opposite to her.

"Are you feeling quite the thing, Rose?" he asked. "You

seemed very *distraite* during dinner. Did you overdo it this afternoon?''

Rose, who had determined to keep up her cool manner with Miles and everyone else, found herself, to her horror, replying spiritedly to him, ''Of course I haven't been over-doing things! Goodness, I was only doing a small pastel drawing of a Christmas rose, not painting the Sistine Chapel ceiling!''

Why ever was it that he had this dreadful effect on her? She could only be glad that the impromptu and rowdy game of Blindman's Buff going on around them meant that no one was taking the slightest notice of them.

Miles began to laugh. ''That's more like it,'' he exclaimed. ''To what, then, is owed your unwonted reticence this eve-ning?''

''A lady is known by her reticence and her self-control,'' Rose replied, mortified to the extent that she was even cooler with him.

''Not if her name is Caroline Lamb, she isn't,'' was all that he had to say to that.

''So you have been comparing me with her?'' Rose felt more mortified than ever.

''No, you goose, but you must admit that you were most unlike yourself during and after dinner.''

''Perhaps because I didn't like myself much before and felt that I needed to change.''

''Well, for my part,'' he teased, ''I prefer the unreformed Rose to the new one.''

Rose wished that she was one of those hoydenish young women who were allowed the liberty of striking at their beaux with their fan. But she hadn't got her fan with her, and he wasn't her beau, so why should she think he was?

Because, you goose, she told herself, echoing him, he is behaving exactly like one, and if once I thought that it might be an excellent notion to lead him on, I no longer do, and not only because of what Dr Penrose said to me. It would be too dangerous for me by far because I am so powerfully attracted to him. It would have been easier if I had continued to hate him.

Aloud she came out with, "And that is exactly *why* I decided to reform."

"No, Rose, don't say that."

"Why, because—and I must say this—it would be easier for you to seduce the old Rose than the new one?"

Was that what she thought of him? Of course it was. He had given her no reason to think otherwise. More than that, his own feelings were so contrary. First he wanted to protect her and then he wanted to bed her. A moment ago he had been worried for her because of her apparent low spirits and had wanted to help or to comfort her. Earlier her high spirits had been such a challenge to him that the temptation which she presented to him had become stronger than ever. He had never before been in such a pother over a woman.

His feelings for Emily had been straightforward. He had wanted a wife and she had seemed a suitable one. Passionate love had never entered into the equation, and for the first time Miles realised that Emily might have had yet another reason for deserting him.

"Now it is your turn to be quiet," Rose remarked when Miles's silence stretched on and on.

"And I have not been painting the Sistine Chapel ceiling, either," he retorted. "Only sitting next to a most contrary young lady who is as big a mystery to me as the Sphinx, but usually more talkative. I'm struggling to reconcile all the different Roses I think I know."

Rose stood up. "Forgive me, but I think that you are creating your own mysteries, Sir Miles. Now, if you will allow me, I must retire. I have had a long day and tomorrow will be even longer—and we have not yet begun the real Christmas festivities."

"I have distressed you," Miles said, rising in his turn.

"Do not let me drive you away—unless you are truly weary."

"Yes, I am truly weary, and I must be ready for tomorrow's exertions. I bid you goodnight."

She had gone, leaving Miles to stare after her. What a strange Christmas this had turned out to be. He had thought to spend a mild, recuperative few days in the north where he hardly knew anybody, rather like visiting a spa to mend one's health a little—and then return home refreshed.

Instead, meeting Rose Charlton had put paid to that hope.

Before lamenting his sad condition overmuch, he remembered what she had said about Christmas and Misrule and the world being turned upside down. Give Miss Rose Charlton her due, she had succeeded in turning his world upside down—and no mistake!

Chapter Four

Miles did not succeed in manoeuvring Rose into his carriage for the trip to Courtney House on the next day. Anthony and Isabel had both observed, with some misgivings, how much time they were spending together.

Anthony said to his wife, "He may not be aware that Rose's reputation is not of the best—and nor is the rest of the company apparently—so we really ought to protect him. We shall invite her to travel with us. It would not do for him to become *épris* with her, not knowing about the rumours."

Isabel said thoughtfully, "He appears to be fascinated by her. It is he who seeks her out. So far as I can see, Rose does not particularly fix herself on him."

"All the more reason for us to keep them apart. I still wish that you had not invited her, although I am bound to say that she has behaved well so far."

Rose might have smiled ruefully had she heard this conversation. She sat opposite Anthony, willing herself to be everything that was correct—if only for Isabel's sake. She would contrive to be inconspicuous during the visit, drawing as little attention to herself as possible.

Later she was to tell herself that before planning her behaviour for the afternoon she ought to have remembered the old Latin saying, "Man proposes, God disposes'. She had been so busy worrying about Miles Heyward, and how he would behave towards her, that she forgot that there might be others present of whom she ought to be wary.

At first all went well. Courtney House was beautiful because, since it had been built and furnished over two hundred years ago, none of its subsequent owners had thought to add to, or change, anything in it. The house was delightfully true to itself, Rose thought, only to hear Mrs Major Scriven dismiss it as "boringly old-fashioned. One wonders why no one ever thought to bring it up to date."

Miss Courtney led them into a large room with two fireplaces in it, both shedding heat on to her grateful guests who had had a cold journey of it—"but then," as Rose stoutly observed to Mrs Major Scriven who found that yet another ground for complaint, "it is Christmastide, after all."

The long table down the middle of the room, which had once been the medieval Great Hall, was loaded with food and drink. Chairs, settles and benches, enough to accommodate an army, were set about it. One wall was decorated by a superb collection of Civil War pikes, muskets, swords and armour. Beneath them was a long oak buffet, laid out with still more food. Footmen and women servants stood about, drilled by a fat and stately butler who kept a stern eye on them to see that all the guests were satisfied. Overhead hung banners with the arms of the various families who had married into the Courtneys on them.

The portraits of bygone Courtneys, all with the light eyes and sandy hair of the House's present owner, looked down at them from the walls. To enhance the room's antique splendour boughs of holly, ivy and mistletoe had been disposed everywhere, even around the iron chandeliers hanging overhead. The decorations always associated with Christmas had already arrived at Courtney House even if they were not due to appear at Morton Castle until the morrow.

"They say that the Waits are to sing and play carols for us this evening, during an interval in the dancing," Isabel whispered to Rose. "I told Anthony that we ought to have arranged for them to visit us. Since he won't want to be outdone by Miss Courtney he will probably agree."

The guests stood around waiting for their hostess to join them when she had finished greeting all her guests in the Entrance Hall. This she did, entering behind a man bearing a huge silver dish on which a boar's head reposed, an orange in its mouth. He laid it on one end of the table, left empty for that purpose. That done, Miss Courtney bowed to her guests and announced, "Let the feasting begin."

Which it instantly did. Most of those present advanced on the table and the buffet, and with the help of the servants began to fill their plates. Some of the men immediately rushed to the side-table on which wine, port, brandy and sherry, as well as a large bowl of hot punch, had been laid out and began to drink with a will.

Rose was almost mown down in the crush until a strong hand on her arm held her up and led her away from the scrimmage which had developed. She was fascinated to watch her fellow guests losing their usual courtly manners in the face of the bean feast laid out before them.

The hand, of course, belonged to Miles.

"I thought that you needed rescuing," he told her, adding, "You are obviously not accustomed to the loosened manners of Yuletide. If we wait a little the crowd will disperse and since enough has been provided to feed several hungry villages there will be plenty left for us when the first rush dies down."

"You're probably right," she said, "but my Christmases have always been quiet ones. I have never seen anything quite like this. To top all, our hostess referred to our promised meal as informal!"

"I gather that our hostess is famous for the splendour of the banquets which she gives on all the major feast days of the year. A little bird has also whispered to me that she may not be giving many more. It seems that despite the appearance of this magnificent banquet the Courtney finances are on their last legs. There is even talk of her retiring to the Dower House and retrenching heavily. In the meantime, now that the crowd has thinned a little, I suggest that we both visit the table to collect our share of the goodies on show.''

Rose, all her good resolutions about avoiding him flying away, allowed him to lead her to the table and then, her plate having been filled with slices of boar's meat, a chicken leg and various patties, plus rolls and butter, Miles led her to a small table in the corner. ''Where we may eat in peace,'' he said, ''but not before I have fetched you something to drink.''

''Lemonade, please,'' Rose said, feeling that she needed to avoid strong drink in order to keep a cool head.

''No punch?'' he asked her, cocking his head comically on one side. ''After all, it is Christmas.''

Rose relented. ''Only if the cups are small.''

''Understood, madam.''

Rose watched him go, threading his way easily through the group around the drinks table. Oh, if only could she trust him—but, more to the point, could she trust herself? At least in this crowded room—for large though the hall was, it was crammed with people—she was surely safe from him, or from anyone else. So she thought, but though their small table was on its own in a far corner, this was not to save her from the advances of Major Scriven whose nuncheon had, so far, been only a liquid one.

The sight of her, apparently on her own, seemed to have excited him. His wife was already seated at another small table between Anthony and Isabel and he seemed to think that this gave him the opportunity to come and trouble Rose.

''Beauty is left on her own, I see,'' he cried, waving his half-full brandy glass at her. ''How can that be? Are all the swains and bachelors in this room blind?''

He sank into the empty chair opposite to her and put down his glass so carelessly that the liquor slopped on to the polished table top. Next he stretched out his hand and tried to grasp hers when she raised a piece of buttered roll to her mouth.

Rose pulled her hand away. He leered at her, and said, "Come, come, don't be coy, missy. You're in no position to play the innocent, are you? Particularly when I see that your erstwhile lover, Attercliffe, is here. Has he come to claim you?"

Attercliffe! Was he here? He must be one of Miss Courtney's guests. Of course, his mother had been a Courtney, and living out of the great world as his hostess did, she would not know that he was not now received anywhere. And how had Major Scriven come to learn about the rumours that had involved him and Rose—to her detriment?

Rose's appetite, which had been whetted by the superb array of food, disappeared completely. She only had one idea in her head and that was to turn tail and hide somewhere. Had she known that Attercliffe was to be present she would have invented a migraine, something, anything, in order to avoid a visit to Courtney House, so that she would be saved from meeting him.

Could she do that now? Could she ask Miss Courtney if she might retire to a private room in order to rest, giving the excuse that she had been overcome by a sudden indisposition? On the other hand, to do that would mean admitting guilt, that she needed to hide, that her reputation was so blown upon that she was not welcome in decent company.

All the time that her busy mind was going round in circles the Major was chattering suggestively to her. Had Attercliffe betrayed her to him—and if it were not Attercliffe, then who? Once she might have thought that it must have been Miles—but not after the fashion in which he had been treating her lately. Rose looked wildly round the room, ignoring the Major, willing him to go away. She saw Miles coming towards them, a footman behind him, carrying their drinks on a tray. Was he to be her unlikely saviour?

But no! Behind the footman was Attercliffe himself, look-

ing older but not so debauched as she might have expected
after so many years. Had he seen her? Rose prayed not—but,
of course, he had. It seemed that she was to be spared nothing.

Miles arrived at the table. He stared forbiddingly at the
Major, whose presence was obviously distressing Rose, and
who, although the hour was yet early, was already barely
sober. Miles ignored him while the footmen put their drinks
down on the table, and then sat down in the chair next to
her.

Rose's face was so white and stricken that he thought that
this time she might really be feeling ill, unlike on the previous evening when he had teased her. He handed her her
punch in its small glass cup with an engraving of Bacchus
on the side and, still pointedly ignoring the Major, picked up
his own drink and toasted her with, "*Was Hael*, Miss
Charlton."

Rose offered him a watery smile, at which, still ignoring
the fuming Major, Miles murmured in an effort to restore her
normal cheerfulness, "I have to inform you, Miss Charlton,
that among we topers the correct reply to that ancient toast
is to cap it with *Drink Hael*."

"Really." Rose managed another watery smile at this and
offered him the traditional response, "*Drink Hael*, then."

"Bravo, Miss Charlton," was his reply and they drank
their punch together.

Attercliffe had by now reached their table in time to hear
the Major snarl at Miles, "What's all this Miss Charlton,
Heyward? Everyone's well aware that it's Rose and Miles
with you in the day, and darling and dearie in the dead of
night."

"Can you think of any reason, Miss Charlton, why I
should not knock him down for you?" exclaimed Miles savagely.

"Only that the few remnants of the good reputation which
I might still have left would disappear forever," returned

Rose, her lips numb, "and of what use would that be to me? Although I thank you for the offer."

Major Scriven gave an ugly laugh. "Oh, don't try to bam me, either of you. Attercliffe's valet told mine of your unsavoury reputation." He was about to say more but Attercliffe interrupted him with, "This is neither the time of the year, nor the place, Scriven, for you to be retailing ugly and lying gossip in public."

"Oh, that's rich," bawled the Major, "seeing what your reputation is—and the lady's…"

This time he was stopped, not by Attercliffe verbally interrupting him, but by his seizing the Major by the collar, swinging him round and leading him away, through the fascinated onlookers, remarking over his shoulder to Rose, "Allow me to relieve you of the presence of this troublesome fly."

Miles and Rose stared after him, until Miles, on turning to look at her, thought that she was about to faint.

"Rose, you really do look ill tonight," he said, his own face white and concerned. "Would you like me to ask Miss Courtney if you might retire to somewhere private?"

Rose murmured dazedly, "By no means. My presence here has already caused a most unpleasant scene which has resulted in most of the assembled guests staring at me. To retire after that would be the outside of enough. It would almost certainly be seen as an admission of guilt and I should immediately become a social outcast. Allow me to try to eat and drink as though nothing has happened. If you find that you no longer wish to remain with me, I shall quite understand."

Miles bit back an oath. "I have not the slightest wish to leave you on your own to suffer the stares and gossip which will surely follow Scriven's disgraceful conduct. What I *do* wish is that I might have been able to protect you myself but Attercliffe forestalled me by bodily removing him. I have to confess that, although I know what game the Major might be playing, I am not sure of Attercliffe's.''

Rose, remembering what had happened between herself and Attercliffe eight years ago, was equally surprised by his behaviour. Whatever she had expected from him it was not that. For him to be her protector was as unexpected as his arrival at Courtney House.

As for Miles, *his* wish to protect her was the only good thing about the whole ghastly incident. It was not what she might have expected from him when they had met again at Morton Castle. She had no notion what had caused his change of heart and she could only hope that it might be permanent.

On the other hand he might yet, on mature reflection, feel that he did not wish to be on friendly terms with a woman whose reputation was so blown on that a man, even if he were in his cups, could insult her publicly. If only she could disappear so completely that she might never be seen again, as a wicked fairy had done in one of the pantomimes which she had seen at Drury Lane. Not that she was a wicked fairy, but in the eyes of the world in which she lived she might just as well be.

Miles, though, was facing his true feelings about Rose Charlton for the first time. He was, despite everything, in love with her so deeply that if he could have challenged Major Scriven to pistols at dawn in order to dispose of him forever, he would have done so on the spot. He was stopped only by his knowledge that this would merely serve to hurt Rose's reputation even more.

He no longer believed that she was a mermaid, or a light-skirt, or a barque of frailty or any of the words which described a fallen woman. Something in her manner told him that she was brave and true. He would do anything to save her from the unpleasant gossip which would surely follow Attercliffe's presence and the Major's open demeaning of her.

"You are right not to wish to retire," he told her. "It would not help matters. I will do all in my power to see that you are not exposed to further public insult."

"For which the verdict will be," Rose told him, "that I have you in my toils."

"What better toils could I be in?" Miles asked her. "Courage, my friend, the devil is dead, as the old soldiers used to say, so as to shame his memory. Whether the devil's name be Attercliffe or Scriven I will leave you to judge. Eat your nuncheon so that no one will think that what has passed has distressed you, and when you have emptied your plate, I will fetch you some of the more exotic-looking pastries, as well as a glass of Madeira. I need to see the roses back in your cheeks—and not white Christmas ones either."

His kindness almost had Rose in tears. She tried to do as he had asked, and while she struggled to clear her plate he kept up a steady line of banter about everything around them. Gradually she had ceased to be the object of curious stares. Attercliffe was talking to Miss Courtney. The Major and his wife seemed to have disappeared. Other topics besides Miss Rose Charlton's reputation were now the subjects of gossip.

Rose did not delude herself that the matter was over. Neither Anthony nor Isabel would forgive her for being a cause of scandal at their friend's grand party. Indeed, when Miles went to fetch her the promised pastries and Madeira, Isabel came over to her, her face frozen.

"Well, I see that it was as Anthony feared. Your presence here has created a fine brouhaha. Major Scriven was bawling about your fallen state, even while Miss Courtney's footmen were taking him to the stables to cure his drunkenness with a pail of water, before putting him to bed until he is fit to leave.

"The damage, however, has been done. I have suggested to Miss Courtney that you should retire to one of the upstairs suites to remain there until it is time for us to return home. All things considered, it would not be right for you to take part in the dancing. She fully agrees. She will arrange for you to be fed and cared for until we leave. I hope that you will be commonsensical enough to agree to this offer.''

Rose said drily, ''Of course, I must accept her offer. You have left me with no alternative.''

Isabel gave a short laugh. ''You have made me look a fool before Anthony. We shall have to decide what to do with you when we return home. Were it not Christmas Eve tomorrow you could leave for home in the morning, but as it is I will not have it said that we cast you out at Christmastide.''

''And the Major?'' asked Rose steadily. ''What of him? And Lord Attercliffe, is he to be banished?''

''That is no business of yours, but Major Scriven is an old friend of Anthony's and drink misled him. He will, I am sure, regret his behaviour when he is sober, but do not expect any apologies from him. As for Lord Attercliffe, he is our hostess's cousin and it would not do for him to be harshly treated. Ah, here comes your maid with one of the housekeepers to help you to your room. I will talk to you again later.''

Without causing yet another commotion, Rose could do no other than she was bid. Miles was still at the drinks table, awaiting his turn so that she could not even tell him adieu and thank him for his kindness. She followed the two women without a backward glance and consequently did not see him return with her pastries and a glass of Madeira—only to find Isabel Morton sitting in her place.

Miles put the plate and the glass down. ''What have you done with Rose?'' His voice was cold and Isabel flushed a little.

''Miss Courtney felt that, considering everything, it would be best if Rose retired to a private room. She asked me to plead illness for her.''

''Did she, indeed? And how long is it proposed that she stay there?''

"Until we go home. We dare not risk any more scenes for Miss Courtney's sake."

"And for yours, I suppose."

He knew that by arranging this the pair of them were dealing Rose's reputation a death blow. He wanted to say that he would leave Courtney House at once and Morton Castle on the morrow, but that would, he knew, only serve to damage Rose even further.

He left both Isabel and the food and drink without a further word. He desperately wanted to see Rose as soon as possible. A few coins offered to one of the footmen might succeed in finding out where she had been sent to remain in purdah, as it were, until the evening was over.

He would not arrange that at once, but would allow a decent interval to pass while he walked and talked to those around him, even to the Courtney woman, whom he was sure that Isabel Morton had suborned, but who was guilty of as much unChristian cruelty as she had been.

One of the footmen proved to be as obliging as Miles could have expected. He knew exactly where Rose had been exiled. "Up the main staircase and to the right. The poor young lady has been taken to one of the better suites for a nice lie down, the housekeeper said, since she was feeling ill."

Miles tapped on her door, but no one answered. Had Rose been left on her own? Was she perhaps asleep? He opened the door carefully to find himself in a tiny entrance hall with an open archway to the right. He could hear two voices. One of them was Attercliffe's.

He froze. Could the damaging stories about her be true after all? Had she and Attercliffe really been lovers? It might be ungentlemanly of him to eavesdrop, but he neither walked away, nor entered the room. Instead he stood quite still in order to listen to what was being said.

Attercliffe was speaking. "No, I won't leave," he was

saying, "until you have heard what I have come to say. You must understand that it is my guilty conscience which has brought me here."

This apparently did not mollify Rose for she replied with a break in her voice, "Please go. Have you not done enough harm to me already? Think of the gossip it would cause if it became known that you had followed me here to speak to me in private."

"But privacy is what I need. For if I said this in public, no one would believe me. Only you and I know the truth. May I not ask you for your forgiveness, so that, having it, I might sleep in peace again? I am well aware that nothing I can say will ever cancel the great wrong I did you when I was a mad boy. My only excuse is that I wanted so desperately to marry you, not only for your fortune, but because you were the young woman I had always dreamed of. My bad reputation, my poverty, everything about me, meant that if I had asked your father for your hand he would have laughed me out of the room.

"That was why I tricked you and kidnapped you. The world does not know, nor wish to know, of your total innocence. It prefers to believe that you were my willing accomplice. A scandalous story is always more titillating than the truth—that I respected your innocence on that mad drive north towards Gretna…"

"Why are you telling me this," cried Rose desperately, "telling me what I already know?"

"To purge myself, and so that you might know that I truly loved you then—and love you still. My one regret is that when, inevitably, what I had done became known, I could not convince those to whom scandal is meat and drink of your innocence, nor silence the servants who knew—or thought they knew—the truth and passed it on.

"Not long afterwards something odd happened to me. I fell seriously ill and as I recovered from it I came, for the first time, to examine my wild behaviour towards others and,

A Christmas Rose

in particular, towards you. In consequence I began to feel deeply ashamed of it and to understand how my selfishness must have hurt you. I am well aware that however remorseful I am, however much I may regret my behaviour, I shall never suffer as much as you must have done.

"I have tried to live a good life since then and I would like you to know that it was not I who revived and set in motion again the rumours about what happened eight years ago. I have worked hard and restored my family's fortunes, and now I would like to try to repair the damage I did to you. Marry me, Rose, so that together we can face down the world."

Miles began to start forward on hearing this, but stopped himself. He needed to know what Rose's answer would be.

"Marry you!" she exclaimed. "No, Lord Attercliffe, if indeed you are truly repentant I can offer you forgiveness, as a good Christian should, especially at Christmastide, but I do not wish to see or hear from you again. It is no exaggeration to say that for the last eight years my life, through no fault of my own, has been blighted by your wicked selfishness. Please leave me immediately. You say that your conscience has brought you here to ask me to forgive you, and by offering to marry me you hope to make up for the unhappy past, but it is too late. You cannot erase that past, or the lies that you told to my father."

On hearing this, Miles advanced into the room where Rose was facing Attercliffe.

"Yes, leave us both," he said, "at once. I can't call you out, for I want no further scandal to hurt her, either for what you did eight years ago, or for what you are doing now. Just go. Nothing that you can say can ever be sufficient reparation for what you did."

The face Attercliffe turned on him was one of shame.

"I truly meant what I said—and my offer to Miss Charlton."

"So you say. But your word has been shown to be worthless. Do not try to defend yourself—you have no defence."

Attercliffe opened his mouth, but, faced with Miles's implacable gaze, he hung his head and walked out of the room. But before he left he said, his voice shaking, "I shall never forget you, Rose."

Rose, who had stood proud and firm during the whole dreadful encounter, once Attercliffe had gone, sank down, shivering, on to a sofa. "You heard?"

"Nearly every word, I think. Oh, Rose, why, once I came to know you, did I ever doubt you?"

"Everyone doubted me, so that was no surprise. The surprise would have been if anyone had believed me. Even my father and my grandfather thought that I had been Attercliffe's willing accomplice—so why should you be different?"

"You rightly shame me by what you say. You must, however, understand that since I have come to know you I have also come to believe that the woman I have begun to love could not have behaved as gossip—and Oliver Fenton—said."

She said wearily, "I could defend myself, tell you that Oliver Fenton was mistaken, but I shall not do so. It never answered in the past, so why should it answer now?"

It had taken, she thought, Attercliffe's confession of his guilt to convince Miles of her honesty—and, for the moment, that was not enough. She had come to love him, but after her encounter with Attercliffe all that she wanted, nay, all that she needed, was to be alone.

"Please leave me, Sir Miles Heyward. I wish to be solitary."

Her use of his full name cut Miles to the quick. He had wanted to comfort her, but he could see that she did not want to be comforted, by him—or by anyone.

"You ought not to be alone," he said at last, "not after

that encounter with Attercliffe, following on Scriven's appalling behaviour.''

"I am tired," Rose told him, "of everyone around me knowing what is best for me. For once allow me to be the judge of that. It is surely not too much for me to ask."

Miles thought that she was wrong, but he could also see that she was at the end of her strength and, if he pushed too hard, he feared that she might break down completely; he was not sure what consequences might flow from that.

"Very well, if that is what you wish."

"I do wish—and reflect, you must not be found here alone with me."

"I will go, Rose, but believe me, this is not my last word. Tomorrow, when you have recovered from the shocks of today, you might think differently when we talk again."

"Perhaps."

Rose turned her face away from him. All that she wanted was to sleep, to forget, to try to heal herself, and she could not do that until she had returned to Morton Castle. She could only imagine what Isabel and Anthony might have to say to her on the journey back. She would not, she vowed, try to justify herself. Attercliffe's confession had come too late to help her. She remembered that he had boasted to her father that he had made her his willing mistress on their journey north to try to persuade him to be allowed to marry her and thus save her reputation.

"After all, she will become Lady Attercliffe," he had said, "and that is no mean thing."

She had protested her innocence, but in vain. Tonight she must try to forget the past, and tomorrow…well, what she would do tomorrow would be quite another thing—as Sir Miles Heyward would discover.

Miles bowed to her and left. He had at last acknowledged to himself that he loved her and that meant that he must at all costs protect her. But it also meant that he must leave her at once, since to badger her further would be cruel. He returned to the party by the backstairs so that no one should know that he had visited her in her room. The ball had begun. He sat in a corner, away from everyone, and watched the others enjoying themselves while he worked out exactly how he would propose to Rose after breakfast in the morning.

She had been right to turn him away, he decided. It would have been wrong, as well as tactless of him, to offer for her immediately after Scriven had insulted her and Attercliffe had badgered her with his unwanted proposal.

Tomorrow, he hoped, would be another day.

Chapter Five

The breakfast room at Morton Castle was empty when Miles walked in early on the following morning. It was a dark and sombre day and his valet had informed him that the locals believed that snow was on the way. "Which is only proper at Christmas, they say."

He helped himself to some of the food laid out on the sideboard and allowed the butler to pour him a cup of coffee, although he had never felt less like eating or drinking. A few guests strolled in while he struggled through his meal, but Rose was not among them. He fetched himself another plateful and drank yet another cup of coffee, but he might as well have been eating and drinking straw and water.

He noted that during their absence the previous day the staff at the Castle had decked the room—and presumably the other rooms—with Christmas trimmings, mostly holly, ivy, mistletoe and bowls of Christmas roses. Only his own Rose was absent, and this was a surprise since, like himself, she usually came down early.

Perhaps he had missed her because she had come down even earlier than usual and was either in the library or had returned to her room. He threw down his napkin and set off to find her.

She wasn't in the library. That, too, was empty. The newspapers laid out on the tables were undisturbed. Most people were sleeping late after the previous day's merrymaking. He ran upstairs and tapped on the door of her suite. There was no answer. He rapped again. Still silence.

Nothing for it, but to enter. The suite was as empty as the library had been with no sign that Rose had ever been there.

Suppressing an oath, Miles ran downstairs. Was it possible that she had left Morton Castle? Surely not, the hour was still early—and where would she be going on Christmas Eve of all times? Home, of course, you nodcock! What was there to keep her here? Not even Sir Miles Heyward, apparently.

He might be wrong, but he feared not. At the bottom of the stairs he met a distracted Isabel waving a letter in the air.

"Do you know where Miss Charlton may be?" he asked her.

Isabel moaned back at him. "You may well ask. Anthony had occasion to speak to her about last night's little nonsense on the way home. It was, of course, his duty. And just now, I found this pushed under my bedroom door," and she waved the letter, at him this time.

"She has written that since she has become an embarrassment to us, she would be doing us a kindness if she departed for home immediately, leaving us to enjoy our Christmas in peace."

"Her home is in Nottinghamshire, is it not?"

"North of Mansfield, not far from Newstead Abbey."

"Thank you. You will excuse me if I leave you, too."

"Leave Morton Castle and us, you mean?"

"Indeed. Present my compliments to Anthony, and tell him that I cannot allow Miss Charlton to travel home on Christmas Eve without a proper escort when snow is forecast. I intend to follow her, and when I find her I shall ask her to marry me."

"But whatever will Anthony say, either to you chasing after her or to you marrying her, since her reputation has now been ruined for good?"

"What he might have to say is of no matter to me, nor to Miss Charlton either. May I bid you the kind of Christmas you both deserve. Now, I must leave you—I have no time to waste."

He gave the startled and offended Isabel no opportunity to answer him but tore back up the stairs at top speed to find his valet and order him to start packing immediately, and to send a message to the servants' hall telling his followers to prepare to leave on the instant. He could not lose her now.

Rose's chaise stopped suddenly. It had begun to snow about an hour ago, lightly at first and now a little more heavily. What could be wrong? She was uneasily aware that dashing along the York to London road on Christmas Eve might not have been the most commonsensical thing to do.

John Coachman was rapping on the window in the door. She opened it.

"What is it, John?"

"Beg pardon, Miss Rose, but I think that we ought to stop at the next post-house. The weather is getting rapidly worse. We don't want to be stranded on the road with no means of going backwards or forwards."

She had wanted to be as far away from Morton Castle and from everyone in it as soon as possible, but she could not ignore John's worried face. "Very well. Do you know which one it is?"

"It's a good way yet, I fear. If the weather worsens and we can't reach it, there's an inn not much further along called the Gate Hangs Well, which we could stop at in a pinch. The horses could rest there overnight and be fit for the morning. If the weather improves, that is."

"I leave it to your judgement, John."

"Aye," he grunted back at her. If he had been allowed to use his own judgement back at Morton Castle he would not have started out in such unpromising weather at all, but Miss

Rose had been firm that she wanted to leave immediately, and there had been no gainsaying her.

Rose leaned back against the cushions. It was cold in the chaise and her maid had begun to shiver. The worst of it was that she was beginning to regret giving in to an impulse which had seemed reasonable enough in the early hours of the day. Not only that, her treacherous heart kept reminding her that she was also leaving behind Miles Heyward.

Why could she not stop thinking about him? Now that her anger against Attercliffe had died away she was thinking of Miles more and more. Would she ever see him again? Never before had a man touched her frozen heart so deeply that it had started to melt.

On meeting him again at Morton Castle she had felt nothing but dislike for him because of her memory of their first encounter when he had accused her of leading Oliver Fenton on and then dropping him. Slowly, though, the more she saw of Miles, the more she had become attracted to him, and it soon became plain that, despite her doubtful reputation, he was also becoming attracted to her.

Yesterday he had defended her stoutly, and after that he had wanted to help her when she had been so distressed after her meeting with Attercliffe. Nothing could come of it, she knew, for she could not allow him to propose marriage to her. It would not be right for him to saddle himself with a wife whom no one would receive. It was that, as much as anything else, which had made her decide to leave Morton Castle at such breakneck speed.

She had to hope that he would forget her, although she knew that she would never forget him. It was not the cold which was causing her to shiver, but the thought of the empty life ahead of her.

Anthony Morton had come out to the stables to try to persuade Miles not to follow Rose.

"No good can come of it," he had said earnestly. "Wherever you go, scenes such as that yesterday will be sure to follow her. I cannot say that I am other than relieved that she has chosen to take herself off.''

Miles had shown Anthony his teeth. ''And have you asked Major Scriven to take himself off?'' he demanded. ''After all, it was his drunken folly that started the scenes to which you refer.''

Anthony's silence told him everything.

''I see that you have not. Forgive me, if I leave without further adieux. I need to be on the road if I am to catch Rose before dark and the coming snow storm slow me down.''

With that he jumped into his chaise and was gone. He had left behind a friendship in ruins but, since the friendship appeared to be worth nothing, he could not regret that, but only mourn the kind and jolly fellow which Anthony Morton had once been.

The road south from York was soon reached. Shortly after that the promised snow started to fall. It would serve to slow Rose down and he might hope to catch her up sooner than he could have expected. On the other hand, there was always the chance that her carriage had met with an accident in the storm and ended up in a ditch.

The very thought of it nearly unhinged him. He had to tell himself to show a little common sense and not behave like a terror-stricken maiden lady or a new recruit on the battle-field. He must not worry so much that he missed her while he worked himself into a near-syncope.

He stopped at two post-houses, but there was no sign of her chaise at either of them. Some little distance before he reached the third the snow had become stronger than ever, and it was only by chance that, staring out of the window, he saw Rose's chaise drawn up in the entrance to the yard of a small inn.

The Gate Hangs Well, the creaking sign said. Miles did not need to order his driver to stop, the worsening weather achieved that. He halted before the inn's front door—a light had already been lit beside it—and leaped out. He had found Rose, and, by God, he was going to ask her what the devil she thought she was doing running away from him in this foul weather.

And if that was not quite what the spirit of Christmas ought to be, be damned to it. She had given him such a fright that it would take him some time to recover his equilibrium because what he really wanted to do was first to tell her what he thought of her for leaving him behind and then to kiss her senseless!

Rose was in the inn parlour asking the landlady if she could provide her and her small staff with nuncheon when Miles burst in.

He was all enraged male animal. "What in thunder did you think that you were doing when you set out on such a long journey in foul weather, and on Christmas Eve too?"

Rose stared haughtily back at him. What kind of welcome was that when she had spent her entire morning mooning after him?

"I was not aware, Sir Miles Heyward, that I had to ask your permission before undertaking either a journey or anything else." Her voice was frosty but her eyes shot sparks at him.

"I can understand your wishing to leave Morton Castle behind, but not why you should leave me—and without a word of farewell, too," he fired back at her.

The landlady, who had stood by helpless, now took a hand. "Do you wish me to have this gentleman removed, miss?"

"No," exclaimed Rose and Miles together.

"No," repeated Miles. "Do you really mean that 'no', Rose?"

"Yes—no—I don't know," returned Rose idiotically. The landlady threw her eyes to heaven, before turning to more earthly matters.

"Do you intend to lodge here for the night, sir?" she asked Miles. "And would you and your staff be requiring a meal?"

"If that is possible,"

"We have just enough rooms left to accommodate you if your staff is not too large."

"So your husband told me when I arrived," Miles said, beginning to regret the mixture of rage and relief which had caused him to storm at Rose when he had first seen her. Not that it seemed to have distressed her. The colour had returned to her cheeks for the first time since she had arrived at Morton Castle and she appeared only too ready and willing to spit defiance at him.

What he didn't know was that when he had walked through the door the mere sight of him had been enough to raise Rose's spirits immensely. She had not really thought that he might follow her when she had decided on her headlong flight from the Mortons and all that they stood for. After all, she had refused his kind offer of assistance on the previous day and then had disappeared without a word of farewell to him—so what did his sudden reappearance tell her?

She hardly dared to think. Instead she said to the landlady, who was asking her whether she wished to eat her nuncheon with Sir Miles or did she want to take it alone in her room, "Of course, you may serve us together—if Sir Miles wishes that, too."

"Of course I wish it," Miles told her roughly, and assured the woman that he had every intention of sharing his meal with Miss Charlton.

Once she had gone to carry out their orders, he told Rose in no uncertain terms what his feelings for her were. "You don't think I've driven like a madman all the way along the York to London road in order to eat alone when I can eat with you. Besides, I have more than one bone to pick with you," he added, for the anxiety he had felt for her during the drive was still burning within him.

"You mean besides the bones that the landlady might bring us for our nuncheon?" Rose returned naughtily.

"You know perfectly well what I mean. I'm tired of logic chopping, nit-picking and all the nonsense I have had to put up with from you ever since I arrived in Yorkshire." And before she could stop him he pulled her into his arms in order to begin the long-delayed task of kissing her senseless.

For Rose it was like coming home, or the arrival of spring after a long winter, or... And then thought stopped altogether. Thank God, he had come after her—what a fool she had been to believe that he might have been toying with her to help him to endure a rather dull holiday. She shuddered at the thought that her folly might have meant that she had lost him altogether.

Miles suddenly pulled away from her, gasping. The sweet smell of her, her softness in his hard arms and his hard body and his hard... No, stop that! It was bad enough losing his self-control as he had just done without his wretched mind urging his body on into even further excesses in a semi-public place.

"Witch!" he said thickly. "What do you do to me?"

"Who, me?" Rose asked him, her expression wicked. "Correct me if I am mistaken, but I believe that it was you who set about me so cavalierly and not I who assaulted you!"

"Aye, that's the nub of it," he exclaimed. "How am I going to keep my hands off you while we're closeted in this doll's house of an inn, in a room where anyone can come in at any moment?"

"Well, we could try behaving ourselves," Rose told him. "It might help if you sat on one side of the fire and I on the other—at a safe distance, that is."

"I'll attempt to oblige you," Miles muttered, falling into the chair she was pointing at, "but I might find it rather difficult. Now what the devil's up?" he exclaimed as the noise of a loud argument began outside, to be ended only by the slamming of the inn's front door.

Rose had no time to answer him for the landlady had returned with what she called the bill of fare, which was a
grubby sheet with the names of some dishes scrawled on it.

"Forgive the recent uproar," she told them, "only some
folk won't take no for an answer."

Rose and Miles were too engrossed in trying to decipher
the so-called bill of fare to ask her to enlarge on her explanation.

"We'll have the lot," Miles finally told her, "and choose
what we want when you bring it in. You may serve us a
glass of Madeira each to pass the time while we wait. You
would like a glass, wouldn't you, Rose?"

Rose had reached the point where she would have agreed
with everything he said. She could think of nothing more
agreeable than sitting with him before a roaring fire, drinking
Madeira—or anything else he chose to order.

And so the day wore on. After their meal they remained
in the inn parlour and talked—and how they talked. Miles
had not proposed to her, but was behaving, Rose thought,
rather blearily—the glass of Madeira had become two—as
though he had.

He told her of his ambition to retire to the country and
experiment with animals and plants. Rose told him that the
Charlton estate in Nottinghamshire was run by an agent who
had been talking of doing that very thing.

"It's the plants which interest me the most," she told him.

"Excellent," he said, "since it's the animals which I wish
to experiment with."

It was as though, in throwing off the shackles of conform-
ity which had bound them at Morton Castle, they had discovered their true selves. Their ease with one another was
remarkable. Miles had discarded all his suspicions about
Rose's supposed dubious past and Rose was coming to know
the man behind the rather brusque mask which Miles adopted
in company where he was not entirely at ease.

"My estate in Nottinghamshire is well run," she told him,

"but I don't think that my agent, Earnshaw, has much interest in improving the nature of the livestock on it. Grandfather started to carry out some experiments not long before he died, but Earnshaw discontinued them after that."

She did not say that if he married her, Miles would not need to buy an estate. They could settle on hers and they could join together in restarting her grandfather's work. That would have to wait until he—or if he—proposed to her. She was unaware that he was still delaying because he did not wish her to feel that he was bullying her into submitting to him. It was plain to Miles that in her short life Rose had already had to endure a great deal of coercion of a most unpleasant nature. What made it worse was that it had been caused by Attercliffe's lies about her. Nor did he wish her to compare him with Attercliffe, who had kidnapped her and lied about her.

So he kept their conversation light and, in the words of a long-dead poet, they talked the sun down the sky—not that there was much sun outside on the afternoon of December 24th. The wind had got up and the snow had begun to fall more heavily to the degree that if it went on they both thought that they might be stranded at the inn for more than one day.

Before they retired for the night they walked to the window for one last look at the bleak landscape. Snow covered everything but at last it had stopped falling, the moon and stars had come out and the entire world seemed to be in the grip of a deadly cold.

Rose shivered at the sight. "Thank goodness John Coachman urged me to stop. What would it be like to be caught outside in this with nowhere to go?"

Miles nodded agreement. "Best not to think about it."

When, finally, the time came for them to retire, they decided to do so separately—for propriety's sake.

"Although, stranded here far from family, friends, and gossip," Miles said, "who is to know what we are doing?"

"We do," said Rose smartly. She had already lost her reputation once, and she thought that twice might be one time too many. So Jennie, her maid, a candle in her hand, lighted her way upstairs, leaving Miles to retire later.

A fire in a small grate was burning in her bedroom, but it was still cold. A warming pan had been put in the bed, though, with Rose's nightgown around it.

"It's still very cold in here," Rose said, "but it's better than being stranded on the road, eh, Jennie?"

Jennie nodded, "Or hiding in the barn next to the stables since all the rooms in the inn are full, like those two poor devils the landlord turned away because our parties had already taken them. Not that he knows that they've discovered refuge there—that is, if they haven't gone on to find somewhere better. One of the grooms said that they were travelling in a cart which lost a wheel not long before they reached the inn."

Rose, who had been pulling her shoes off, began to put them on again, saying, "Are you telling me the truth? If so, why should not we make room for them? I'm sure that Sir Miles would agree with me."

How could she possibly go to sleep in comfort knowing that two poor souls might be shivering in the barn at the far end of the yard?

Jennie looked doubtful. Rose, her shoes now on, picked up the shawl that she had discarded.

"Do you know which room Sir Miles is in, Jennie?"

"His valet said he's in the one opposite to yours."

"Wait here," Rose ordered, "I need to talk to him immediately," and she walked across the corridor to rap on Miles's door.

It was opened by his valet, Blagg. A surprised look crossed his face when he saw that the visitor was Rose.

"I wonder if I might speak to your master?"

"I'll ask him," Blagg said, and retreated inside. A moment

later Miles appeared. He was in his shirt sleeves, and had stripped off his cravat.

"What's the matter, Rose? You look worried."

She hesitated. What would he make of what she was about to propose? Suppose he refused to help her, what would she do then?

"Could I come into your room? I don't want to talk about this in the corridor."

"Certainly, but for form's sake Blagg ought to remain with us."

"Very well."

Once in Miles's bedroom, in defiance of all the proprieties which governed the world of upper-class single women, and which she had so recently cited, Rose's fears and doubts disappeared.

"Miles, I have just discovered that the noise which we heard this afternoon must have been caused by two travellers being turned away from the inn because between us we had taken all the rooms. Now Jennie tells me that their cart had broken down before they reached the inn. She believes that they may be spending the night in the barn, without food or warmth, in this terrible weather. I know that if we had been informed that two poor travellers were being turned away, on foot, on a night like this, we would have ordered them to be given one of our rooms. Jennie and I could have shared mine."

"Surely," Miles agreed, "common humanity would have dictated that—but what do you propose that we do about it now?"

"That, if you would come with me, we ought to visit the barn to find out whether they are still there, and, if so, ask the landlord to arrange matters as I have already suggested."

Miles, regardless of Blagg's presence, put an arm around her and kissed her gently on the cheek. "I will go, but I don't think that you ought to accompany me. It is very cold outside and the stable-yard is not a fit place for a lady."

"Oh, but I must. Think, it's my fault, even more than yours, that the inn is full. If I hadn't gone haring down the road home like a mad thing, you wouldn't have followed me, the inn would have been empty and the landlord would have been only too happy to accommodate them. I must try to help them—in common humanity—as you have just said."

"Very well, but only if you go back to your room, put on some stout shoes and a warm coat, and join me here in a few minutes when I have had time to arm myself against the winter's cold."

"You don't think I'm refining too much on this?" Rose asked, turning at the door to look earnestly at him. "But I couldn't sleep knowing that some poor unfortunates were out there, almost dying of cold because of me."

Miles crossed the room to put both arms around her this time and kiss her gently again. "No, I don't. It does you nothing but credit to think about others when it is quite plain to me that so few have ever thought about you. While I think of it, put on a scarf too, if you have one."

How practical he was, Rose thought happily when she joined him again. While Jennie had been finding her warm clothes and helping her into them, the Waits had arrived and were standing outside the front of the inn, serenading the small crowd in the bar with the carol "God rest you merry, gentlemen!"

So they, too, were serenaded all the way downstairs and out into the inn yard. They were each carrying a candle in case they needed light. They met no one on the way because all the inn servants, including the landlord and his wife, and their own staff, apart from Blagg and Jennie, were listening to the Waits—and drinking with them, too.

"Perhaps we ought to have spoken to the landlord about what we propose to do," Rose said to Miles as they walked out of the back door.

He shook his head. "If there is no one in the barn then we should look foolish. If they are there, then we can arrange for them to be housed in the inn—and, again in common humanity, they can scarcely refuse us.''

Once they were outside the singing grew faint when they moved further into the yard. As they had hoped, it was empty of people. Their chaises were drawn up, waiting for the morning when their owners would be able to travel on. The stables were full of their horses.

Rose began to fear that they were on a wild goose chase and that she had brought Miles down with her for nothing. She almost began to tell him so, but decided to wait until they had inspected the barn.

The doors to it were shut. Miles opened them. It was a good thing that she had asked him to help her, Rose thought, because she could not have opened them on her own. He left them apart so that the moonlight could flood in to the opening at least, but the far end of the barn was lost in darkness. The flickering light of their candles barely pierced the gloom. Nothing moved, but they could hear rustling coming from the corner furthest away from them.

Miles walked forward, his candle held high, and called out, ''Ho, there, if anyone is taking shelter here, answer me. Know that we come in friendship in order to help, not harm, you.''

For a moment nothing stirred, and then a shadowy form walked towards them. It proved to be a man of middling size, decently dressed in the clothes of an artisan.

''Do you speak truly?'' he asked. ''You are not here to turn us away?''

''No, indeed,'' Rose said. ''We have come to offer you a room and a bed in the inn. I understood that there were two of you. Where is the other one?''

The man gave a half-sob. ''The other one is my wife and, although she is not yet near her time, we fear that she is about to give birth.''

Rose swept past Miles, exclaiming, ''Give birth! Where is she?''

The man waved an arm towards the corner. "Over there. I have made her a makeshift bed to keep her warm, but I fear the cold may yet kill her if the coming bairn does not."

Miles behind her, Rose ran over to where the woman was lying on a crude bed whose mattress was a pile of straw and whose blankets were her and her husband's threadbare coats.

"I dare not leave her," the man said, "even to fetch anything from our cart that might help her. It lost a wheel back on the road. I was fearful that the child might be born while I was gone. It is our first."

Rose, after handing the man her candle, sank to her knees beside the woman, took her cold hand in her own warm one and began to chafe it gently. The woman was young and had doubtless once been pretty, but her face was now the colour of clay. She was moaning and shivering as the cold and the pangs of birth had their way with her. She looked up at Rose and tried to smile.

Rose said gently to her, "You must not worry any more. We have come to take you indoors where you may be warm again and your baby may be born in comfort."

She said to Miles over her shoulder, "She needs to be taken up to my room immediately, and a doctor or a midwife sent for—if there are either in the village, that is. Can you carry her between you?"

"But what will the landlady say?" asked the man hesitantly.

Rose said grimly, "She had better not say anything."

Behind her Miles gave a stifled laugh. Aloud he said, looking at the white-faced husband, "By the look of you both, you haven't had a decent meal today. If you would like me to carry her I'll gladly do so."

"I should be most grateful if you would, sir. I wouldn't like to drop her."

Miles handed his candle to him, saying, "If you will hold that for me, I will take your wife to Miss Charlton's room. By the by, I am Sir Miles Heyward, and if you would be so good as to tell me your name, I shall be able to address you properly.''

''I am Walter Harshaw, Sir Miles, and it is most kind of you and Miss Charlton to help us just as I was beginning to fear that neither of us, nor the bairn when it came, would last the night.''

''It is Christmastide, Mr Harshaw,'' Miles told him, ''and it behoves us to behave as Christians ought to, and do our duty by our fellow men. Now, if you and Miss Charlton will light the way for me, I shall endeavour to carry your wife into the inn and upstairs to her bedroom as gently as possible. After that we shall try to find someone to help her to give birth.''

Rose lit the way for them. Walter Harshaw picked up the overcoats and a small sack containing the rest of their belongings while Miles lifted up his wife and cradled her in his strong arms.

They walked through the yard to the strains of yet another carol and the drunken singing of the patrons of the inn. This time it was ''While shepherds watched their flocks by night''. Once they reached the bottom of the stairs, Rose put down her candle.

''I'm off to the bar,'' she told the two men, ''to tell the landlord and his wife to do *their* Christian duty by giving the Harshaws suitable accommodation, and to try to discover whether a doctor or a midwife is available to help Mr Harshaw's wife give birth.''

''No, Rose,'' Miles called to her, ''wait for me. It is not proper for you to go into the bar on your own.''

''Then damn propriety,'' Rose snorted back at him. ''By the look of her, Mrs Harshaw might give birth at any moment.'' And she shot off towards the bar to do her part in bringing relief from fear for a pair of travellers who had hitherto found no help and no kindness—not even at Christmas.

Chapter Six

Miles had known that it was useless to try to argue with Rose. She had a mind and will of her own and it was one of the reasons why he had come to love her.

Miles lowered Mrs Harshaw into Rose's bed where he and Jennie tried to make her comfortable. Her husband he told to sit in a chair by it while he went downstairs to add his voice to Rose's. He did not need to trouble himself. He had scarcely reached the top of the stairs before Rose reappeared, the landlady panting behind her.

"I've sent one of the lads to fetch the doctor from the village. He shouldn't be long in coming. If I had known that the poor young woman was expecting, I wouldn't have turned them away."

Well, that is what she is saying now to excuse herself, thought Rose, but said nothing aloud, since once the gentry had intervened on behalf of the poor travellers nothing was too good for them. Miles ordered food and ale for Mr Harshaw and warm milk for his poor wife who was now visibly and audibly in the later stages of labour.

It was Rose and Jennie who went downstairs with the landlady to collect some food and extra blankets. It was Rose who helped Mrs Harshaw to drink her milk and held her hand and tried to comfort her while Jennie wiped her face with a warm cloth. She and Jennie undressed Mrs Harshaw and helped her into one of Rose's nightgowns, and tore up one of her petticoats to swaddle the baby in when it was born.

After that they waited for the doctor, and it was he, when he walked into the bedroom and was told the whole sad story, who remarked drily, "Found in the barn, were they? How appropriate at Christmastide."

From then on he said little. Miles and the woman's worried husband were banished from the room while Rose and Jennie were left to be amateur midwives. Rose was a little troubled about Jennie's being present at the birth, but that sturdy young woman told her, "No need to worry about me, Miss Rose. I saw three of my little brothers and sisters born and helped at the birth of the last one. There aren't any secrets in a cottage."

Midnight passed before, after a short but difficult labour, a tiny girl burst into the world. The doctor handed her to Rose, who had tied a towel over her elegant dress and now swathed the little creature in the petticoat that she had prepared earlier before handing her to Jennie to hold.

Jennie, stroking the baby's dark head, reverted to the speech of her childhood, saying, "What me feyther always told me about birthing babies, Miss Rose, turned out to be true: 'You only 'ave to catch 'em. God and Nature do the job for you!'"

She handed the baby back to Rose, who sank into the room's one armchair and looked down in wonderment at the baby girl's scarlet face, at her tiny starfish-like hands. Never mind that from the moment of birth the little creature had been bawling its anger at being born at all, and at having to leave the safe haven of its mother's body, her presence was a small miracle—as is all birth.

So entranced was she that it took the doctor's order to her, to hand the baby to its mother so that she might feed it now

that he had done everything he could for her, to break her
trance.

Mrs Harshaw put the squalling child to her breast. Silence
fell. For the first time she had colour in her cheeks and it
was plain that, painful though the birth had been, its magic
was beginning to work on her.

"I thought that I heard yonder fine gentleman call you
Miss Rose when you came to rescue us. Is that your name,
m'lady?"

Rose agreed that it was.

"If you would be so kind, I would like you to permit me
to call my little girl Rose in your honour."

"No permission needed. It is you who would be honouring
me."

The doctor, who was washing his hands in a bowl of hot
water carried upstairs by the ever-busy Jennie, said, again in
his dry manner, "How apt: a Christmas Rose, no less. If the
Waits were still with us we could have had them celebrating
a birth on Christmas Day."

It was over. Rose went to fetch Mr Harshaw so that he
might see his wife and child and know that all was well. The
landlady had promised to move a palliasse and blankets into
what had been Rose's room so that he might sleep there.
Miles came, too, and was allowed to hold baby Rose for a
moment.

"Another Christmas Rose," he said, echoing the doctor,
when he handed the child back to her mother.

He kissed the smiling Rose on the cheek, saying, "Dear
girl, you were a tower of strength from when we first found
the Harshaws. No hysterics, plenty of common sense and a
willingness to do what you were told when the doctor arrived."

"And Jennie, don't forget Jennie. She was a tower of
strength as well. We took turns to run up and down the stairs
to fetch hot water when it was needed, and she heated up
some soup for the poor creature when her labour was over.

"It was most fortunate that we were in time to move the mother into the inn, and that Jennie had seen babies born and Grandfather had made me assist at the birth of foals as a good countrywoman ought!"

On that, Miles kissed her again. He had already promised Mr Harshaw a position as a farrier on his staff when he had learned that he had run out of work in his own small village and had been making for a town off the York road where he had heard that he might find employment.

Her long vigil might have ended, but astonishingly, Rose had never felt less like sleep as she informed Miles, who was still fully dressed although he had long since sent his valet to his own bed.

"Quite natural of you," he told her. "I was always in a similar state after battle. It is as though great excitement tunes the human body so that it is able to endure more and more of it."

"Like tuning a piano, or a harp," Rose suggested, "so that they will play well."

"Exactly. When it dies down you'll feel like sleeping for a week."

"So, in the meantime I must endure it."

"Yes."

Rose paced restlessly round his room to which they had retired, leaving the Harshaws in hers. "I am to share a room with Jennie," she said. "If she's in the same state, my restlessness won't disturb her. She will most likely be as excited as I am."

Miles shook his head at her. "While you were all busy with poor Mrs Harshaw, I leaned on the landlady. Blagg and I are to share a room in the attic, where impromptu beds have been set up. You will sleep here, and Jennie will have Blagg's original room, thus leaving the pair of you, who have done all of the hard work, to have rooms of your own."

Rose stopped pacing. "You mean that I am to sleep in your room; that I am turning you out?"

"At my request. A quiet room of your own is what you both deserve."

The excitement that had built up in Rose ever since Jennie had told her of the stranded pair in the barn increased. Miles had been only too ready to help her to rescue the travellers when many gentlemen might have disdained such a task. He had thrown off the trappings of his class and had helped the poor artisan and his wife and spoken to them as kindly and courteously as though they had been gentry.

"What do you think that you deserve, Sir Miles Heyward?"

"I? I deserve very little. It was you who started this whole business and have been on your feet all night, not I."

"So, what do I deserve, then? Nothing but a cold, lonely bed?"

Excitement bred recklessness, Rose was discovering. Why should she not have what she most wanted? She had spent several hard hours dealing with the result of love and passion and, far from putting her off both emotions, it had had the effect of making her want to experience them to the full. And if the result should be a child, then what could be better than to hold her own in her arms instead of someone else's?

For once Miles was puzzled. "What are you trying to tell me, Rose?"

"This. That since everyone believes that I am already ruined—even though I wasn't—I don't see why I shouldn't be ruined in earnest. Regardless of whether you wish to marry me or not, dear Miles, I should be delighted if you would consent to ruin me tonight."

Miles said hoarsely, "You can't mean it, Rose."

"Of course I do. I have no intention of ever again entering what is called good society, and if you don't wish to oblige me I shall retire to my country estate to live and die there as an eccentric old maid."

"Good God," exclaimed Miles. "We can't have that. But

before I set about ruining you I ought to propose to you, to make it legal before the fact—or should it be afterwards?''

"Such niceties of English grammar are beyond me tonight," replied Rose grandly. "But by all means propose to me first—if that would make you happy."

He went down on one knee before her.

"Dear Rose, my Christmas Rose, marry me and put me out of *my* misery so that I shan't live and die a crusty old bachelor no one would want to know. As pledge or token of my love for you I offer you this," and he pulled his signet ring from the little finger of his left hand.

"Pray accept it, and say that you will marry me as soon as it can be arranged."

"Of course I will marry you, my dearest Miles. I love you so much and I feared that I had lost my chance with you after I so foolishly ran away early this morning—or is it now early yesterday morning?"

"Indeed, you had not lost me, although it was only when I learned that you had left Morton Castle without telling me that you were going that I realised how deep was my love for you."

He stood up and added, "Now give me your *left* hand, Rose."

Smiling, Rose held it out to him.

He took it and slipped the ring on her thumb, murmuring, "Rose Charlton, with this ring I do thee wed. And, since such a declaration when made by our forefathers meant that we were considered to be legally married, you may come to bed with me tonight, not to be ruined but to consummate our joint love. Let the lawyers and the priest marry us again as soon as I can obtain a special licence."

"And I, Rose Charlton, do take thee, Miles Heyward, to be my lawfully wedded husband, and now, if you can no longer ruin me, bless me in the marriage bed instead."

"Willingly, my love, willingly."

Rose flew into his arms. "Now I need never go lonely to bed again!"

Miles picked her up and carried her to his bed. "If I could do this for Harshaw's wife," he said, "then I can certainly do it for my own."

"Thank you," Rose said, kissing him on the cheek before he laid her carefully down. "I can't wait to find out what being ruined—or being a wife—is really like. Imagination can only take one so far."

"True," said Miles. "I'll try not to be too impetuous, but I've waited for so long to do this, you'll have to forgive me if I go too fast for you. I've wanted to make love to you ever since I first saw you in London and believed you to be Oliver Fenton's betrayer. I immediately burned to take you to bed and betray you myself—in revenge for him, I told myself! I should not have trusted Oliver; good friend though he is, I should have remembered that he's given greatly to exaggeration." He smiled ruefully. "I think that my anger with you when we met again was really anger at myself for wanting a known ladybird. I only lost it when I came to know you better."

Rose's loss was her clothes: she was soon as naked as Mother Eve. Their disappearance was accompanied by sighing, stroking and kissing—some on parts of her body, Rose found, of which no lady ever spoke. It was these which had the greatest effect on her.

She obligingly helped Miles to turn himself into Adam before the Fall—to discover that his body was even more magnificent unclothed. What almost frightened her was her first sight of a fully roused man—except that she had the most extraordinary desire to stroke him there, but refrained, until later on in their loving, he said thickly, "Touch me there, Rose, as I have touched you."

Which she promptly did—to learn that, in the height of their passion, he seemed to be as abandoned to everything as she was. She was well aware that what they were doing was no new thing for him, even if it was for her, and had consequently had expected him to be more in control than she was, but no such thing. Instead, he suddenly seized her stroking hand and muttered, "No more, Rose, no more, you are ready for me now, so I must be ready for you. I shall try not to hurt you."

His words had the most powerful effect on Rose: she felt a sudden rush of joy. He must truly think her to be virgin, despite all the *on-dits* and rumours that he had heard and had originally believed.

She lifted her arms and clasped him to her the harder, saying, "Oh, Miles, I love you so," and as she spoke he entered her for the first time. Rose choked back the inevitable pain and bore it valiantly until, without warning, pain turned into pleasure and for the first time she experienced the delight of total and complete union with the beloved as Miles joined her in her ecstasy.

Afterwards, exhausted by their loving, and their long day, they lay quiet in one another's arms.

Rose sighed. Miles raised himself on his elbow.

"No regrets, I hope, nor too much pain either. I should not have been so swift with you…"

"Neither," said Rose, turning her head into his broad chest. "And you?"

"Who, I? Not at all." He did not tell her that to find her virgin, as she had always claimed to be, had been for him his most crowning moment during their love-making. He was her first love, no doubt about that, and for the strong man he was, it was almost humbling for him, in more ways than one.

"I shall not make love to you again tonight," he whispered. "We have had a hard day and you must be allowed to rest after your initiation into married pleasure."

After that Miles rolled her on to her side, and put an arm around her, whereat Rose promptly took his hand. His last words to her, before the deep sleep after such great ecstasy overtook them, were, "If tonight were to result in a child, how would you feel?"

"Delighted," she whispered back sleepily. "To have both a birth and a conception take place on Christmas Day would be a fine thing, would it not? Of all the seasons of the year Christmastide is the best one for us to celebrate renewal and birth since it is the time when winter begins to die so that spring may be born. As Christ was born on Christmas Day, and the Harshaws' baby girl."

After that, they slept.

Miles was the first to wake on Christmas Day morning and Rose's last words to him still echoed in his head. He rose from the bed, gently, trying not to disturb her. They had rolled a little apart while they slept. For the first time since he had met her again he thought that the tranquillity on her sleeping face told a true story: it could not have been assumed to enable her to face the world.

He pulled on his night-shirt, which still lay where Blagg had left it, walked across to the window and drew the curtains a little. Outside the sun was shining. Water was dripping from the eaves of buildings: a thaw had obviously set in. With luck they could be on their way south after they had broken their fast.

"Miles," said a sleepy voice from the bed. "I feared that you might have left me."

He moved over to sit by her.

"Not I. I would not desert you after last night."

"I shall have to desert you," Rose murmured. "Whatever will Jennie think if she comes to wake me and finds that I have not been in my own bed all night? I don't wish to shock her."

Miles began to laugh. "I don't think you're in any danger of doing that. I have to tell you that I believe that she and Blagg have been sharing a bed back at Morton Castle—and probably last night, too. From something Blagg said to me I fancy that there will be two weddings being celebrated when we marry, not one.''

Rose remembered what Jennie had said about there being no secrets in a cottage the night before.

''All the same,'' she said, ''I feel that I ought to leave you before she does arrive. And I ought to look in on the Harshaws as well and see how the mother and the child are faring. Before I go, I must tell you that I've been thinking about our future.''

''Have you, indeed, Lady Heyward? And here I was thinking that you were sleeping.''

''You woke me. I know that you hardly made a sound, but I knew that you had gone all the same. The bed suddenly felt empty. But that is not to the point. The thing is I have been thinking that now that we are married, you have no need to buy a landed estate. My own is large enough for us both to experiment with—me with the plants and you with the animals. If we need a larger one, later on, that would be a different thing, of course.''

Miles bent over and kissed her. The temptation to make love to her again was strong, but he thought that it was much too soon after her initiation last night. She needed time to heal and they might have a long day ahead of them.

Instead, he said, ''I can see that I have a practical wife, not one who will expect to spend all her money on bonnets and dress.''

''Oh, I shall expect those, too,'' Rose said, teasing him a little after the way of happy lovers. ''And now I must leave you to dress and be ready for breakfast.''

''Before you go,'' Miles said, ''I trust that it is agreed that we leave together if the weather is fit for us to travel. I shall insist on escorting you all the way to your home. After that I shall go post-haste to London to obtain a special licence and return to make all the arrangements to be married in your parish church. We may have to delay the wedding a little for we must invite my mother and her husband to be present. Our public marriage must not be seen to be hugger-mugger.''

Rose thought that this news might please Dr Penrose, who had been so worried about her.

''You do not wish to return to your own home in London—or be married from there?''

''My own home?'' Miles shook his head. ''Since my mother remarried, I don't have a home, only a house which might as well be empty for all the pleasure I take in it. The bride should be married from her own home and, from what you have said, you have asked me to share it with you. My house is in London and I have no desire to live there ever again. We might pay a visit now and then, but otherwise I wish to be a countryman—as I believe that you wish to be a countrywoman. Is that so?''

Rose scrambled out of bed to begin pulling on her clothes which lay on the floor where they had been thrown in their haste to consummate their informal ''marriage'.

''That is my wish. I don't like London much, either. It's a nasty smelly place. Not that the country doesn't smell, too, but it's of the earth earthy—which is quite different.''

Miles gave her another kiss. ''Thank goodness for that. Do you think that we shall always agree with one another so heartily?''

''I doubt it,'' said Rose, ''but my hope is that we shall be friends as well as lovers.''

''Well said. Let us always bear that in mind.''

''There is another thing, dearest Miles,'' Rose said mischievously, ''which we ought also to bear in mind. If my manifest misconduct causes us not to be received by society, I know that we are sure to be besieged by our real friends who will visit us to confirm in their generous minds how well we are doing.''

Miles kissed her and said, ''Now, my darling Rose, don't take more than your share of opprobrium. I must admit that we have *both* been guilty of gross misconduct, so you may rest assured that those jealous friends who still harbour evil thoughts about us will descend on us to confirm that we are doing as badly as they always feared and hoped!''

''Splendid,'' exclaimed Rose. ''I can see that our future life will not be without its excitements. Speaking of future lives, ought we not to do something for the Harshaws?''

''As to that, I have already offered Harshaw a post on our staff. He says that he is a skilled farrier and a country household can always do with one—or more. Now that we intend to settle in Nottinghamshire we shall have to arrange for them to travel to your home as soon as Mrs Harshaw and the baby are fit to travel.''

It was Rose's turn to kiss him. ''What a splendid notion. We couldn't simply leave them here to fend for themselves— and you are right about farriers…they're always wanted in the country and I'm sure we can find him plenty of work.''

She was now fully dressed again, without Jennie's assistance, even if her clothes did bear the stains of last night's varied experiences.

''I'll see you at breakfast,'' he told her when they parted at the door, ''and then we must prepare to leave. The weather looks as though it has changed.''

''Fair weather.'' Rose smiled when she kissed him a temporary goodbye. It would not be long before there were no goodbyes for them. Together they were ready to travel into their new life, and what better time could they have in which to prepare for the future, and forget the past, than Christmas Day.

''Joy to the World'', the Waits were lustily singing outside the village church when at last they drove home with joy in their hearts as well.

Author Note

When my editor first asked me to write a Christmas short story she recommended that I focus on one of the de Burgh brothers, the seven bachelors who made their debut in *Taming the Wolf*. But having grown quite protective of these medieval knights, I protested that I wanted each one to have his own book. So she suggested that I write about the patriarch of the rowdy brood, the Earl of Campion himself. At first I was taken aback, having never envisioned a romance for the father of the seven strapping de Burgh boys. But I realised that Fawke de Burgh was one of the wisest and most appealing of my characters and, as such, deserving of his own love story. And the Christmas season, full of warm and wonderful traditions, even during the thirteenth century, provided just the setting.

To all those who have been following the de Burgh books, I hope you find this a worthy addition. And to those unfamiliar with the series, I hope you enjoy this introduction to the family as much as I enjoyed writing it.

Deborah Simmons

THE UNEXPECTED GUEST

Deborah Simmons

Chapter One

His sons were not coming home for Christmas.

Fawke de Burgh, Earl of Campion, stood with his hands clasped behind his back, facing the evidence that swirled before him. Alone in the solar, he had opened the shutters to one of the tall, narrow windows, only to be buffeted by a blast of chill air and its accompanying snow. The weather was worse than in living memory, and he could only shake his head at its fury. Travel during the winter was never easy, but no one would be fool enough to tackle the frozen roads in the week past, marked by a blizzard such as he had never seen. And Campion would not endanger his family simply to indulge a father's whimsy.

Still he could not deny his disappointment, for he had become accustomed to a Yuletide surrounded by his offspring. It was the only time they were all together these days, and Campion had yet to meet one son's wife and see his newest grandchild.

Perhaps the holiday would have been more bearable if so many were not away, but out of his seven sons, only two were here at Campion Castle, the most meager gathering yet. And although he loved them all, the earl knew that Stephen and Reynold were those least likely to cheer him. A clever lad, Stephen had so far squandered his talents in too much wine, while Reynold, cursed with a bad leg, went through life with a grimness that belied all his accomplishments.

With a sigh, the earl shifted, welcoming the bitter wind that reflected his mood. He had never expected all of his sons to stay at Campion, but neither had he thought so many would settle elsewhere. Who would take over when he was gone? His heir was Dunstan, but the eldest de Burgh was busy with his own demesne, in addition to his heiress wife's holdings. Both Geoffrey and Simon had recently taken wives and were content to live in the homes that marriage brought to them. Robin was overseeing one of Dunstan's properties in the south, and Nicholas, eager for new adventures, had joined him there.

Campion was proud of their achievements and their independence, and yet he knew a certain melancholy at their absence. Not only would he miss them, but the holiday itself would not be the same. Such celebrations were the venue of women, as Campion, who had buried two wives, knew well. In the past few years, Dunstan's lady had made sure the hall was decked in greenery and all the traditions observed, but without her, who would see to it?

They had managed to drag the Yule log inside during a break in the weather and, of course, there would be feasting, but who would take the time to make a Christmas bush and insist upon all the games and gifts and songs? Campion pictured himself stepping into the breach, but he could not rouse much enthusiasm for the prospect, especially since Stephen and Reynold would little appreciate his efforts.

The sound of footsteps made him lift his hands to the shutters. It would not do for the Earl of Campion to be seen mooning out the window like a dispirited lad. Worse yet, he did not care to have a servant hurrying to shut the cold away from him as if he were enfeebled. Lately he had noted a certain subtle fussing over him that did not sit well. He might not be as young as he once was, but he was lord here, and he could still hold his own against his knights, if not his brawny boys.

Campion's fingers stilled at the sight of dark movement among the swirling white outside, and he leaned closer, but the snow obscured his vision of the land below. Although it was probably nothing, he would send a man out to check the grounds, he decided, just as the sound of his steward's voice rose behind him.

"My lord! My lord! Ah, there you are! Have you seen them? Someone is at the gate, a small party, struggling against the elements."

Not a trick of the eye then, but arrivals in these conditions and so late in the day? It was nearly nightfall. "Let them in," Campion said. Closing the shutters, he turned even as he wondered who would be abroad so recklessly. If it were one of his sons, the earl's enthusiasm for the company of family would be tempered by dismay at such a misjudgment. But who else would be about? Certainly no enemy, even one foolish enough to attack the famous stronghold of Campion, would dare the elements, while pilgrims and anyone else with any sense would be inside.

Perhaps a messenger from court, he mused, but such missives were ill news more often than not, and he left the solar with a distinct sense of unease. Still he knew his duty, and he would welcome any traveler who braved this weather to reach the haven that was his home. He moved down the winding stairs into the great hall, where he gestured for a servant to light additional torches and called for food and lodging for those who would soon enter.

The steward, having delivered his message to a waiting knight, returned. "My lord Reynold has gone to meet them," he noted, and Campion knew that his son would see that those at the gate made it to the hall no matter what the conditions outside. Despite the leg that pained him—or perhaps because of it—Reynold's will was stronger than any of the others.

"Shall I have the hot, spiced wine brought out?" the steward asked, and Campion nodded, tamping down his annoyance at such mundane questions. When Dunstan's wife had lived at the castle, she had served as chatelaine and handled all the details of food and household so well that Campion missed her woman's touch.

In more ways than one, the earl thought, frowning at the thought of the Christmas ahead. Someone would have to place the holly and ivy and bay about the hall in celebration of the season. And although the castle was cleaner than before Marion's tenure, Campion saw that the walls could use a good scrubbing. After Epiphany, he would set the servants to a thorough wash, he decided. Meanwhile, the Yule log burned in welcome in a hall that was spacious and well-appointed, and visitors, this night, would be grateful for any kind of shelter.

Outside he heard horses, while nearby the murmur of voices rose expectantly. Among them he recognized that of Wilda, one of the female servants, who eyed the entrance anxiously. Always superstitious, Wilda was staring at the doors with great significance, and Campion smiled. Not only did Wilda hold firm to the old belief that the first person to cross the threshold after midnight on New Year's Day was a harbinger of the year ahead, but she thought that those who appeared on Christmas Eve gave an indication of the holiday's happiness.

The arrival of a dark-haired man was thought to be lucky, and since Campion had been blessed with seven such sons, the comings and goings of his own family had provided plenty of omens of good fortune during winters past. Of course, he did not put faith in such nonsense, but his household was more peaceful when the credulous among it were appeased.

And so he watched for Reynold, who was well aware of the servants' expectations, but when the doors were thrust open, it was not his son who was first to step over the threshold. Several people burst inside, shivering and stomping with the cold, and in the lead was a slight figure in a voluminous cape that fell back with a movement to reveal a swish of skirts. No man at all, but a woman, Campion realized, as the servants gasped softly. While they all stood gaping, she flung back her hood, and a mass of black curls spilled out over the green mantle of snow-dusted wool.

"Humph. Well, at least she's got dark hair," Wilda muttered, and Campion swallowed his astonishment to step forward. Although he put no credence in forecasting the festivities based on his guest's coloring, nonetheless he was as surprised as anyone to find a woman about in such foul weather and on Christmas Eve.

"Father, may I present Lady Warwick, who is seeking shelter from the storm," Reynold said, stepping forward.

"Lady," the earl said with a nod. "I am Campion. Welcome to my home. Please sit down and rest from your journey." A small nod of a pale oval face made Campion push his own heavy chair toward the hearth. She went into it without complaint, and he stood beside, studying the other members of the party.

There was another woman, not dressed as finely, who might be an attendant, several men-at-arms and a handful of male servants. No other man was in evidence, and Campion wondered if some disaster marked his absence and the party's presence in his hall. As his own servants took wet cloaks and brought blankets for the group that huddled near the fire, Campion's gaze returned to the dark head by his side.

The mass of hair was rather amazing, for few except young unmarried ladies left theirs down. And even damp, the black curls were such as Campion had never seen before, so thick and rich that he was tempted to reach out and test one fat lock. Stifling the odd urge, he watched the heavy mane slide over one slender shoulder, his attention drawn downward only to arrest itself suddenly, for the lady was removing her boots.

Obviously they were wet and chilling her, but Campion was momentarily taken aback. Surely she would rather disrobe in private, and he leaned forward to offer her a chamber in which to do so. But his mouth seemed strangely unable to work as her slender hands tugged at the hose beneath her hem. Campion caught a glimpse of pale skin, the curve of a well-turned ankle and the instep of a small arched foot, before he recovered himself and straightened.

He slanted a quick glance at Wilda's back, glad that the superstitious woman had not seen Lady Warwick's toes, for a barefoot person was not welcome at the Yuletide fire, according to some ridiculous belief. Perhaps because the sight was so unnerving, Campion thought as he sought to regain his own composure.

It had been a long time since he had entertained a woman outside of his own family, so perhaps he was out of step with current manners, Campion told himself. Certainly the circumstances warranted swift action, for the whole party might well be frostbitten. It was his own reaction that bore censure, Campion thought ruefully. He had no excuse for his staring or for the slow, seeping warmth that had invaded him at the sight of a little bare flesh. By the rood, he was much too old for such nonsense!

"We have readied a chamber for you, my lady," he said, his voice a hoarse rasp that made him clear his throat. Reluctantly he peeked at his guest, but she had already tucked her feet beneath her and was taking a cup of spiced wine from a servant.

"Thank you, my lord. I admit that a warm bed would be most welcome." The statement was uttered in a serious tone that held no subtle inflections, so why did it conjure visions of linens heated by his own body? Campion looked away. Perhaps he had been too much in the company of his randy son Stephen of late. And just where was Stephen? Warming a bed, no doubt, and not his own, Campion thought, his lips thinning into a grim line. He had not taught his boys to live like monks, but neither did he approve of Stephen's careless dalliances.

"Thank you for taking us in, my lord," Lady Warwick said, and Campion's attention was drawn to her once more. A woolen blanket had been draped over her shoulders, and she held the wine in both hands to thaw her fingers, pink without the covering of her wet gloves, but she seemed to be feeling better, for she lifted her face and smiled, causing Campion to take in a startled breath at the sight.

She was lovely. The fire suffused her cheeks with life, and now he could see clearly the smoothness of her skin, the thickness of her black lashes...and her eyes. They were a most unusual shade of blue, almost the color of spring violets, and Campion stared again before he caught himself. No wonder his family had begun fussing over him, for only a fool or a dotard would be so dazed by a pretty face. A *young* pretty face.

He returned her glorious smile with a dignified nod. "You are most welcome, of course, but may I ask how came you to be traveling in this foul weather?" *There. Now he had command of himself as he should.*

She drew herself up, and Campion saw a strength that belied her years. Her violet eyes shone with a determination born of possession, of a maturity that made him reassess her age. She was no girl, he realized, but a woman. Still she was no older than most of his sons. Where was her husband?

"I was on my way to celebrate Christmas with my cousin when we were driven to ground by the storm," she explained. She met his gaze unflinchingly, as if daring him to pass judgment upon such a foolhardy scheme, but Campion said nothing. Often he found it wiser to remain silent while others spoke, and in this instance his judgment was correct, for she soon continued.

"Truth be told, it was not so treacherous when we started," Lady Warwick admitted. Although she was aware of her error, the firm set of her chin told him that she would take no rebuke from him, and Campion felt his lips stir. "We were forced to seek shelter last night at a public inn, and I daresay were plagued with bodily pests for our trouble. We had hoped to reach our destination before Christmas Eve, but, as you can see, we must throw ourselves on your mercy, my lord."

Lady Warwick took no pleasure in seeking assistance, that much was obvious, and Campion had to admire her spirit, although he still had reservations about her single-minded journey. "I am happy to offer a place to stay for you and your company, but what of your husband? Is he waiting with your cousin perhaps?" he asked.

At Campion's question, Lady Warwick's expression became positively mutinous. "I am a widow, my lord, and have commanded myself and my household for many years," she said in a haughty tone he suspected was intended to put him in his place. He bit back his smile, for if the most arrogant and fierce of men had failed to subdue him, this stubborn young woman was certainly no threat.

"I see," Campion said, keeping his thoughts to himself. The men in her party moved over to the trestle table to partake of some food, but he motioned for a servant to set her portion upon a nearby stool.

"Thank you," she murmured a bit stiffly. At his silence, she seemed to relax and, setting down her cup, she reached for a portion of cheese. "Your hall is the most beautiful that I have ever seen."

"Ah, but sadly unprepared for the holiday," Campion noted. "I fear we lack a woman's touch, and my sons will not be bringing their wives in this foul weather. In truth, I was uncertain what sort of celebrations the season would hold, so your arrival has been most timely."

She looked a question at him as she nibbled daintily.

"Guests will surely enliven what might have been a rather quiet twelve days of festivities," Campion added. Despite her reluctance to seek help, she must see that there was no shame in accepting his hospitality. Travelers were welcomed any time of the year, but most assuredly at Christmas.

Violet eyes widened as she swallowed hard, and Campion leaned forward, concerned that she might choke, but she straightened and held up a hand as if to ward him off. "No. I...oh, but we cannot stay. I mean, we would not wish to impose upon you for such a time."

"But you surely cannot think to travel in this weather?" Campion asked in surprise. Already she had admitted the folly of her journey; to attempt it again would make her devoid of common sense.

"Oh, it will probably clear tomorrow."

Campion gave her a jaundiced look, and her gaze slid away from his, making him wonder if there was something to her trip other than what she had revealed. Even if the snow stopped, it already covered the roads, as she well knew. Her speech and bearing marked her as an intelligent woman. Why would she risk her life to pay a visit?

Campion was not a man to pry unless she made her business his own, but if Lady Warwick thought to leave on the morrow, she was mistaken. The stubborn woman was liable to end up frozen to death in a drift, should he accede to her wishes. And no matter how accustomed the lady was to making her own decisions, here at Campion, he ruled.

Still, he had not done so by acting unwisely, and so he kept his own counsel, hoping that after a good night's rest, Lady Warwick would be better able to see reason. In the meantime, he made her as comfortable as he could, offering her more food, more wine, another blanket....

"Greetings!" The sound of Stephen's voice made Campion glance across the hall. The handsomest of his sons appeared, looking no worse from his apparent frolic except for a slight tousling of his hair. At the sight of the guests, he flashed a smile that could melt the coldest of hearts, and Campion was caught between pride in the boy's charm and dismay at his poor use of it.

"What have we here, Father, visitors upon this Christmas Eve?" Stephen asked, moving closer.

"Lady Warwick, you have met my son Reynold. This is my son, Stephen," Campion said. "Lady Warwick will be staying with us until the weather abates," he explained. To his amusement, she lifted her chin as if to protest, but Stephen stepped toward her and bowed low, demanding her attention.

"My lady. It is indeed a pleasure to be graced with your presence." Stephen's rather smug look suggested he anticipated the usual feminine response to his attractions, but Lady Warwick only nodded in greeting, as if he held little interest for her.

Stephen's dismay at her less than enthusiastic response was almost palpable, and Campion had to curb his smile as he turned to study the lady more thoughtfully. She was an interesting woman—beautiful, intelligent, confident and too discerning to be swayed by Stephen's rather jaded appeal— certainly a rare guest in his household.

Stephen did not give up easily, however, and managed to seat himself on the stool, placing her tray of food on his lap, where she would have to reach for it. Campion frowned. His sons were too old to receive rebukes from their father, and yet, he just might have to speak to Stephen, who seemed to be growing more heedless by the day.

"Have you been traveling far, my lady?" the boy asked, carving a piece of cheese and offering it to her on the point of his own knife. It was very nicely done but for the drawl in Stephen's tone that told Campion his son was up to something.

"No, not very far," Lady Warwick said as she gingerly removed the cheese with her dainty fingers. Her answer was oddly evasive, and Campion wondered if she sought to avoid the intimacy Stephen was forcing upon her or if the question itself disturbed her.

"Ah, but how is it then that I have never met you? Just

how close do you make your home?'' Although Campion frowned at Stephen's silky sarcasm, he, too, would know more of his guest.

''I live at Mallin Fell, at the manor there.''

Campion hid his surprise. That was no simple day's journey even in the best of times, but several days' ride to the east.

''Ah,'' Stephen said as she nibbled at the portion of cheese. ''I am not too familiar with that area and know of no Warwicks there. Who owns the holding?''

The lady bristled. ''I do. Now if you will excuse me, my lords, I would see my rest.'' Eliminating the opportunity for any further questions, she rose to her feet, and Campion had a glimpse of slender ankle as she stood, obviously having forgotten her lack of footwear. But her attendant appeared at her elbow with fresh slippers and she slid them on swiftly.

''Wilda, see Lady Warwick to her chamber, please,'' Campion said, before Stephen could offer to escort her. The servant did his bidding, and he watched Lady Warwick move toward the stairs. Although not tall, she held herself so well that her very bearing drew respect. Indeed, she might have been a queen or an abbess or any other powerful woman— but for that rich mane of hair. It fell wantonly down her back to her waist and flowed when she walked…

Campion's inappropriate thoughts were interrupted by a snort and a thump as Stephen took the vacated chair with a disgruntled expression. ''Haughty wench,'' he muttered. ''She's probably some kind of man hater.''

Reynold grunted from his place near the hearth, stretching his bad leg out before it now that the lady was gone. ''Just because she didn't fall into your lap, like every other female?''

Stephen scowled. ''If you're so clever, tell me this—how is it that a young, beautiful widow with a manor and lands, no less, remains unwed?'' he asked, lifting a dark brow.

Reynold shrugged, obviously uninterested in such things. "She is not that young."

Campion glanced at his son in surprise, for surely Lady Warwick was not much older than Reynold himself. He again wondered at her age, for Reynold obviously saw the maturity that belied her youthful face.

"Perhaps she is barren," Stephen mused.

"Stephen!" For once, Campion reprimanded his son.

"Well?" Stephen said, sliding him a sullen glance. "What else would keep her from another marriage? Unless she's a shrew, of course, which might be a possibility, considering the set of that pretty little chin."

Campion rose to his feet. He had no intention of watching Stephen sulk because the lady had not swooned over him in the manner of most others of her gender.

"She's too old for you anyway," Reynold muttered as he rubbed his thigh. The piercing cold outside had probably done little to help it, but Campion knew better than to comment.

Stephen snorted. "She isn't any older than I am. And, anyway, there's nothing wrong with a more experienced woman. And being a widow, she ought to know exactly what she wants," he added lewdly.

"Apparently, it isn't you," Reynold commented.

Choking back a laugh, Campion coughed to cover the noise and headed toward the stairs. Any woman who ignored Stephen promised to enliven the hall, and the earl found himself looking forward to discovering more about the intriguing Lady Warwick. His steps to the great chamber were lighter than before, and he realized, with some surprise, that his heart was more buoyant, too.

Perhaps the Yuletide wouldn't be so dull after all.

Chapter Two

J oy Thorncombe, Lady Warwick, eyed the thin light filtering through the shutters with dismay. Not only had she slept far too long, but the gloom that seeped into the chamber did not bode well for travel. Lying there comfortable and warm in the huge, elaborately carved bed, she felt tempted to stay where she was, to revel in the luxury and relative security of Campion Castle. But she would not trust herself to the hospitality of a man, even one with such a sterling reputation as the earl, and so she rose swiftly, calling for her attendant.

"Roesia, get up! 'Tis late, and we must be on our way."

"Oh, my lady, must we? I've never slept half so well in my life," Roesia said, stretching slowly. "This place is wonderful!"

Joy could hardly argue. The room was beautiful, furnished with chests and a settle and even some kind of soft carpet to cover the tiles and with a wide hearth to stave away the chill. It was at once both cozy and elegant, and the thought of returning to a frigid ride along frozen roads held no allure, but the need to reach her destination pressed upon her as she reached for her clothing.

"Could you believe the size of the hall and these chambers? Fit for a king! And what about the food that they brought us, even though supper was over? That spiced wine was delicious, and did you try those little tarts with the dusting of sugar?'' Roesia asked, sighing with the memory.

''No,'' Joy answered, oddly piqued at her attendant's enthusiasm for Campion. At Mallin, they did not have enough money to buy all the expensive spices that were used in such delicacies, but they ate well enough—simple fare that was probably better for the digestion, Joy thought righteously.

''And the hot bath, practically waiting for us here in our own chamber!'' Roesia added.

''With servants aplenty to bring it,'' Joy noted, but she had to admit that the gesture had been a thoughtful one, and more than welcome when they were sodden and chilled from their efforts to find shelter. The memory brought her thoughts grimly back to the journey ahead, and she dressed swiftly.

Roesia moved more slowly. ''I could grow accustomed to this sort of life,'' she muttered as she laced up her gown.

''As could anyone, I'm sure,'' Joy answered in a dry tone. The de Burghs were wealthy beyond her imagining. And yet, the castle inhabitants, even those who served, seemed genuinely kind and welcoming. Perhaps it was the Christmas season that moved them to such benevolence, Joy thought with a trace of asperity. But whatever the motive, she was not accustomed to charity, and so she remained resolved to leave as soon as her train could be readied.

It was with that purpose in mind that Joy made her way down the curved stairway to the great hall, but on the bottom step she halted in surprise at the sight that met her eyes. Last night in the dim light of torches and candles, the vaulted room had been shadowy and huge, but now… Joy drew in a deep breath, for she had never seen anything like it. It was vast and bright and clean, with painted walls and tall windows, with cupboards and settles and chairs and so many trestle tables that Joy blinked in astonishment.

And everywhere people rushed to and fro, from those dressed in the finest clothing to the lowliest garb. Men and women talked and smiled, their voices creating a constant din, while around them children dashed, laughing and squealing. Servants were busy with flagons, ale flowed and cups were raised in salute, while the scents of cooking food and spices drifted in from the kitchens.

"What madness is this?" Joy whispered.

Behind her Roesia laughed softly. "''Tis Christmas Day, my lady. Or have you forgotten?"

Joy *had* forgotten, and she felt an unaccountable sadness at the knowledge. But the celebrations she had known were nothing like this. Although she had always done her best to observe the traditions and provide for those at Mallin Fell, here all was on a grand scale, far beyond her meager efforts. There was simply more noise, more people, more food, more laughter and more happiness than Joy had ever imagined. She told herself it was an illusion, a trick wrought by wealth and power, but when she glimpsed her host approaching, the man looked disturbingly real.

Had he been this tall last night? Joy wondered, keeping her place upon the step so she need not crane her neck upward when he reached her side. Had he been this regal, this graceful, this…handsome? Joy swallowed hard as the Earl of Campion dipped his dark head toward her in greeting, his very being emanating authority and strength, yet when he spoke it was with a gentleness that she felt right down to her bones.

"My lady, may I wish you a good Christmas and bid you join our celebration," he said, smiling pleasantly.

"Thank you," Joy answered, her mind vainly groping for a more intelligent reply. The earl's gaze held her, and for a moment she had the absurd notion that he could see right inside her. The idea brought her wayward thoughts back to her purpose and she lifted her chin, determined to politely refuse his welcome and be on her way.

Usually Joy, set upon an objective, was formidable, despite her dainty frame. Indeed, Roesia often said that when determined, her mistress was an irresistible force. However, neither one of them could have ever anticipated the Earl of Campion, who, for all his cultured manners, took on the appearance of an immovable object.

He simply would not budge, Joy realized as he led her to a chair at the great table, yet he did so in a quiet, elegant way that disguised his high-handedness so well that another woman might not have recognized it. Although Joy was not deceived, she was forced to admit that she liked his style. No matter what she said, Campion smiled and nodded, as if in agreement with her, and then insisted that she stay for the feast.

She told him that she must go, but he would not hear of it, and he turned aside her every protest with a graciousness that was neither bullying nor condescending. As they argued in a most civilized manner, Joy wondered if the earl ever lost his temper or if he even possessed one, for he seemed to be the most composed of men. He would make a formidable enemy, she suspected, and the knowledge made her reluctant to continue her protest.

Even as Joy reconsidered her position, it became apparent that the meal was about to begin, and she knew she would be churlish to delay it with her departure. When she saw the faces of Roesia and her men, only too eager for fine food and some holiday cheer, Joy found she could not refuse them. With a lift of her chin, she nodded to Campion, her manner poised despite her capitulation.

"Very well, but only for the feast. Then we must go," she said. Campion's answering smile was nothing more than a courtesy, and yet Joy felt a warmth that she could not explain, as if he were truly pleased by her presence. She told herself it was nonsense, but she could not deny that the earl had a way about him that was very appealing. His paternal air was deceiving, Joy realized, as she studied him more closely, for he was not old. Indeed, he was still young and vigorous, and there was something about him that she found attractive.

Smiling at such foolishness, Joy shook her head, but her

gaze followed Campion as he rose to announce the beginning of the feast and to introduce his guests. Joy stood and murmured some pleasantries, though she could not help feeling a little awed as she looked down the long line of trestle tables filled with castle residents, knights, servants, villeins and freemen from the vast lands of the de Burghs. A great, deafening shout rang out as they raised their cups, and then the boar's head, the traditional Christmas delicacy, was carried in to much fanfare.

Roesia's words echoed in her head. *I could grow accustomed to this.* Although Joy had never paid much attention to food, she could not ignore the taste, the variety and the sheer size of the courses. Certainly there were more than the twelve special dishes called for by the holiday, as platters of beef, mutton, turkey and cheeses were accompanied by sauces, mustard, apples and nuts, and followed by frumenty, posset, mince pie and pudding.

While she ate, Joy studied the great hall and its inhabitants. The household was predominantly male, and when Campion spoke to her of his seven sons, she was not surprised. There was no chatelaine, and no ladies-in-waiting. The few women who sat at the lower tables appeared to be wives of the many knights, while farther down there were those who were villeins or married to freemen.

Joy sat on the earl's right but found herself sharing a trencher with his son Stephen. A more typical example of his gender, Stephen was spoiled and arrogant, and but for the looks they shared, she would hardly think him Campion's son. The other son in residence, Reynold, was also little like his father in demeanor. He was quiet and rather bitter looking. Foolish boy, Joy thought, as she saw all that he had before him. He should be thankful for his lot instead of ruing a slight limp, but wasn't that just like a man?

Lost in her thoughts, Joy was startled when Stephen leaned close, brushing against her breast as he cut her meat. "Thank you, but I can do that myself," she said, putting him in his

place with a cool smile. Although he moved back an appropriate distance, the boy sulked for most of the meal, drank
too much wine and then began taunting his brother. Joy felt
like smacking him on the head and ordering him to behave,
the spoiled churl.

Finally he took an interest in her attendant, and though Joy
would not wish such a fellow on Roesia, she enjoyed the
relative peace that came with the engagement of his interest
elsewhere. Peace and prosperity. It was evident in every filled
cup, in each voice raised in speech or song between the
courses that filled the groaning tables. There was no desperation here, no worries over harvest or money or allegiances,
Joy noted with a twinge of envy.

And yet none of the revelers misbehaved. The loud voices
never erupted in anger or drunken debauchery, for Campion
set the tone for the hall. He was the calm, solid center of it
all, radiating a power and strength that few men could wield
on the battlefield, let alone seated in a chair at the head of a
feast table. Joy had always disdained men of rank as bullies,
but here was a true lord, a man who ruled through wisdom
not force.

Looking around her at the happy faces and then back at
the man who reigned over all, Joy knew a brief yearning to
be a part of this place and its people. She had always thought
of the de Burghs as mighty knights, but now she began to
wonder if she were not seeing the real family now. It encom-
passed all of the earl's subjects, drawn together here in a
realm of his making, where honor and goodness reigned.

Perhaps she had partaken of too much spiced wine, Joy
thought ruefully, or more likely, too much of the Christmas
spirit. It pervaded the hall in a way that made her think such
warmth was present year-round, when she knew that no home
could be as wonderful as Campion Castle appeared to the
eyes of an outsider. Visiting here was like a trip to some
fantastic land of plenty, but as pleasant as it might be, her
brief sojourn had to come to an end. And soon.

Despite the temptations of the Yule hearth and friendly people, the promise of singing and other celebrations that would drag the feasting on most of the day, Joy felt the press of time, urging her to be gone. And so she leaned close to Campion's chair, a finely carved oak piece that she immediately recognized as her seat of the night before. He had given her his chair, she realized, swallowing an odd lump in her throat at the gesture.

"My lord," she began, but he cut her off with a smile.

"Campion. Please call me Campion."

"Campion, I would thank you for this wonderful meal, but we must be on our way," Joy said firmly. Instead of dismissing her with a wave of his hand, as she expected, the earl bent toward her. He probably did so in order to be heard above the noise, but he was so near that Joy could see the strands of silver in his hair and the fine lines that fanned out from his eyes on his sun-darkened face.

And what beautiful eyes, Joy marveled. They were not as dark as she had first thought, but a light, clear brown that seemed to hold the wisdom of the ages in their depths. Joy felt herself drifting toward them, as if drawn by what she might find there—mysteries, truths, peace and something unknown. A blush rose in her cheeks as she jerked backward suddenly, aware of a strange, unsettling sensation.

Campion appeared not to notice. "Surely my home is not so lacking in Christmas welcome that you would refuse my hospitality?" he asked. Joy took a shallow breath and shifted warily as she tried to recapture her concentration. She had never learned the subtle game of convincing an arrogant man that her will was his idea. Indeed, she had been accused often enough of being unnaturally forceful, of not knowing her place, and worse.

"Nay, my lord, but I have dallied too much already at your fine table and must hurry to my destination," Joy explained. She forced a smile that she hoped was cajoling, but too many years as her own mistress probably made it more intimidating than anything else.

Campion studied her silently, and if he had been any other man, Joy might have known a twinge of fear. One could never be too careful with the volatile members of the opposite gender, to whom an unprotected woman was often fair game in terms of property, money or desire. But it was hard to impute Campion with such motives. Indeed, he was the first man Joy had ever met who seemed wholly comfortable with himself. He had lands, wealth and power aplenty, and the very thought of the calm, collected earl suddenly succumbing to fleshly urges was nearly laughable.

So why wasn't she laughing? Instead, Joy felt an odd sort of warmth at the very notion. Campion's head was tilted toward her slightly, his attention almost a tangible thing, such was the intensity of his regard, and Joy suppressed the impulse to squirm underneath the direct gaze of those enigmatic eyes.

"I understand your wish for a swift journey, but I fear that you will make little progress in this weather," the earl finally said. "I'm sure you do not want to repeat your experience of last evening, yet the conditions are little better today, for the villeins and freemen who journeyed only as far as their own farms this morning were full of stories of the fierce elements."

It was no rebuke, but a gentle reminder, and Joy frowned. A glance toward the tall, narrow windows showed the light was still thin and pale, a sign that the sky had not cleared, and she knew that yesterday's drifts had been nearly impassable. The need to be off, and soon, warred against the temptation to linger here in the stronghold Campion had carved for himself, an island in a stormy sea of troubles, where the world didn't seem to intrude.

But Joy had never been one to hide from her duties or lean upon a man, even one as elegant and powerful as Campion. She lifted her chin, resolved to depart, yet even as she would speak, the earl leaned toward her once more, as if imparting wisdom for her ears alone.

"Forgive me for speaking plainly, Lady, but in this weather, you are more likely to die upon the road than reach your destination," he said. Joy opened her mouth to protest, but at his somber look, so fraught with reason, she thought better of her speech. He was right, of course. She had let her fierce determination cloud her judgment.

Joy looked around the hall, at Roesia flirting with Campion's boy, at her men talking so easily with the knights of the castle, drinking their ale in warmth and comfort, and she felt a villain. Should she order them out, they would loyally do her bidding even to their death, and, as the earl reminded her, that was a distinct possibility. All too well, she remembered the blinding snow and the fear that they might not reach shelter before the horses reached the limits of their endurance.

Only a fool would dare such forces again, Joy thought, ruefully. Although no fool, sometimes she was so accustomed to taking charge, so intent upon a goal, that she could not see anything else. It was both her strength and her weakness.

"Lady." Campion's low voice startled her, for Joy had nearly forgotten his presence. When she turned toward him, she wondered how that had ever happened, for her senses hummed with awareness at his nearness.

"I cannot let you leave in such conditions," he said. His expression was gentle yet implacable, and Joy bristled. Did he truly think to stop her? "Tell me why you must hurry, and I will do my best to help you in any way I can," he added softly.

Joy glanced away from his probing gaze. "I wish only to be in familiar surroundings during the Yuletide. And although your offer is very gracious, let me assure you that I have taken care of myself for many years," she said.

"Obviously," Campion answered, his lips curving

slightly, and Joy found her outrage seeping away. It was hard to remain angry with a man who had a sense of humor, especially when he was in the right. Joy had always thought males the far more stupid of the two genders, no matter what the Church's doctrine on the subject, for it was usually men who fought each other, who were ruled by their lusts for power and such.

Yet she could not imagine the Earl of Campion being ruled by anything. Here was a man to admire and even emulate, Joy decided, coveting some of his calm composure. For years, she had done her best to maintain her holding, making informed decisions with a clear head, but she knew there was a part of her nature that was given over to impatience and argument, which she did her best to subdue.

She saw no such imperfections in Campion. Indeed, it was difficult to find any fault with the earl. Although Joy had never been inclined to take much note of a man's appearance, she could not deny that she found him handsome. His face was narrow but strong, his dark hair sleek, and the streaks of silver in it only added to his innate dignity. It was obvious he was a knight, for his lean muscles were evident beneath the fine fabric of his tunic. Joy's gaze lingered momentarily along his broad chest before skidding away.

"Very well. I will accept your generous hospitality for another night," she murmured, trying to rein in her unusual thoughts.

"Not another night. You must stay for the entire Yuletide," Campion said. When Joy glanced at him in alarm, she found his manner serene, not threatening. "I have already told you of my sons and their families and how the weather has prevented them from joining us this Christmas. And since these same conditions have conspired to bring you to Campion, I charge you with staying in their place and bringing joy to our holiday," he said.

Joy stared at him in surprise. "How did you know?" she asked, wondering if the earl was omnipotent, if his eyes could truly see another's soul and the secrets hidden there. Or had he some knowledge of her, some word of which she was unaware?

"Know what?" he asked, his expression puzzled.

"My name. My name is Joy."

"How lovely, but I knew it not," he said, in a charming yet genuine manner that chased away her momentary fears. "I meant only that we wish for visitors at this time of year, to add to our happiness." His smile was oddly wistful, and Joy was rocked by a sudden, sharp realization.

He was lonely.

She looked about her at the vast hall filled with people, at Campion's sons and knights and servants and villeins, and she wondered how the man could want for anything. Yet he did. She knew it as surely as he now knew her name, and the knowledge made this man not so omnipotent, but oddly human. And it was that glimpse of vulnerability that swayed her far more than warnings of foul weather ever could.

Joy glanced back at Campion, at the polite smile that curved his lips, and she wanted to ask him outright if he missed his family. But would the earl, so dignified and poised as he faced her, admit to such a frailty? Joy wondered. She doubted it, and somehow she found his elegant veneer frustrating, as if that tiny peek had whetted her appetite for the true Campion. She let herself meet his gaze and wished that she could see behind those enigmatic eyes to the man who dwelled within.

"Only if you let me do something in return for your generosity," Joy said finally. "You have complained of the lack of greenery and such Christmas trappings. You must let Roesia and I hang some bundles upon the walls and help to organize the feasting, as your son's wife would do, were she here."

"If you wish, but I will hold you to no such bargain," Campion said. "You shall do only as much as you will and take Marion's place only when you wish," Campion said.

Although he sent her a courteous smile, Joy felt oddly discomposed, as if all between them was not settled to her satisfaction. Perhaps it was caused by the earl's slow, confident smile that told her he had harbored no doubts about his powers of persuasion. Or perhaps it was dismay at her own unusually impulsive agreement, a decision based more upon emotion than logic.

However, Joy suspected it had more to do with his final words, for she wanted to be considered his equal, not as his relative. And, although she could not have said why, she especially did not want to be mistaken for his daughter.

Chapter Three

The day after Christmas dawned bright and clear, much to Campion's disappointment. After the gloom of recent weeks, he should have been glad to greet the sunshine, but his thoughts immediately turned to his guest and their bargain. Would she remain to honor it? His instincts told him she was a woman of her word, but he sensed, too, that she was not telling him everything.

What did it matter if she stayed or went? Campion chided himself, and yet he could not deny a particular fascination with the beautiful Lady Warwick. She was intelligent and competent, no simpering maiden, but a forthright woman with opinions on every subject. He smiled as he recalled the lively debate she had brought to his tired hall during the long day of feasting.

The old place was looking a bit livelier, too, for she had already hung some greenery, tied with brightly colored cloth over the doors, and had promised more. He chuckled at the memory of how she had bedeviled his sons until they had braved the snow to gather branches for her. Stephen had grumbled and called her the Christmas Commander, but Campion had admired the way she took charge without being loud or brash. He could well use her firm, but gentle aid year-round.

The thought gave him pause. Ever since Marion left he had missed a woman's fine hand, the presence of a chatelaine who would make her own decisions without deferring to him. Idly Campion wished that he could convince the capable Lady Warwick to tarry after Epiphany, but she had a journey ahead that she had already interrupted and her own manor to attend. Why would she forsake it for Campion? And she could hardly remain at the castle indefinitely unless she joined the family, he mused, but the idea of her marrying Stephen or Reynold somehow made him uneasy.

His mood suddenly soured, Campion listened to a servant's report upon the dairy and the extra butchering required for the holiday, but his thoughts were elsewhere and he finally dismissed the fellow with an absent wave before hurrying toward the hall. He realized, even as he made his way down the stairs, that the anticipation seizing him surely exceeded what was warranted by the presence of guests.

His relief, too, was excessive, but it rushed through him, nonetheless, when he saw her. She was seated in the massive chair next to his own, just as if she belonged there, and Campion knew a distinct sense of satisfaction at the sight. Even Reynold, looking more grim than usual as he left the hall, could do little to disturb his odd feeling of contentment.

"Hail, Father!" Stephen said with a courtly bow, and Campion wondered, not for the first time, how his wayward son could carouse all night and then rise in the morning, looking no worse for it. "We're going skating," Stephen said, lifting aloft a set of sharpened animal bones.

Campion saw that several knights and a couple of their ladies were already donning their cloaks, and he knew that the weather would be perfect, crisp and clear after the recent temperatures, which ought to have turned the pond that lay outside the castle walls into a heavy sheet of ice.

"But I cannot convince our lovely guest to try the sport," Stephen said. Turning toward Lady Warwick, he bowed again. "I fear she is reluctant to trust herself into my care, but I will not let you fall, my lady. Come," he cajoled in his most persuasive tone. Although Joy shook her head firmly, Stephen pressed her, leaning close until Campion stepped forward.

"Perhaps I shall join you," he said. Stephen swiveled toward him to stare in surprise, and Campion could see the question in his son's gaze. It did not reach his lips, however, for Lady Warwick's attendant took the opportunity to seize Stephen's arm.

"I would be most grateful, if you would teach me, my lord," she said, flashing him a smile, and Stephen's momentary dismay was lost in an answering grin.

"Of course, mistress, I would be happy to teach you everything I know," he purred, and Campion shook his head as he watched them go. Although people were already crowding the hall, the earl found himself alone with Lady Warwick at the head of the high table, and he fought back the urge to apologize for his son. Stephen was old enough to handle himself, even if his behavior had veered wildly of late.

"Do not tell me that you really intend to strap these outrageous things to your boots!"

Campion turned his head to see Lady Warwick with an amusing expression of distaste upon her lovely features as she fingered the narrow bones. His attention caught, he smiled down at her.

"Yes," he said, and the word hung in the air in a manner that forced him to clear his throat. "I learned to skate when I was just a boy."

"But, why?" she asked, her dark brows tilting together as if truly bewildered, and Campion laughed.

"For the simple pleasure of it," he said, his mind drifting against his will to other pleasures that he had been too long without.

Lady Warwick looked dubious still, and he reached out

to take her hand. "Come, I will show you," he said, leaning over her. It was a simple gesture, an innocent one, but the feel of her small fingers in his own was oddly enticing, and when his gaze met hers, he felt a moment's disorientation, just as though those violet eyes were calling him home.

It was over too swiftly for Campion to draw any conclusions, for she tugged her hand from his with an awkward air of confusion. "I don't think so. I am not one for games or frivolous activities," she explained with an air of dismissal.

Campion wondered just what she considered frivolous. She looked so serious, her dark head bent, her hands in her lap, that he frowned. Had she lost her sense of fun with her husband's death, or had she never been given the chance to cultivate it? Either way, he was determined to gift her with an hour of play.

"It is not dangerous. You need not fear injury," he said softly.

As expected, her chin lifted. "I am not afraid of hurting myself."

"Then come," Campion said, straightening. His words were a challenge, and as he suspected, Lady Warwick could not resist. A twitch of her lips told him that she was well aware of his tactics, but then a slow smile spread across her face that nearly knocked the wind from him. Joy was not merely lovely, she was breathtaking, and Campion simply stood staring at her for one stunned moment.

"Very well," she said, rising to her feet, and Campion found himself wondering about her late husband. Had the man appreciated his bounty, or had he been too often away to entertain his young wife? Had he been a man of intelligence who thrived on his wife's wit or an oaf who condemned her as stubborn and willful? Campion had always been interested in people, and he told himself that therein lay his curiosity even as he suspected he was becoming far too fascinated by Lady Warwick.

After they had donned their gloves and cloaks, Campion led his guest through the great doors of the hall into the bailey. The air was cold, and he drew a deep draft, enjoying its crisp flavor. Beside him, Lady Warwick eyed the brewery and various buildings with approval, and Campion felt an intense pride in his demesne that he had not known in a long time. Indeed, he felt better than he had in years as they followed the path of trampled snow, and when they reached the pond, he stopped to admire the scene, made singular by the winter's unusual amount of snow.

Around them, the world was covered in white, fluffy mounds that curved over a hillock and topped the gnarled oaks whose branches dipped beneath the heavy burden. And stretched ahead lay the water, shimmering in the sunshine yet solid as stone, for upon it several of those from the castle skated, along with some of the freemen from the village.

His land, his people, Campion thought, with a certain happiness. And beside him, his unexpected guest. He turned to see that Lady Warwick had thrown back her hood, revealing the thick black curls that fairly gleamed in the light. Her cheeks were pink with cold, her lips curved into a gentle smile that echoed his own wonder, and Campion savored the joy of the moment, of pleasure shared and anticipated. He urged her over to a large rock, where they donned their skates, but the rest of the group was too boisterous, so he led her to a more secluded area of the pond, where dark branches hung close to the frozen water.

Considering that he could not remember the last time the pond had frozen, let alone when he had skated its surface, Campion was surprised at the ease with which the skill returned. Sweeping ahead in a long curve, he returned to halt before his student and held out his hands. Although she gripped them, her initial steps were unsteady, so Campion slid an arm around her as he drew her onto the surface, keeping a solid stance while she struggled to find her balance.

He moved forward, taking her with him, and Lady Warwick swayed precariously, flinging an arm around his waist to grip him tightly. Campion took his time, adjusting himself to her tentative efforts as he began a gentle march across the ice. They proceeded slowly, while he murmured advice and encouragement until, at last, his companion seemed to be able to stand without difficulty.

"Why would anyone want to do this?" she asked, but she followed the question with a laugh, and Campion could see she was enjoying herself. Skating might be a foolish pleasure, but life was too short not to make the most of each and every one of them, and Campion was glad to serve as her teacher. As she gained confidence, he took them farther across the ice, gliding smoothly for a long moment before he glanced down at her face.

That was his mistake, for the look of wonder there nearly took his breath away. Her violet eyes glittered above pink cheeks and pale skin, her delicate mouth was drawn wide in a white smile, and Campion faltered. Lady Warwick shrieked and they swung around, grasping wildly at each other, before regaining their balance, both of them laughing at the near calamity.

They were facing each other now, hanging on to each other's arms, and a sudden sway of Lady Warwick's body made Campion bend his head near. Suddenly he was aware of the scent of her, womanly and inviting. His lips brushed against a thick lock of her hair, and the sleek softness affected him in more places than he cared to admit.

With a low grunt of dismay, Campion gingerly set her away from him. They had been too close, and he put some space between them, sliding his hands down to hold her own. She was becoming more adept now, and he glided backward as she followed him forward. In this manner, they circled their small area of the pond, hidden by the curve of the water and the drape of the snowy trees, until Lady Warwick was laughing with delight.

"See how well you skate!" Campion said. "You like it."

"Yes, I like it," she said in a low, breathless voice that made him clear his throat. He let go of her hands, and she shrieked in protest but continued on her own.

"Look!" she cried, obviously delighted with her new skill, and Campion watched in admiration as she gained speed, moving into a long curve. He thought of the women he had known since he had buried his wives, fancy ladies of the court who were interested in money and power but not in a rowdy family of growing boys, women only too eager to pursue a wealthy widower but far too elegant to dash about on a frozen pond.

Lady Warwick was different, Campion mused. If she enjoyed this, then wait until the flowers were in bloom and…he drew up short. Joy wouldn't be here come the spring, he realized, and he felt the slow seep of disappointment into his bones. His smile faltered, and he glanced away at the white hillside where Campion rose, its golden towers no longer as shiny as they once were, the haven it provided somehow lacking.

"Oh! But how do I stop?" Lady Warwick's cry brought Campion's attention back to her, but it was too late. Her eyes wide, she was heading straight for him, arms flailing, and even though he reached out to slow her, she was an irresistible force that knocked him off his feet. He fell backward, and they both landed in a heap on the ice, laughing as they struggled to sit upright.

"Are you hurt?" Campion asked, relieved when she shook her head in response. Despite their spill, he had never felt better, for this little jaunt had him pulsing with life, but it was not only the skating that affected him.

Joy was on his lap, beautiful and young and full of energy that seemed to feed his own, and suddenly he was assaulted by images and urges better suited to his randy son Stephen. He felt in the grip of something inexplicable, as if possessed, and to his horror, the pressure of her small derriere on his lap made him hard, painfully so.

Campion's hands shook as he lifted them to her face, and he wanted nothing more than to bury his fingers in her heavy hair, to draw her close, to kiss her lips and more…to slake this frantic thirst with her body. He dared a glance at her eyes, expected to see a reflection of his own shock, but instead she simply stared back at him, violet depths wide and precious as gems. The world stilled, the air around them so hushed that Campion could hear her breath and feel its warmth against his skin, as temptation warred with honor within him.

A shout from across the pond made them both start and, grateful for the distraction, Campion rose, sliding her from his lap and helping her to her feet. His hands fell away, and he didn't know whether to laugh at his own folly or apologize. He could not recall a situation so awkward, but then he could not recall ever being in the grip of so fierce a desire.

Desire.

Joy blinked, drawing her trembling fingers back to her sides as she tried to regain her lost composure. For a moment she had been struck motionless by a blossoming heat that could surely melt the ice beneath her. And it had been so sudden, so unexpected that she had not even recognized the sensation for what it was.

Desire.

She had always scoffed at ladies who sought liaisons with men, for they did little to refute the Church's claim that women were ruled by their lusts. As a clearheaded female capable of managing her own affairs, Joy had held herself above such nonsense. Certainly she admired a handsome form as well as the next woman, but she had never been prompted to act upon such admiration. *Until now.*

Joy shivered at the thought of her position upon the earl's lap, her initial laughter fading in the face of his warmth.

She had felt the strength of his power, of a protection such as she had never known, and then the slow curl of awareness, of his nearness. Her heart skittered, and she rubbed her arms as if to ward off the unusual reaction.

"Are you cold? Let us return to the castle," Campion said, looking maddeningly unaffected by their near embrace. Perhaps she had imagined the excitement in his enigmatic gaze, for now he evidenced nothing more than a polite interest in her welfare.

Joy nodded, eager to take a respite from the earl's heady company, and she moved shakily toward shore as she sought an explanation for her peculiar response to him. Campion was just a man, she told herself. He walked and talked like any other…except that his voice was so deep and husky that it managed to both soothe and rouse her, and he moved with an appealing grace possessed by no other, whether gliding over the frozen pond like something out of a dream or striding across his hall.

Joy swallowed hard, wondering why this man, among all of his gender, should affect her so. Of course, he was handsome. All the de Burghs were accounted dashing and good-looking, though Joy had not been particularly impressed by the attributes of Stephen and Reynold. They could not hold a candle to their father.

But it was more than his pleasing countenance that attracted her. His power, perhaps? Joy considered that as she sat down to remove her skates. The straps were tangled, and she struggled with the wet leather until a pair of hands pushed her own aside. Campion knelt before her, and Joy's eyes widened as she stared at his dark head. His fingers, without their gloves, were as elegant yet forceful as the rest of him, and Joy felt a renewed warmth at his touch. When his palm slid up to cup her ankle in an intimate hold, her whole body blazed in reaction.

Perhaps it was the way he carried himself, Joy thought, as he made short work of removing her skates. Power sat upon his shoulders so easily, as if nothing could shake his quiet strength, and yet he was not arrogant. It was a confidence born of honor…and of knowledge, she decided, as he helped her to her feet.

Joy had often condemned members of the male gender as fools, but Campion was truly intelligent, with a mind open to differing opinions. Not only did he have a great store of book learning, along with his vast life experiences, but he possessed some kind of innate wisdom that shone in his eyes, which Joy found extremely provocative.

All that was very fine and cerebral, but how to explain the jolt of awareness she felt at his nearness, the rush of heat to parts of her that had never known any warmth? Joy felt the loss of his touch like a tangible thing as he moved beside her to walk the snowy path. She shivered again, for though she wished to shrug away those sensations or deny them, Joy had always been truthful with herself. And the truth was that for the first time in her life she wanted a man.

So startled was she by the admission that she halted in her tracks, staring blindly at the broad back of the male in question. The very notion of her being seized by over-wrought desires ought to have been horrifying, shocking at the very least, but instead of gasping, Joy choked back a laugh. For what could possibly come of her wanton yearning?

Of all the men in the land she had surely chosen the only one who possessed far too much honor to succumb to passions of the flesh.

All through the feast, Joy watched him, trying to discover why Campion, of all people, should suddenly provoke her heretofore nonexistent ardor. But by the meal's end, she was no closer to answers than she had been when sitting in his lap upon the ice.

The want was just *there*, thrumming in her blood whenever she looked at him, and when she did not, it grew more insistent, like an unsatisfied craving. Never before had a man aroused such interest in her, and being of a curious nature, Joy was driven to closer scrutiny.

And the more she studied him, the more interested she became. Everything about him became noteworthy: the way the strands of silver streaked his dark hair, the way his dark green tunic fell across his broad chest, the width of shoulders that were imposing and yet not intimidating. Campion was not a man to wield his power recklessly, and that knowledge was almost as exciting to Joy as his physical form.

Her gaze dipped to his graceful wrists and long, slender fingers, and she flushed with heat as she remembered the feel of them over her own. Strong. Protective. Exciting. How could the sight of a man's hands, regal in repose, thrill her so? she wondered. It was absurd, and yet, undeniable. This incredible new feeling had seized her just as surely as the Christmas spirit had hold of all else in Campion's hall.

Indeed, Joy might have thought her desire some kind of strange consequence of the season or her luxurious surroundings, but she felt no such thrill when she looked upon Reynold or Stephen or any other man present. It was only Campion who affected her so. Of course, she rarely met men of the earl's rank, but those she had known had annoyed her more often than not. Not so Campion.

Joy felt giddy as a young girl, as the young girl she had never been, while she sneaked peeks at his elegant countenance. In the space of two days' time, it had become familiar to her, achingly so, like a favorite book one could not bear to put away. Even as she looked on, a child approached the earl's massive chair to speak with him, and Joy held her breath, but unlike most of his sex, Campion did not rebuff the girl. He leaned forward to answer her with a gentle smile that filled Joy with heat and song, as if the celebration around her echoed in her very being.

Not for the first time, she realized that when Campion

gave someone his attention, he gave it full measure. He did not fiddle with his cup or glance away or evidence impatience of any sort. The earl did nothing idly, but focused himself wholly upon his audience, large or small, man or woman. And when that powerful regard was turned toward her, Joy felt she was the center of his world, the single most important person alive.

It was silly, of course, and at first, Joy had found the sensation rather disturbing, but now she coveted that concentration, wanting it for herself with a selfish yearning. *Wanting* Campion. Ever it came back to that, Joy realized, as her gaze drifted over his powerful form once more, dropping to the hands that rested upon his knees.

Joy wondered what they would feel like upon her, not in the companionable manner of her skating lesson, but as a man touches a woman. She no longer held any illusions about romance, but she had to admit to a curiosity about such things, recently fired by Campion. Her limited experience left her at a loss, and so she imagined touching him, instead, sifting her fingers through his hair, exploring beneath his tunic to the hard body below.

Joy shifted, restless in her seat as she took the fantasy further, envisioning herself in the earl's bed, sharing untold mysteries in the darkness of the night. How would it feel to have those strong arms around her without the fear that he would steal anything of hers, including her independence? Here was an honorable man, a man of the world who might teach her a thing or two.

As Joy sat there, lost in pleasant illusions, an idea evolved slowly, insinuating itself into her mind until she gasped with the audacity of it. And then she wanted to laugh in delight, excitement and relief surging through her, along with a low curl of warmth. Could she?

Why not?

Turning her head slightly, Joy studied the Earl of Campion with a new intensity. By all accounts, he was a man of honor who held himself apart from the common dalliances of others of his gender. She had heard no gossip about him, no rumors of lemans or mistresses, and the knowledge was both pleasing and daunting, for what made her think she could change his mind?

Her own formidable will, Joy decided with a smile. Roesia often complained about it, but Joy was driven, and when she wanted something, she usually achieved her goal. She had poured herself into Mallin Fell, turning the small demesne into a stable, if not highly prosperous, holding. And she had managed to keep it, against all odds.

And through the years, she had asked little enough for herself. Certainly she had never complained, considering herself well-off compared to most of the female population. Joy was accustomed to work and always thought of her people first, but now she found herself wanting something for herself, and the more she thought about it, the more determined she was to have it, despite the slight twitching of her conscience.

There had been few pleasures in her life; how wrong could it be to want to wring something from this holiday? To know a man's touch for the first time in her life? To finally discover the great mystery? Joy had been glad enough on her wedding night when her boy husband had turned away from her, no more eager than she to consummate their marriage. And she had known no regrets when he had died before growing more into his manhood, leaving her untouched.

A virgin widow.

But now her status seemed ludicrous, and the more Joy considered it, the more she became determined to remedy the situation. She was a curious woman, after all, a seeker of knowledge, so why shouldn't she want to learn from the wisest man she had ever met? With seven sons, the earl ought to know what he was about in the bedchamber, Joy realized, flushing at the thought.

She lifted her chin as she became resolved. Just this once she would take from a man. They owned the world, had harried her most of her life and owed her more than she could ever claim. It was time she got something worthwhile from their gender and past time she discovered what she had denied herself, Joy thought, with new determination. This Yuletide she would give herself a gift.

Campion.

Chapter Four

After the feasting, Joy escaped to the solar, ostensibly to bundle Christmas greenery. In reality, she needed to think. Now that she had made her decision, she had only to execute it, but the methods involved in luring a man into her bed were something she had never taken an interest in before. Certainly, with someone like Stephen, she would not need to have a plan, just breath in her body, she thought with a grimace. But Campion was no randy rogue. He was a mature man seemingly unaffected by her presence.

Joy frowned, considering all that she had seen of courting behaviors, but those were usually among the lower orders, and she could not imagine plopping herself on the earl's lap with a giggle. Indeed, the idea was so horrifying that she dropped the sprig of holly she had been tying and bent to pick it up. Roesia and Stephen had brought in plenty of bay and holly when they returned from skating, and she and Joy were now gathering it into bunches of twelve to decorate the hall.

Idly Joy wondered if Roesia's trip to the pond had been as interesting as her own, and the thought made her pause. Laying the sprig in her lap, Joy slanted a speculative glance toward her attendant. Although younger than herself, Roesia had more experience dealing with men, claiming an appreciation of them that Joy had always disdained, yet now that knowledge might come to good use.

"Roesia, how do you go about making a man...notice you?" Joy asked. The question, although put forward casually enough, caused her attendant to spill her evergreens, scattering small boughs upon the tiled floor.

Eyeing her with a puzzled expression, Roesia knelt to retrieve her work. "Excuse me, my lady, but I thought you asked something about gaining a man's attention!" She laughed, seemingly amused at her own folly, but the sound died away when she looked at Joy's face.

"You are serious? I was not mistaken?" she asked.

Joy lifted her chin. "I have always sought to increase my store of knowledge by learning from others, but if you are unwilling to share your—"

"Oh, my lady!" Roesia interrupted. "Oh, this is wonderful! But I thought you were resolved against marriage!"

Joy frowned. "I am resolved against it."

"But, you said—"

"I said I was interested in the arts of seduction, not imprisonment," Joy said with a sound of disgust.

Roesia blinked at her in bewilderment. "Surely, you aren't talking about becoming a man's...mistress!" she objected. "You, with all your high ideals about women and all!"

"No, I most certainly will not become a mistress. I won't be around long enough to qualify as that," Joy answered, shifting in her seat uncomfortably at the reminder of her more vocal views. "I am thinking of a simple dalliance, the kind that happens all the time at court and even among my neighbors."

Roesia gaped at her openmouthed, and Joy bristled. "You are always prattling on about the pleasures to be found in a man's arms. Now would you deny your words?"

Roesia shook her head. "No, my lady, but I enjoy a good kiss or two now and then and maybe even a tumble with the right fellow, while you've never even looked at a man!"

"Well, now I am," Joy replied with a righteous expression.

"And that's all to the good, my lady! But a woman like you wasn't made for a quick toss. Why, I thought you couldn't stand Stephen...." Her words trailed off as she studied Joy. "Oh, my lord, it's Campion! 'Tis the earl himself who has caught your eye!" Roesia said, lifting a hand to her throat as if she found the discovery shocking.

"And what, pray tell, is wrong with Campion?" Joy said in a dangerously low tone that warned her attendant to watch her speech.

"Nothing, my lady. Truly, nothing. Lord, what a man!" Roesia said with a sigh of appreciation. She seemed lost in thoughts of the earl for so long that Joy scowled at her, and Roesia gave her an apologetic smile before sobering. "But he's totally different! You can't take a man like that to your bed and wake up unchanged."

"Whatever do you mean?" Joy asked, genuinely puzzled. Of course, she wanted the experience to change her. She wanted, at last, to be a woman, in every sense of the word.

Roesia flushed. "You're talking about simple lust, my lady, but it's not always easy to separate your heart from the rest of you." At Joy's questioning look, she threw up her hands in exasperation. "What of love, my lady? Not all your fine ideas or stubborn will can protect you against it."

"Love!" Joy scoffed. She had always thought that so-called romance was a bunch of foolishness conjured by wandering minstrels in order to trade upon the good graces of the lady of the castle. "I fear it not!" she said with a laugh.

Roesia simply shook her head. "And what of Campion? He's not like Stephen, eager to get under any woman's skirt! I know more of men than you, my lady, and I tell you that he's not the sort to take a woman to his bed unless he loves her. Do you think he'll just perform like a stallion and then let you go?"

Joy stiffened at the implied threat to her coveted independence. "He will have no choice," she said, "for I am my own woman. He can make no claim upon me."

Roesia sighed as if put upon by a poor student. "My lady, you don't know a thing about males, if you think that. For all that he looks gentle eyed and calm, the earl has a fierceness in him. Else how could he have ruled these lands and built this dynasty of his? And I would think you ought not give yourself to him unless you mean it. Forever."

Just as Joy opened her mouth to argue, Roesia gave her a hopeful smile. "If you've got your sights set on the earl, why not wed him? That would solve all our problems! And I can't say I'd mind living here," she added with an admiring glance toward the castle's luxurious furnishings.

"I will not marry again," Joy said. She had hated being torn from her home to wed a stranger, had resented her lanky boy of a husband, and, after his death, had come to prize her independence. Men controlled everything about a wife—her money, her property, her very life. Even friendships between women were discouraged, for a wife must keep her mind upon her duties.

Since the Church decreed that God had made womankind subject to male control, a woman who acted for herself was believed to be possessed by the Devil. And the courts were no more favorable than the Church. If a wife killed her husband, she was executed for treason because her husband was her master, while a man could buy a pardon should he be moved to such violence against his spouse. While men ruled, they conspired to keep women as less than chattel, and no doubt would do so until the end of time, Joy thought bitterly.

"Well, Campion is no boy forced upon you by relatives. He's a man, with power aplenty to control his fate, and marrying him would be wholly different. No more worries over the harvest or holding your demesne or *anything*." Roesia sighed at the notion, and Joy felt a bitter guilt at the lean years. She had done her best to run the small household and bit of lands surrounding it without help from anyone, but she had precious few funds and there was always something to eat away at them.

Oblivious to her thoughts, Roesia smiled wickedly. "And since you've a taste for the earl, you could ease it every night, or day for that matter!"

Joy frowned at her attendant's exuberance. "As appealing as that notion is," she answered dryly, "I am hardly ready to give up my life for it."

"But the earl's not like most men! He thinks differently, having read so many books and all. And you don't see him treating anyone badly."

It was true. Campion seemed so wise, so…understanding, but as her husband, he would still own her, and Joy refused to submit to anyone's possession. She had struggled to make a life for herself at her small manor, a life in which she had all that she needed.

As if reading her thoughts, Roesia glanced about the well-appointed solar, a far cry from the close quarters to which they were accustomed. "And this castle is the most beautiful place I've ever seen, with so many lovely things. Why, living here would be like living a dream," her attendant said.

"For you, perhaps. But for me it would be bondage, of a sort, and I am not bargaining away my freedom for a few pieces of furniture and delicacies upon my table."

Roesia sighed as she reached for a ribbon to tie around her bundle of greenery. "You're a hard woman, my lady. I just hope that you won't one day rue those precious views of yours, for they won't keep you warm on a cold night."

Her words turned Joy's thoughts toward Campion, and she imagined his strong body heating hers, holding the chill and all else at bay. It was a tantalizing notion, but one which she dismissed with a frown. An extra fur would work as well, she told herself firmly. And it would be a lot less trouble in the bargain.

Irritated with her attendant, Joy had finally returned to the hall, where she had spent the evening desultorily weaving the rest of the greenery around a wooden frame into a kissing bush. Roesia had been no help at all. In fact, the woman who had perpetually urged her to find a man now refused to aid Joy in interesting one. Capricious creature!

Although Campion had presided over the light supper served earlier, he had disappeared since, and Joy knew a sense of disappointment, along with annoyance at herself. When had she ever cared about a man's movements, as long as they did not jeopardize her home? Perhaps since she had decided to learn the fine arts of seduction, she thought with a wry grimace.

But without her victim's presence, she could only sit back and stew, a very disturbing sensation that made her wonder just how much she was investing in this little plan of hers. It was near sunset, and the holiday revelry was winding to a close as the villeins and freemen who had spent the day at the castle prepared to take their leave.

Stephen was acting the gregarious host, and Joy debated whether to ask him or his brother where their father had gone. While part of her rebelled at seeking out her prey, another part declared such knowledge necessary to the fulfillment of her plan. Racked by the unaccustomed confusion, Joy finished the bush with an impatient gesture.

She looked up, prepared to call a servant over to hang it, only to find Stephen standing in front of her. Too close. There was nowhere to go, and the massive chair was too heavy to slide backward. Besides, it was not in her nature to cede ground to a man, so she simply lifted her chin and gave him a questioning look. To her annoyance, he placed his hands on the table on either side of her, effectively hedging her in as he loomed over her.

"Beautiful, work, my lady. Shall we try it?" he asked, in a low voice, tilting his dark head toward the bush. And before Joy could answer, he lowered his mouth to hers.

The mistletoe that was lodged among the evergreen

boughs, ribbons and nuts was supposed to promote the kiss of peace, but this was no friendly brush of the lips. Stephen's was a kiss of seduction, his lips moving expertly over her own, and Joy, a stranger to such things, made the mistake of gasping in surprise. To her astonishment, Stephen seized the opportunity to thrust his tongue into her mouth. He tasted of wine and bitterness. The cold calculation of his movements fueled her outrage, and Joy pulled back at the same time that she lifted her knee.

Although she had little experience in kissing, she knew how to protect herself, and she heard Stephen's yelp of pain as she slipped from his embrace. Watching him warily, she saw him teeter precariously before plunging toward the table. Only the innate de Burgh grace saved him from smashing his handsome face into the worn wood, and Joy spared him no sympathy.

Reynold grunted in amusement, and Stephen turned his head, his handsome face surly, but Joy lifted her chin, meeting his glare with her own until he shoved away from the table. His easy smile returning, he bowed his head toward her. "Touché, lady," he said softly, before turning to go.

"Coddled whelp," Joy murmured, but she held her ground until he disappeared up the stairs, then she sank back down into her chair with a sigh at the vagaries of fate. She did not want the son's attention, but the father's! It was only after her gaze fell upon the abandoned kissing bush that Joy realized she ought to thank the errant de Burgh, and a slow smile crept over her face.

Stephen had given her what Roesia would not—a clue to the art of seduction—and Joy seized upon the tempting idea, hoping that her efforts went far better than Stephen's. As the plan took root she ignored her own trepidation and rose to her feet, walking toward the servant who was removing the last cups of ale from the trestle tables.

"Wilda?" Joy asked. At the woman's wary nod, she

smiled. "I wondered if you knew where Lord Campion might be."

"Taking a bath, I gather, though why the men of this family feel such a need to be clean I will never know. Why, it's not natural!" the servant confided, before realizing that she might have said too much. She glanced away, her eyes downcast as she reached for another cup. "Probably something he read in those foreign books of his," she muttered.

"Or a man's sport," Joy said dryly. She knew that oftentimes male bathers had women attendants, which could lead to more than washing.

Wilda immediately shook her head at the implication. "Oh, you won't find anything of that here, my lady!" she declared. "His lordship and all the boys are good men. Oh, Stephen's a bit of a rogue, but how can he help it when all the females adore him?"

Joy could have argued with that, but she was relieved to learn that the earl was as honorable as she had judged him.

"Lord Campion ought to be back down soon, for he likes to keep an eye on his hall, to make sure the celebrating doesn't go on all night," Wilda noted with a grin.

"I see," Joy answered. "Thank you. I think I will wait to…speak with him."

"You do that, my lady!" Wilda said, returning to her work. Turning, Joy walked slowly back to the high table, where she idly fingered the kissing bush. Around her the festivities were coming to an end, servants cleaning away debris and dousing candles so that soon the massive vaulted space was in shadow. Taking a seat in Campion's chair, Joy watched Reynold usher out a few straggling knights before he sought his own rest. Then some of the servants began making up pallets on the other side of the room, so far away that they disappeared into darkness.

Night was coming at last to Campion. Where was the earl? Joy knew an odd sensation that she ascribed to anticipation, not to overwrought nerves. But when, at last, she heard footsteps, she flinched, suddenly regretting her impulsive decision. Turning, she saw Campion standing on the stairs, surveying his domain, and the very sight of him flooded her with warmth. Any doubts she had entertained fled swiftly as she rose to her feet.

"Campion." It felt wonderful to speak his name, but Joy knew a possessive need to discover his first name, his true name, and whisper it to him in the dark of his chamber. She shivered.

"Lady Warwick. I am surprised to find you here so late," the earl said. Concern colored his voice, and Joy wanted to be rid of it—and all else that stood between them.

"How do you like it?" she asked, moving aside to reveal her work. Campion looked at her, and for a moment, she saw a glimpse of vulnerability behind those all-knowing eyes, a dazed look of slumbering…something. But then it was gone, replaced by his maddeningly courteous demeanor.

Courtesy be hanged, Joy thought with a mutinous glance. She wanted to scream and shout and drag a reaction from Campion that was more than polite welcome, that was impolite welcome, that was even a small measure of the overwhelming heat she felt in his presence. Instead, she gestured toward the table. "Here. Come see your Christmas bush," she said. "What think you of it?"

Campion stepped forward, his movements fluid, his tall form cast in shadow, and Joy swallowed. As he studied her creation, she inched closer. When he turned his head to find her next to him, he cleared his throat, staring down at her with a certain intensity that gave her hope. "Lovely," he answered.

"Do you think so?" Joy asked, her breath quickening at his nearness. Even in the dim glow of the remaining candles, she could see his broad shoulders, the elegant way in which he held himself. She wanted to reach out and touch him. "Then we must make use of it," she murmured. A surge of power ran through her that she would never have associated with the role of seductress, and she liked it well.

Campion lifted his brows in polite query. Too polite. "A kiss," Joy demanded.

Surprise glinted his eyes. "Certainly," he said, and to Joy's chagrin, he did not look one bit excited by the prospect. He was at his most dignified, the earl, and he bent his head as if to brush her cheek, but a glancing touch of peace was not what Joy wanted. She was blossoming in her new role, and at the last moment, she turned to meet his lips with her own.

They were warm and firm and so very delicious that Joy grabbed onto his tunic to pull herself closer. She tried to remember just how Stephen had managed to get inside her mouth, but it was awfully hard to keep her mind on her task when she felt so odd, all fiery and alive. Campion went still and for a moment, Joy thought he would push her away, just as she had done to his son. She made a low sound of protest, but then his mouth opened over hers, his arms came around her and his breath mingled with hers in exquisite union.

Joy moved against him, her arms circling his broad chest as his tongue meshed with hers, for Campion took the kiss beyond Stephen's calculated efforts. No cool display of expertise was this, but a passion that rivaled her own. One of his hands moved behind her head, as if to hold her in place, while the other stroked her back, lower and lower still, until it closed around her buttocks and lifted her. Joy felt the hot, hard length of him rub her stomach, and she wiggled against it, wanting more. It was shocking and primitive and so exciting that she cried out in glorious surrender.

And then it was over. Just as suddenly as it had been unleashed, Campion's potent ardor was restrained once more. Joy, whimpering a protest, realized that he was setting her away, gently but firmly. She had but a glimpse of his stricken expression before he turned his head away.

"Forgive me. I had no right, no call to—" He broke off,

and when he swiveled toward her, she saw that he had assumed his usual dignity. "You must seek your chamber. It is late, and you are without your attendant."

That is the idea! Joy wanted to scream. "But—"

"There is no excuse for my behavior."

"But—"

Someone moved at the entrance to the kitchens, and Campion, with seemingly preternatural recognition, called softly, "Wilda, would you please escort Lady Warwick to her chamber?"

"Yes, my lord," came the reply, and Joy wanted to shriek in frustration. So much for her seduction attempt! But what could she do? Tell Wilda to mind her own business? Press the earl back upon the high table and force him to appease her desires? The very notion grated and, lifting her chin, Joy went, chagrined at her rejection.

But even as she stalked away, she knew that for one precious moment she had felt the earth move, and she had moved Campion, too, whether he willed it or not.

Campion arose early after a uneasy night filled with images of his guest which, while enthralling, left him feeling guilty and ashamed. Even in the broad light of dawn, the memory of their embrace plagued him, and he groaned. What had possessed him? He could not recall ever acting so impulsively, so *wildly*. It was simply not his nature. Perhaps he was growing old. Old and mad!

He stayed in his chamber, unwilling to face the frantic revelry of the season, at least until the feasting began again, but he found himself pacing the length of the room with a restlessness he had not known in years. It was in this state that Reynold found him, and his son's innocent inquiry after his health suddenly annoyed him beyond endurance.

"I am fine," Campion muttered. *A fully functioning man,* he felt like adding. *A man who realizes what he has been missing and now must fight the craving for what he cannot have.* He stood at the window, hands clasped behind his back, and stared out at the bleak landscape below, enjoying the chill wind upon his face. *Mayhap it would cool his hot blood.*

Behind him he heard Reynold take a seat on the settle near the hearth. "'Tis looking more like Christmas in the hall," his son said.

"Yes," Campion answered. *Thanks to his bargain with the guest he had treated so poorly last evening!*

"Already the knights have made use of the kissing bush."

At Reynold's mention of the greenery that held the mistletoe, Campion felt a flash of heat scald his cheekbones. The memory of Lady Warwick in his arms, his hand buried in her thick hair, made him clear his throat.

"That is as it should be, as long as the revelry does not get out of hand," Campion said. He was a fine one to talk, he thought, for, as lord, it was up to him to set an example for his subjects. Last night he had set a poor one, should anyone have seen him with Lady Warwick in the shadows, and the knowledge that his actions may have injured his visitor's reputation made them doubly regretful.

"Stephen tried it out first," Reynold said in a deceptively careless tone that made Campion turn to look at him. "With the lady herself."

Campion stiffened. "Lady Warwick?"

Reynold nodded. "You know Stephen, always one for the ladies, whether they want him or not."

Campion held his tongue for a good long moment as he tried to divine Reynold's meaning. "Are you saying that Stephen *forced* himself upon our guest?" His fury mixed with his own shame, for had he not done the same?

"Well, he didn't hurt her. In fact, she hurt him. First, she drove a knee into his groin, and then she practically knocked him face-first into the high table. It was quite amusing, although I suspect his pride was injured more than anything else," Reynold said.

Campion was glad he had not been present, for it had been

a long time since he had brawled with one of his own sons, and right now he had an overpowering urge to thrash Stephen. "Where is he?"

Reynold shrugged. "Off with someone who is not so immune to his charms."

"When he reappears, I will have him apologize," Campion said, more to himself than Reynold. Then, remembering Reynold's presence, the earl eyed his son carefully, wondering at his motives. The boys had always held together, keeping each other's mischief from their sire. Why had Stephen's actions suddenly compelled Reynold to speak? "Thank you for telling me," Campion said.

Reynold shrugged and rose to his feet. "Lady Warwick seems well able to take care of herself, but I thought you should know that she came away from the encounter looking as if she had just tasted some rancid meat." Reynold grunted in amusement and turned to go, leaving Campion staring after him.

Had Lady Warwick looked the same after she left him last night? No, he could still hear her low cry of pleasure, feel her pressing against him. Or was that only what he wished to recall? With a frown, Campion knew he owed his guest an apology, not just for his son, but for himself. What must she think of the de Burghs? he wondered with a shudder.

Campion found her in the solar with her attendant, sewing small figures, presumably for the kissing bush, and he felt guilty for their bargain, especially considering what had come of her handiwork. Standing in the doorway unobserved, he took a moment to admire the guest who had wrought so much havoc among the de Burghs.

Although young and beautiful, Joy looked far too somber to arouse such passions, making Campion wish that he could remove the line that blotted her brow and the tension in her mouth. What mysteries lay behind her serious demeanor? He would ease her cares, if only she would confide in him, but she kept her own counsel, and with such fierce independence that he would not presume to intrude.

Then, as if his perusal alerted her to his presence, she glanced up to see him, and Campion was rewarded with a smile that struck him so forcefully he hardly noticed her nod of dismissal to her attendant. "No, Lady, you need not send Roesia away," he protested as the woman passed him, leaving him alone with Lady Warwick in the cozy room.

Unnerved, Campion drew upon his dignity and approached his guest, bowing his head in greeting. "Lady, I have just had some grievous news," he said. At her startled expression, he moved forward to halt in front of her.

"Nay, nothing tragic," he said gently. "But, nonetheless, it is disturbing. I heard that Stephen treated you ill last night, and of course, my own actions were inexcusable. I want you to know that Stephen will apologize and that our family is usually not so poorly behaved. As a guest in my home, you should be inviolate, safe and secure from any sort of imposition, and I assure you that nothing of the kind will happen again during your stay."

Instead of thanking him tearfully, Joy shrugged off his words. "I am becoming accustomed to the childish antics of your sons, but I will be pleased to hear Stephen's repentance," she said. Campion was nonplussed, but then when had this woman ever behaved in a predictable fashion? As if to prove his theory, she stood, giving him a smile that he could only describe as roguish. "As for you, I will accept no apology."

Campion felt stricken until she stepped closer. "But I will take another kiss." To his astonishment, she lifted her hand to reveal a small sprig of mistletoe, which she dangled above them. He stiffened in dismay. Surely this lovely young woman did not mean she wanted him to... He was most puzzled, for why would she reject Stephen in one breath and tease him in the next? She waited expectantly while Campion struggled for a polite reply.

"My dear lady, I am most…" *What?* Flattered? Surprised? For once, he was at a loss for words. "Tempted. However, after last night, I think you will agree that it would be wiser to refrain from these holiday rituals with Stephen or myself."

"I am not interested in Stephen," she said.

She spoke in that direct way of hers, her violet gaze challenging, and if Campion didn't know better he would think she was proclaiming her interest in…himself. "Lady," he said, chiding her gently. "You cannot know what you are about. You are a young and vibrant woman, while I…I have sons older than those you have met, seven sons in all, and grandchildren!"

"Ah, so that means you are no longer interested in women?" she asked, her lips tilting in an echo of his own chiding expression.

Campion frowned. "Of course not. I find you most attractive." Intriguing, *arousing.* "But surely you would prefer someone your own age, like Reynold or Stephen." Although Campion nearly choked on their names, unwilling to urge the lady toward either son, he was determined to be sensible and to make his guest see reason.

At the mention of his sons, she dropped all pretense of teasing, granting him the direct gaze he so admired. "Stephen and Reynold are still boys, despite their ages, and we both know it," she said, before turning to move gracefully toward the hearth. Stunned, Campion felt he ought to defend his sons, but he suspected she was all too right in her assessment. Although full-grown knights, in some ways, those two were like children, neither one mature enough to stand on his own.

Silently Campion watched her circle the room, each step charming and assured, until she paused before the window. "I've had a boy, and I find I'm more interested in a man," she said, turning her head toward him, and Campion's mouth went dry.

Never before had he been treated to such bold speech. Oh, there had been ladies at court, with their subtle and not-so-subtle pursuits, but most of their intrigues had left him cold. Lady Warwick spoke with a forthrightness that left no doubt as to her intent, yet somehow her words were not brazen, nor were her actions. He could not imagine that she did this with any degree of regularity, and that knowledge was even more daunting.

Already Campion felt his body respond to the desire implicit in her words, and he took a deep breath in an effort to control it. As the man, elder and more experienced, it was up to him to put a stop to this nonsense. Surely she was too young, too unworldly, to know what she was doing.

"Lady—"

"Joy. Please call me Joy."

"Joy." Her name slid far too easily off of his tongue, for he had swiftly come to think of her as bringing joy to his holiday, along with other more complex emotions. Although she seemed at once too serious and too willful for so frivolous a title, Campion thought the name suited her. *Joy*.

"And you are called?"

Campion stilled, stunned for a moment at her request. When he spoke, he did so automatically, without pausing to consider the wisdom of granting her such an intimacy. "Fawke," he said slowly.

"Fawke." She echoed his name in a low voice that skittered along his nerve endings to rouse both his lower body and the heart he had thought better schooled after all these years. How long had it been since someone had called him by his right name? Standing there, watching the slight figure who stood at his solar window, Campion had the sudden, eerie sensation that he was meeting his fate, and all that he might do would simply delay the inevitable. He shook the feeling aside and cleared his throat, striving to regain his reason.

"Joy, you can hardly be serious about this…" *Infatuation? Dalliance? Simple kiss?* Again Campion was at a loss for words.

"And why not?" she asked, over her shoulder. Campion watched the gentle sway of her black curls and felt his body tighten treasonously. "I was wed at age sixteen, an arrangement to keep property in the family. He was thirteen." Her tone was flat, but Campion sensed her resentment and added his own. Although such alliances were not uncommon, he did not approve of marriages involving children of either gender.

"Not a year later, he was gored by a wild boar, and I've been a widow ever since. During all that time, I have never had any desire to remarry, nor any desire to dally with a man." As the startling revelation of her words struck him, Campion found that she had turned to face him once more, her chin lifted in the familiar expression of defiance. "So don't tell me what I want or don't want. I'm a grown woman. I know my own mind."

What Joy would have done or said next, Campion didn't know, for at that point his steward entered, anxiously wishing to consult with her about some petty detail of the feast. Something about candles? Effortlessly sliding into the role of chatelaine that had been assigned her, she moved toward the man, her soft replies barely discernible to Campion, whose mind was still focused on something else entirely. As if aware of his thoughts, Joy gave him a nod and a smile before following his steward from the room with a grace, confidence and allure unequaled.

Campion stood there staring after her, feeling as if his mouth were hanging open from their encounter. Joy wanted *him?* Joy *wanted* him. He drew a deep breath, tamping down the elation that swept through him and replacing it with a more appropriate response.

He had not held his earldom by succumbing to impulse or irrational behavior, no matter how tempting. Unlike his son Stephen, Campion did not engage in brief liaisons, and despite the admiration and attraction he felt for his Christmas guest, he had nothing else to offer her.

The truth was that he had no intention of taking another wife and, even if he did, Joy was too young. Too beautiful. Too alive. Too stubborn. Too *everything*.

Chapter Five

After what happened in the solar, Campion kept a careful, if cordial, distance from his guest. Despite her protestations otherwise, Joy was a headstrong young woman who could not be expected to make the best judgment, and in this case, she was simply not thinking clearly. Campion had a wealth of experience with avoiding temptation, and he knew better.

But he could still enjoy her visit, and he did, delighting in her company. He had decided that Joy was too somber, and in keeping with their skating lesson, he was determined that she learn to enjoy herself while visiting his demesne. Just yesterday, he had encouraged her to join in the games that were part of the Christmas celebration, and tonight, having learned that she did not play chess, he was taking great pleasure in teaching her.

And Joy was an adept pupil. Already, during their second game, she was evincing a remarkable talent for the strategy necessary to win. Really, she was a fascinating creature, Campion mused as they sat before the hearth, the chess table between them. Concentrating on her next move, her dainty fingers hovering over the pieces, she was more beautiful than anyone he had ever seen.

Campion knew that ''fair'' was used to describe women with blond tresses, but surely not one of those ladies could rival Joy with her dark locks hanging loose and heavy. His son Dunstan's wife had fuzzy brown curls, but Joy's were black as night, the sleek long locks seeming to possess a life of their own as they fell clear to her waist.

For all the delicacy of her features, she was a strong-willed, capable woman. And despite her bold speech, there was a subtle air of innocence about her that Campion found very attractive, as if she had missed out on so much of life, including the activities she deemed frivolous. Had she suffered a hard existence? Her clothes were fine enough, her train well manned. Joy was a puzzle, and one he would enjoy unraveling, if he had the time.

And therein lay the cause of Campion's unease, for already it was the fifth day of Christmas, with only seven remaining. Although Joy seemed to enjoy their play well enough, what would happen when she left? Would she return to a life of toil? Campion found his thoughts more and more occupied with her departure and the future that would follow.

Of course, it was only natural that he be concerned with the welfare of one of his guests, but Joy was not the sort of woman who would answer questions about her situation. She was intensely private, another trait he admired, yet he found himself wanting to penetrate that privacy, to establish an intimacy with her that no one else could claim. In a paternal sort of way, Campion told himself, even as his gaze followed the brush of her slender fingers against her bishop.

"Very good!" he said, when he saw her placement of the piece. "You are an excellent student."

Her answering smile nearly stole his breath, and Campion swiftly moved his own piece and tilted back, putting some distance between them. But Joy only leaned closer, her voice so low that he had to bend near to hear her.

"It occurs to me that if you are so determined that I learn all these games of which you are so fond, perhaps there is another manner of play you can teach me, that would be even more pleasurable, for us both," she said, her violet eyes like pools under those thick lashes. Her husky whisper caused an immediate reaction in Campion's body, but he cleared his throat, ignoring the provocative suggestion.

"Watch your queen," he advised hoarsely without daring to look at her. Despite his best efforts, Campion was plagued by unseemly urges when Joy was present, and inappropriate thoughts when she was not. Her teasing comments did not help, and he was becoming thoroughly exasperated with himself.

He had loved both of his wives. He had been very young when he wed the first time, more mature when he married Anne, and yet he could not recall feeling this…unsettled by a female. His wives had both been gentle souls, but Joy, for all her fragility, was not. Her look of cool composure hid a fiery spirit with a core of steel. A fit wife for any man, Campion thought, before catching himself.

Obviously he had been without a woman too long. Indeed, there had been no one since his last visit to court, for he did not believe in the misuse of women and would provide an example for his sons. Yet there was something about Joy that affected him like no other. He began to feel like a randy boy, more true to Stephen's nature than his own! He did not believe in allowing passions to rule one's life and so had long ago suppressed such yearnings, yet now, it was as if his dormant desires wished to make up for the years of celibacy as soon as possible. With Joy.

It was aggravating…and vaguely exhilarating.

"Check," she said, warning of her intent to capture, and Campion looked up in surprise to see her sly smile. She was referring to the chessboard, of course. Then why did he have the impression she meant something else entirely?

Stephen glanced at the cozy scene by the hearth and frowned at his brother Reynold. "She has him rattled," he muttered.

"Who? Father?" Reynold let out a rough sound that was the closest he came to laughter. "Campion is never rattled."

"Yes, he is," Stephen argued. Reynold was too young to recall his mother's death and Campion's long vigil in her chamber, but Stephen remembered it as a chilling time when even his all-wise father seemed to be lost. He shrugged off the memory and took a drink. "I've seen it before, but I never thought to see it again. He hasn't been shaken from his usual stoicism for years. Until now. Until *her*."

Reynold snorted. "You're just piqued that the lady won't notice you."

"Well, I have to admit that there's something wrong when a beautiful young woman pays more attention to my father than me," Stephen said, with a nod toward the duo by the fire. "I wonder what she's up to."

"Nothing," Reynold scoffed. "Do you think that any woman who is interested in Father must have an ulterior motive? You're daft!"

"He's a powerful man," Stephen mused. "While I'm nothing but a younger son with no prospects."

Reynold snorted. "If you would get your head out of your wine cup long enough—"

"Don't start on me, when you should look to yourself," Stephen snapped.

Reynold grunted but did not rise to the bait. "Father is still a handsome fellow to the ladies. Haven't you heard Marion coo about him enough to know that? Just because he's lived like a monk these past years doesn't mean he is one."

"A scary thought," Stephen commented. "Surely you cannot be suggesting that the almighty Campion might have needs like the rest of us mere mortals?"

Reynold muttered a low oath. "Can't you see *anything* around you except yourself?" His gaze swung toward the hearth and then back to Stephen. "He's lonely, and she's good for him. Leave them be."

With a black look, Reynold shook his head and left the

table, much to Stephen's disappointment. He never would admit as much to a soul, but he found himself missing Simon, who could always be counted upon for a good quarrel until he fell for a sword-wielding Amazon in the Forest of Dean. Reynold, who did not suffer an excess of bile, was simply not as much fun.

And as for his insinuation that Campion felt the same as less exalted beings, Stephen doubted it. He glanced toward the fire and shook his head before lifting his cup to drink. Still she had the earl rattled, there was no doubt of it.

It was the sixth day of Christmas, and Joy's frustration was mounting. Although she sensed that Campion was not indifferent to her, he maintained a strict decorum that left her no opportunity to test his remarkable restraint. She had hoped for another cozy game of chess, but tonight he had talked her into playing hoodman's bluff, and so she was standing in the midst of the hall, blindfolded, while the other players turned her around several times.

Laughing at a momentary dizziness, Joy felt her tension ease. Although she could not imagine engaging in such nonsense at home, here at Campion everything, even the most foolish of pastimes took on a magical glow, whether from the season or the castle. Or Campion. At the thought of the stubborn earl, Joy smiled. The object of this game was to find and identify someone without the aid of sight, and she knew just whom she would seek.

Ignoring the loud encouragement of those close by, Joy moved away from the crowd, for she knew Campion would be on the periphery, watching quietly with those enigmatic eyes. He would not be jostling others or frantically hopping about for attention. Campion would be still, his power leashed with dignity.

"You're heading for the kitchens, lady!" someone called, and indeed, Joy recognized the odor of food drifting toward her. Her outstretched fingers brushed against something, a man's chest, but the softness of it made her turn away. There was no softness about the earl, except inside him, where goodness and honor and gentleness dwelt. Much laughter and teasing ensued when she passed by the man, and her hand next found the wooden screen that stood at the end of the hall near the entrance to the buttery and the kitchens.

There she stopped as a faint whiff of something else caught her attention, and suddenly the game and its noisy participants all faded away. In the darkness there was only herself and the man she had sought, whose scent she recognized as well as her own. She could sense his presence, his strength, and smell the familiar flavors of him: clean clothing, the spicy soap that he used and that which was his alone. She had known it before in the darkness of the hall by the kissing bush, and now she reached unerringly out to it again.

Joy was aware of the sound of the crowd, but only as an irritating rumble, for she was focused solely on the earl. One more step and she felt his heat, her hands lifting to rest upon his broad chest, and she stood there, wishing that she could remain where she was always, that he would draw her into his arms and hold her. Keep her.

Someone pulled off the hood, but Joy stayed in front of Campion, and amid shrieks and cheers, the game continued, moving away from the dim area at the end of the hall. Drawing him with her, Joy backed behind the carved screen that would hide them from prying eyes.

There, in the sheltered shadows, Joy tried her hand at a new game, one far more dear to her, as her fingers slid up Campion's chest into the sleek softness of his dark hair. She stroked it with wonder, despite his stillness and the intense regard of his brown eyes.

Along with the usual warmth that came with his nearness, Joy felt something more, a sweetness that seemed to fill her, pressing behind her eyes until she wanted to weep with the pleasure of touching him. Roesia's warning came back to her, but she wondered if it was not too late to heed her attendant, for she already had come to care for this man.

Recklessly Joy raised herself up on her toes and touched her mouth to his, and it was even more wonderful than she remembered. The kiss was an exploration, a greeting well met that nonetheless sent heat surging through her, and her arms slipped around his waist, anchoring her to his strength.

After a moment's hesitation, Campion kissed the corner of her mouth, her eyelashes, her brows and the line of her jaw, murmuring her name in a tone that she had never heard before. It was a whisper that spoke of awe and desire, and Joy responded with abandon, pressing her body against his and welcoming his lips with her own. She recognized now the hard ridge of his manhood against her stomach, and she wanted nothing more than to feel all of him, around her, inside her, as part of her.

"Let us go to your chamber," she urged breathlessly against his cheek, but he stiffened even as she spoke. Joy could sense the withdrawal of his passion, and she whimpered in protest. Still he set her away. Even in the shadows, she could see the glint of his eyes, shining with wisdom and ardor withheld.

"It would not be right," he said.

"But I want you. I...I care for you," Joy said. At her faltering confession, his expression softened, and he reached out to stroke her hair in a gesture of comfort that only made her need more.

"Nay. 'Tis but a passing thing, and I would be a rogue indeed if I were to take advantage of it," he said.

His words made Joy bristle, and she shrugged off his hand. "Do not speak to me as if I were a child, Fawke, for I am not! I am a woman full grown, a widow who has maintained a holding for years! Why do you not credit my decision? Do you think I'm a fool?"

"No, of course not," he said in gentle placation that only made Joy angrier.

"Then why do you dispute me? Why can't I know my own mind? If I chose Reynold, would you fault me?" Joy saw the flicker of emotion that crossed his face, and was well glad of it. She wanted to hurt him, to punish him for denying her.

"No," he said softly, then he turned away, releasing a heavy sigh into the shadows. "The problem, as you've divined, bright lady that you are, is with me. I loved my wives, but after I buried Anne, I vowed never to put myself in such a position again."

Stunned by his admission, Joy came up behind him, placing a palm against his broad back. She had glimpsed a vulnerability in this strong man, but she had never imagined that he had forsaken women to avoid the pain of another's death. How could she argue against such emotion? She slid her arms around his waist and rested her cheek against him.

"Foolish man, you are always complaining about my age," she muttered into his tunic. "Now see how it can only be to your advantage, for I will surely outlive you anyway!"

Campion stiffened, then turned toward her, and Joy was afraid her audacious response had been too much. But he only shook his head and started laughing, a deep rumble of merriment that gladdened her heart. It seemed the perfect opportunity for a kiss or more, to lay claim to this man and convince him to join her in bed, but his admission gave her pause.

She might care for him, but Joy was still intent upon leaving, and although it was hardly the same as dying, she wondered if Campion would be hurt by her defection. He valued loyalty and honor, as did she, so why did she feel that her plans to go were both disloyal and dishonorable?

And so when their moment of quiet intimacy was disturbed by servants bringing the wassail from the kitchens, Joy said nothing, caught in a coil of her own making as surely as Roesia had predicted.

* * *

Jostled to his senses by the wassailers, Campion held out his hand to Joy, whose sudden, stricken expression made him rue his words. He should never have talked about his grief for Anne! It was an ill-mannered man who spoke to one woman of another, and yet, his wives were a part of him and Joy should know it. Perhaps it would remind her of the differences between them.

But even as he tried to hold on to them, Campion felt his objections slipping away. Other men his age took young wives, oftentimes to give them heirs, and although he had plenty of those already, Campion knew no one would fault him for marrying a woman of Joy's years. It was more difficult to rid himself of his refusal to love again, but already she had somehow slipped beneath his reserve to nudge at his heart—and elsewhere.

As his fingers closed over hers, Campion felt the surge of arousal that came simply from touching her. Would that he could lead her upstairs to his chamber! She had offered herself up to him, and his body clamored to accept, but he held firm to his honor.

It would not be right. There was too much standing between them, even more yet unknown, and Campion couldn't shake his feeling that she was keeping something from him. Nor could he completely dismiss his initial impression that Joy was not the best judge of what was best for her.

So, instead of taking her to his bed, Campion escorted her to the chair beside his own, where the rousing game of hoodman's bluff was coming to an end. A glance over the table told him that the revelers were growing weary and that Stephen, slumped in one of the chairs, was drunk. It was not surprising these days, especially with the added festivities, but Campion saw the reckless gleam in his eye and frowned.

He had reason to be proud of all his sons, Stephen included, but right now his patience with the boy's antics was running low. And, along with the exasperation, he felt a familiar guilt that he had somehow failed his son. Perhaps if there had been more of a woman's presence in the household, he thought, and his eyes traveled, unbidden, to Joy.

She spoke of wanting him, but for how long? Barring more ill weather, in only a few more days she would be gone, and they had not talked about extending her visit. Although he ought to be relieved to see the end of his temptation, all he felt was a wrenching despair, as if the lady represented his last chance for her namesake. Joy.

Campion realized that his own perusal had drawn Stephen's, and he felt a sudden, unreasoning proprietorship. *His Joy,* he thought, even as he recognized the reaction as rather barbaric. He had told her often enough to choose another, and now he wanted to deny it, to shout his possession to the world. Only great force of will kept him in his seat.

One of the wassailers stopped by his chair, wishing him prosperity in the coming year, and although Campion turned and smiled, his thoughts remained with those at the high table. He wondered from whence came his passion, for he could not recall ever feeling so deeply, so violently.

"You're going about it the wrong way, you know," Stephen drawled, making Campion wonder what his son was up to now.

"What?" Joy's soft reply followed, and Campion listened intently even as he nodded at the fellow raising his cup in song before him.

"You'll never lure Campion into marriage by pursuing him." Stephen's snide comment made the earl jerk his head toward his son, the wassailer forgotten.

"I have no interest in marrying the earl," Joy replied, and the rebuke that Campion was forming for his son died on his lips. *She didn't want to marry him?*

Stephen continued just as if Joy had not spoken. "He's too noble to marry a pretty young thing like you. Now, if you were in desperate straits, in need of a husband to protect you, then you can be sure the honorable earl would do the right thing, no matter what his personal feelings,'' Stephen said, sneering.

Both stunned and appalled by his son's words, Campion nonetheless recognized the truth of them. If Joy needed him in some way, he would gladly seize the excuse to make her his, and the knowledge did not sit well upon his shoulders.

''Why not plead your case, Lady Warwick?'' Stephen said, inclining his head toward Campion. ''Why not tell him the truth?'' he asked, his mobile mouth moving into a hard line. ''Why not explain that you left your home, rushing into a snowstorm, in order to avoid the arrival of your uncle, who has been pressing you to marry again. Another cousin of his, perhaps? Someone you liked no better than your first husband?''

Campion's gaze swiveled toward Joy. Did Stephen speak the truth of things? Few monied widows were allowed to remain so for long, if they had male relatives or liege lords who would benefit from their remarriage. A widow with no children and a decent holding would be worth a nice settlement, and Campion had wondered at Joy's freedom, but her strength and assurance had fooled him. He had thought her wholly independent, not a woman under siege.

No wonder she had turned to him.

Campion felt a stir of disappointment. He had thought Joy's desire for him was genuine, if misguided, but now he saw her overtures for what they were: the actions of an intelligent woman trying to save herself from another bad marriage. He could hardly blame her, nor did she lose his respect, but for a long moment, he knew a sharp pain, a prick of more than his pride. But it was swiftly overwhelmed by his sense of honor. Here was a lady in distress, a lovely, educated, capable woman who sought his protection. And he had denied her.

''Was it just happenstance that led you here, or were you hunting better game?'' Stephen drawled. ''Perhaps someone who wouldn't care that you might be barren?''

Surprised at the rage that rose within him at Stephen's taunt, Campion surged to his feet and laid his hands on the table. "That's enough." It was all he trusted himself to say.

Stephen swung his gaze around, as if he had all but forgotten his sire's presence, and was even more stunned by the rebuke. Their gazes locked for a long moment until finally, with a low grunt, Stephen picked up his cup and drank. Around them, the silence was deafening, and Campion gestured for the wassailers to begin anew. When they did, he once more took his seat and turned his attention to the woman beside him.

"Is it true?" he asked gently. Joy's head was bent, her face obscured by her luxurious midnight hair, and Campion had the horrible suspicion that she was weeping.

She quickly disabused him of that notion, lifting her chin to reveal a fierce expression. "Perhaps. But what if it is?" she asked, as if in challenge. "'Tis not the first time Hobart has harried me to take a husband, and I'm sure it will not be the last. But do you see me wed? Nay."

She rose to her feet, magnificent in her controlled fury, and whirled toward Stephen. "Since 'tis my business and not yours, Stephen de Burgh, I will keep my own counsel, but let me assure you that I am fully able of handling my uncle and have done so for years. Dare you imagine otherwise?"

The look she gave Stephen made him squirm in his seat, a feat few could manage, and without waiting for a reply, she turned on her heel and stalked from the room with a dignity that stole Campion's breath. He had been right all along. Not only had she kept something from him, but she was too much for him. Too beautiful, too willful, too independent and too passionate—for him to resist.

He knew what he must do.

Chapter Six

Campion awoke on the eve of the new year with new purpose. He had learned long ago that choosing one's moment was vital, and so he had not pursued Joy when she left the hall the night before. She was a stubborn woman, more so when angry, and he gave her time to recover from her outrage in the hope that she would be better able to see reason, come the new day.

As for himself, Campion had made his own decision, for in the face of Joy's dilemma, his resolve not to marry again had fallen by the wayside. He told himself he was doing the honorable thing, but it was the threat of another taking his place that spurred him to action. The mere thought of Joy going to someone else's bed, of marrying a man of her uncle's choosing, was enough to rouse his blood to a fever pitch. *His Joy*.

No longer startled by such violent sentiments in connection with his guest, Campion did his best to wrestle them into submission, cloaking his passion in dignity. He had prepared his arguments and, confident of his success, he sought her out.

She was in the solar with her attendant, and Campion took a moment to admire her beauty before he was discovered. Roesia immediately rose to leave, and Joy, eyeing him with something akin to alarm, voiced her protest. But it went un-heeded, and soon he was alone with the woman who would be his wife.

The rebellious look she gave him boded ill, and Campion knew a sudden, swift disappointment, for he missed the wel-come he had once seen in her expression. Had it been an illusion, as Stephen claimed? Campion only knew he wanted to bring it back, fool that he was. When she pursued him, he had decried it, but now he missed his bold seductress. *His Joy.*

"I apologize once more for any distress that my family has caused you," he said softly, cursing both Stephen and himself. But Joy only shrugged and turned away, a move-ment that struck Campion painfully, and he moved to sit before her upon a low stool.

"Why did you not confide in me?" he asked, without ac-cusation.

"Do all who tarry here share their most personal problems with the lord of the land?" Joy answered with a bitterness that dismayed him.

"Nay, but neither do they offer themselves to me, a far more personal act, wouldn't you say?" Campion replied.

She flushed and frowned. "I have spent long years holding on to that which is mine against the encroachment of men, so you will pardon me if I was wary of trusting you at first sight. What if you were the kind who would send for Ho-bart?"

Campion shook his head, understanding her reluctance and yet smarting from it. "But now, surely, you must know I would do nothing to hurt you," he said.

She laughed at his words, an unhappy sound that made Campion flinch. Had he hurt her? How? Surely not with his rebuffs? "Joy, I...I was just trying to do what was best for you," he explained.

Her chin lifted, and her violet eyes flashed. "And how could you be certain what is right for me? You may have ruled wisely and well for a lifetime, but you are not omnipotent, my lord. You cannot possibly know everything!''

Campion stilled, astounded, not for the first time, by her perception. She was right, of course. Years of making decisions, of running his demesne, of ruling over the disputes of his people and the well-being of his family had left him all too accustomed to proffering answers whenever questions were presented to him. Had he become pompous and all-knowing? Campion made a low sound of apology as the realization struck him that this time, perhaps, he had been wrong.

He reached out to take her hand, to tell her so, but all the fine arguments he had prepared vanished in a swell of foreboding. ''Marry me,'' he said, the words released hurriedly as emotions buffeted him. He needed time to think upon her words, to take a good, long look at himself, yet his blood was beating out a demand that he do something now, before it was too late.

But it was already too late. As Joy shook her head in denial, Campion knew he had rejected her once too often, sealing his fate, along with her own. She pulled her hand from his and stood, as if to dismiss him.

Lifting her chin in the familiar gesture of defiance, she faced him, and Campion could see that her anger was barely controlled. ''I want no proposal born of pity,'' she said. ''I have already suffered one marriage arranged for reasons other than affection, and I will not be a party to another, thank you very much.''

'''Tis not an offer born of pity, nor one I make lightly,'' Campion answered grimly, but she shook her head, backing toward the door, and he felt the situation slipping away from him. For the first time in years beyond count, he was not in control.

''And what of your uncle?'' he asked, desperate to stay her.

''I'll evade him. It's a game we play and none of your

concern.'' The look of contempt she gave him made him surge to his feet.

''And what about your feelings for me? Are they so easily forgotten? What of that which you asked of me? Were you going to share my bed and then leave, without so much as a word?'' Campion asked, risking his pride with the question.

Joy's eyes widened, her expression stricken, but she nodded. ''Yes,'' she whispered, and before he could respond, she hurried through the doorway, as if she could no longer bear his presence.

Her answer so shocked him that Campion made no move to follow. Instead, he sank back down upon the stool in unaccustomed confusion, mind and body in a turmoil such as he had little known in his life. Anger and hurt and disbelief warred together as he stared after her, unwilling to accept what had just occurred. He had ruled his demesne long and well, there being little over the years that was beyond the reach of his will.

It was a humbling experience to be so thoroughly thwarted, and yet Campion's only regret was the loss of what might have been. *But what of me?* he thought in the stillness of the solar. *What of my joy?*

The Earl of Campion could not remember ever being so uncertain. Deeming it best to let the passions that had flared in the solar cool before he spoke again with Joy, he had retired to his chamber, where he hoped to bring his jumbled thoughts and emotions to order. But when one of the villeins reported a block of ice had broken off, threatening to dam the river, he was glad for a chance to go out and tackle a task with which he was familiar.

He would speak again with Joy when he was finished. Meanwhile, he took pleasure in riding his favorite destrier and directing the movements of the men who were breaking up the frozen water. He even got down and lent a hand, despite Reynold's protests, for if his son could aid them without complaining about his bad leg, then Campion would do well to work, too.

He was wet and cold and feeling his age when at last they returned to the castle, his thoughts firmly fixed upon a hot bath. It was only after he was clean and dry and fortified by a hot cup that his thoughts turned once more toward Joy.

Obviously Stephen was wrong, and Joy was not after his money, else she would have agreed to marry him eagerly. Why, then, had she pursued him so diligently? No matter what her bold speech, Campion sensed that she was not a woman to make free with her favors. She had too much the air of innocence about her for that.

Then why? Campion could come up with only one conclusion. Joy truly had wanted him and cared for him. The knowledge settled like a warm ember around his heart, firing his blood and rousing him to action. Surely all the disagreements between them could be resolved somehow, for didn't he return that regard?

No, he thought ruefully, *regard* was too mild a name for what he felt for Joy, and he was determined to tell her so, to persuade her by any means possible that she belonged at Campion, by his side. And with new resolve he went below to look for her.

Down in the hall he found Stephen still at the high table, for he had not gone to the river, dismissing the need with a clever remark. Obviously the boy was still sulking. As Joy must be, Campion decided, for she was not among the revelers, nor in the solar. "Have you seen Lady Warwick?" he asked, glancing about curiously.

"She's gone," Stephen replied.

"Gone?" Campion echoed, uncertain he had heard his son correctly.

"She left before the meal, soon after you went out to break up the ice."

Joy was gone? Campion ignored the rapid pounding of his

heart as he tried to make sense of his son's speech. "But where did she go?"

Stephen shrugged carelessly. "I know not. Perhaps back home to face her uncle or on to another demesne to work her wiles on a new lord."

Campion stiffened. "You mean, she has packed her things and taken to the roads, with her train?" At Stephen's nod, the earl leaned forward, palms spread upon the table in an effort to control the emotions that swept through him. "Why didn't you send word to me?"

Stephen shrugged again. "I knew not where you were along the river or that you would even care to be notified. And far be it from me to involve myself in the affairs of the lady, who warned me well to stay out of her business," he added with a sneer.

"But why? Why would she leave so suddenly?" Campion asked in astonishment, throwing up his hands. Joy was a strong woman, not the sort to cringe and sneak away like a thief in the night. What had driven her to flee?

"She probably didn't like being found out," Stephen drawled.

His son's taunt drew Campion up short, and he leaned upon the table once more. Staring long and hard at the son who so sorely tried his patience, he realized that it was time he spoke. "Aren't you too old to sulk like a boy just because a pretty woman doesn't fancy you?" he asked.

Stephen's head came up swiftly, his eyes glittering. "And aren't you too old to be chasing after a skirt?"

A long moment of silence passed between them until finally Campion answered calmly. "No. I am no doddering invalid. I am a man. What of you, Stephen? What do you call yourself?"

At the question, Campion saw his son's hand tighten around the ever-present cup of wine until the knuckles grew white. Then, without a word, Stephen knocked it aside and swung to his feet. He stalked away, leaving Campion alone at the high table with Reynold, who watched Stephen go with a somber expression.

"He is angry because you bested him in a contest for the lady's affections. It wounds him, for he is well proud of his way with women. 'Tis all he has," Reynold murmured.

"No. You're wrong," Campion said, as he too stared after his errant son. "'Tis not all he has, but 'tis a pity he thinks so." Although it pained him, Campion knew there was nothing he could do for Stephen until the boy decided for himself that he was more than a careless charmer.

With a sigh, Campion swung his gaze toward the window. Outside, the sky was clear, but the shadows were lengthening. Although the snow had begun to melt with the recent warmth, the roads would still be half-frozen and muddy and difficult. Was she all right? Immediately, the knowledge returned to him with the force of a blow.

Joy was gone.

And for all his wealth and power, there was nothing he could do about it. She was a grown woman with no ties to Campion, a guest who was free to leave as she might will, and he had to accept her decision. But she had come into his life like a force of nature, stirring up his safe and staid existence until he felt so good that he wanted to reach out and grasp life in his hands. *And he didn't want to let go.*

Campion had thought to make her see reason, to talk her into taking him as her husband, but wisdom and reason were what had made him refuse her in the first place. They were no use to him. Nor were all his vows to honor and protect a lady in distress. He saw them now for what they were: convenient excuses to have what he wanted without any of the attendant guilt.

To have *Joy*. And now that she was gone, Campion saw too well his mistake. He had been thinking with his mind, patiently deliberating when he ought to have listened to the rest of himself, to the heart that was thundering a protest in his chest, to the desire that she had stoked to a fevered pitch.

Joy was a fire in his blood, and now it ran cold with the want of her. How long ago had she left? he wondered as he whirled around.

Reynold met his panicked gaze and spoke haltingly. "Mayhap she wanted to be married for her own sake, not any other reason," he said, and the stark look in his eyes made Campion pause. Reynold disdained romantic love, and yet, his words held a yearning for someone to see beyond the limp that loomed so large in his own mind.

As Campion should have seen beyond his own image of himself as too dignified, too powerful to succumb to the charms of a beautiful young woman. Dignity be damned! It was time he admitted that he lusted after Joy in a shockingly primitive manner, that he not only admired her but loved her with a frightening and powerful strength, the like of which he had never known before.

But he had pushed her away. Would she believe him now when he admitted his feelings? Shoving aside the doubts of his mind, Campion seized upon the determination of his heart. It was time for action. He strode for the door, calling for his sword and his steed.

"Where are you going?" he heard Reynold ask from behind him.

"I'm going after her!" he shouted over his shoulder. And, he was coming back with her, Campion decided, a smile beginning to curve his lips. It had been a long time since life had thrown him a challenge, and now he found himself taking up the gauntlet with relish.

For Joy.

Campion flung open the doors to his great hall with a stubborn willfulness that even the woman squirming in his arms could not match. He had found her still upon his lands and, without stopping to argue, he had lifted Joy from her horse to his own. When they reached the entrance to the hall, she had balked, and so Campion had simply thrown her over his shoulder.

"Campion! Have you lost your senses?" she cried from behind him, but he dismissed her shouts and the pummeling of her small fists against his back with a grunt of enjoyment. He felt more alive than he had in years. He barely noticed the cheers from the servants, whether delighted at his retrieval of Joy or anticipating the First Foot of the new year as a harbinger of good luck to come.

Campion needed no such omen. He knew that his life had taken a turn that would provide him with joy aplenty, for he held it in his arms. And despite his wiggling burden, he climbed up the stairs with an effortless stride to stalk straight into the great chamber.

He suspected that he ought to kick the door shut, but that seemed a little too violent for his taste, so he carried his prize to the bed, tossing her onto the wide expanse before returning to close and bolt the heavy oak entrance. When he faced her once more, Campion smiled at the sight of Joy, here in his room, alone with him. Since the night of her arrival, he had pictured her in his bed, and he knew a soul-stirring satisfaction to finally have her there.

She was a tangle of cloak and skirts, her mass of heavy black curls falling over her shoulders to her waist, and Campion had a tantalizing glimpse of one slender ankle. As he watched in silence, she struggled up on her knees and lifted her small pale hands to push back her unruly mane. Campion stiffened at the thought of those delicate fingers running through his hair, touching his body. *Soon.* He felt an exhilaration such as he had never known before, as if she alone had tapped some wildness he had long held in check.

"What are you doing?" she demanded, and Campion girded his loins for a pitched battle.

"I'm taking the matter out of your hands," he replied, smiling at his own words.

Her mouth formed an *O* of astonishment that made him

feel absurdly pleased before she managed to recover her usual poise. "See here, Fawke, if this primitive display is fueled by some misguided sense of honor—"

Campion felt his grin widen, and he reached down to unclasp his sword. "Oh, I guarantee you that honor has nothing to do with it," he said. His gaze never left her as he dropped the weapon and moved forward, and he thoroughly enjoyed the shocked expression that came over her face. Joy had always been the aggressor, trying his control with her guileless attempts at seduction, but now it was his turn, and when he kicked off his boots and approached the bed with deliberate purpose, her violet eyes widened in surprise.

He reached her and lifted his hand to test one long, dark lock between his fingers while delighting in Joy's speechless, breathless stare. "I'm afraid you were under a mistaken impression when you left here in such a cowardly manner," he murmured, his gaze never leaving hers. The words made her lift her chin, as he intended, and her eyes flashed.

"Cowardly? I—"

"Don't ever run from me again," Campion said. It was not a threat or a plea, only a statement of fact, but, being Joy, she opened her mouth to argue. He didn't let her, distracting her with his movements as he leaned over her to slip her cloak off and away.

"Because you are mine, Joy," he said, answering any unspoken questions. "*My Joy.* Whether you will it or not. You started this between us, and now I've a mind to finish it," he said, his voice a low rumble as he lowered his mouth to take hers, *to make her his wife.*

She tasted as rich and ardent as he remembered, more so, in fact, for this time they were both unfettered by restraint. He pressed her back into his bed, losing himself in the hot pleasure of her kisses, his hands in the thick heaviness of her hair, his body in the soft embrace of hers.

He had been right about Joy's passionate nature, for she quickly displayed her eagerness, fumbling delightfully as she tried to remove his tunic, and stroking his chest in wonder, just as if she had never touched a man before. Her movements excited him beyond measure, and Campion, too, felt as if all were new to him.

Although he had loved both his wives, he recalled his nights with them with a gentle warmth that little resembled this frantic heat. Joy was bold in her demands, pulling at his clothes, stroking his skin, rubbing her breasts against his chest, as she moaned her pleasure in a manner that drove his own passions to a fevered pitch. He could not get enough of her, and nearly tore her gown in his haste to have her naked beneath him.

Just a few days ago, Campion might have been horrified by his actions, but his blood was running too fierce, too freely, to hesitate. Joy was not satisfied with tender caresses and suddenly he wasn't, either. She had unleashed something inside him that made him mad for her, a certain madness that would not be eased by sweet kisses and light touches, but that craved a deeper, unbridled union.

In the throes of this blessed madness, Campion kissed her throat, her breasts, her stomach, while his hands roved over her smooth skin, exploring every curve and hollow. When at last he nudged her thighs open, Joy cried out in welcome. And when he cupped her there, he felt her teeth rasp against his shoulder in response.

Campion groaned, seizing her hips in his grasp, his fear of hurting her the only thing that kept him from taking her with a wildness he had never imagined. But as he waited, poised above her, his body shuddering with the force of his restraint, he realized that Joy was no gentle virgin, but a widow. Relief swamped him, sweeping away the last vestiges of his control, and with a lusty cry, Campion drove himself into her body.

Too late he felt the give of her maiden's barrier and her jerk of pain, for he was already buried deep inside her. And his pleasure was lost in his shame at this rough handling.

Lifting his head, he looked down at her flushed face. "Joy?" he whispered.

She gazed up at him, her violet eyes wide but holding no rebuke. "I suppose now would be as good a time as any to tell you that my marriage was never consummated."

With a groan, Campion rested his forehead against hers, trying to think of something to say to soothe her, to apologize, but his usual eloquence deserted him, for the rest of his body clamored for something other than words. And then he heard the soft sound of her laugh.

He lifted his head once more. "Forgive me," he murmured, just as she said the same, and Campion felt his own rumble of laughter, a robust release that made him marvel at lovemaking where humor and ardor could exist together. Joy might be the virgin, but he felt she was teaching him afresh. And there was still so much to share with her, he realized, as his body suddenly reminded him of its position inside hers.

He kissed her hair and her ear and her throat, reveling in the taste of her salty skin, while she made soft sounds of delight, her laughter fading away when he rolled onto his back, so that she rested along his length. "Better?" he whispered.

"What?" She lifted her head, an expression of disbelief on her delicate features. "I'll die if it gets any better," she answered breathlessly, and suddenly all amusement left him as he moved, joining her in that sentiment. His efforts at long, slow thrusts were hampered by her impatient movements and her low moans of encouragement, until finally he gave in, burying himself inside her with uncontrolled passion, giving himself up to his joy until her guttural cry brought on his own shout of pleasure.

In the relative quiet of the aftermath, Campion left her resting upon him, her slight weight negligible, and he held her close as exhaustion claimed him. His new bride would either be the death of him or revitalize him beyond his wildest dreams, he thought with delight, but when her silence lengthened, his mood shifted.

"There is something else I forgot to tell you," she murmured, and Campion stiffened as she lifted her face to meet his gaze, her black hair an inky curtain around them. What now? he wondered, with no little alarm, but then she gave him a shy smile endearingly at odds with her former wantonness. "I love you."

Campion sucked in a breath as the strength of his own feelings threatened to overwhelm him. "And I love you, as I have never loved before," he whispered, knowing it was true.

Joy's violet eyes were wide and soft, and she leaned to press a kiss upon his mouth. When she pulled back, however, she tipped up her chin, and Campion nearly groaned at the sight that surely boded ill.

"I must say that as much as I enjoyed your rather barbaric efforts to win me, don't think that I'll stand for such tactics very often," she warned.

Campion frowned. "You'll marry me, Joy," he said, using his most regal tone.

"Yes," she murmured.

"Good," he said, sighing with relief. "Then there won't be any more primitive displays."

"Except in the bedchamber," Joy noted with a sly smile that roused his blood once more. Campion groaned.

"And there is one more thing," she said. Her dainty fingers played with the hair on his chest in a way that made it difficult to concentrate on her words. "You might have guessed that the rumors about my being barren are a little premature."

Startled from his contemplation of the feelings she was inducing in his body, Campion lifted his head and laughed aloud. Everything about Joy was a joy, he thought, his arms tightening around her. But she was not yet ready for more love play.

''I hope you are not set against more children, just in case,'' she said, a hint of vulnerability showing in her violet eyes.

''Oh, I would welcome more babies,'' Campion said in all truth. He knew a sudden exhilaration at the notion and laughed again. ''But is the world ready for more de Burghs?''

Epilogue

New Year's Day dawned clear and shiny as a piece of silver, just as if the Earl of Campion himself had decreed it, and Joy wondered for a moment if the man had dominion over the weather itself, causing it to strand her here to serve his purpose. The thought was not quite as improbable as it might seem, for had he not won dominion over her, a feat seemingly as impossible as ordering the snow and ice?

Yet as she stood in the great hall, watching the preparations for the feast to follow her wedding, Joy could summon no regrets. Roesia had been right. There was no stopping love and, having known it, she would sacrifice all for it. But Joy did not feel she was forfeiting anything in exchange.

Indeed, she was not giving up her independence so much as she was gaining a partner, joining forces with Campion in a union that would not stifle, but enrich her. Suddenly her world was bright with promise, not only of sharing a bed and a life with an incredible man, but of children of her own, a dream she had long ago dismissed as impossible.

For the first time in her life, she was part of a family, and what a family it was! Around her the hall was humming with the congratulations of the servants, genuinely happy at the news of the betrothal. Even Stephen seemed resigned if not enthused about the marriage.

''I suppose there's no help for it,'' he had said with a shrug, and lifted his cup in salute. ''But I refuse to call you mother.''

And Joy had laughed, her heart too full to argue as she waited for the priest and the guests to arrive. Although word had gone out, inviting all within the bounds of Campion's lands to attend, none had yet entered the hall, as if they were awaiting some sign. When Joy had asked why, Wilda informed her that none dared to be the First Foot of New Year's Day. Apparently the first person over the threshold was responsible for the whole year in some way that Joy did not fully comprehend. And since she and Campion had arrived before midnight, all were watching the doors for the first official entrant.

Just as Joy grew impatient with such nonsense, there was a great commotion outside, as if the approach of many horses, while someone shouted about a party at the gate. Wedding guests? Remembering her own unforeseen appearance, Joy did not know what to expect, and she found herself watching nearly as breathlessly as Wilda. Although she cared little enough for superstition, this was her home now, and all who entered here would affect her.

A hush fell over the hall while each servant stopped to look, and then the great doors were flung open, and in strode a huge knight, followed by several others, and Joy knew a moment's fright. Frozen in place, she watched him doff his helm and shake out his dark hair—oddly familiar dark hair— and then a cheer rose up around her as all greeted the man's appearance as a good omen of the year to come.

And then Campion was hurrying forward to embrace the massive creature amid the cries of his people. ''My lord Wessex!'' they shouted. Wessex? Was this Campion's eldest son, Dunstan? But even as Joy tried to identify the man, she was surrounded by others until she felt buffeted by a sea of humanity: tall, dark-haired men, a variety of ladies in elegant costume, squalling infants, servants and outriders, all talking excitedly while the dogs barked their own loud greetings. It was an impossible din, and yet Joy could not help smiling.

It was Campion's family, and never had she seen such a wonderful, happy reunion. She tried to hang back amid all the poignant greetings, but to her astonishment, she too was embraced, by a petite, brown-haired lady. "Hello! I'm Marion, Dunstan's wife," she said, and promptly gave Joy the most beautiful smile she had ever seen, complete with two dimples. Joy smiled back, uncertain how to respond until she felt a familiar arm pull her close and the warm solidarity of Campion's body.

She leaned against it, no longer deeming herself weak for taking the comfort it offered, for this family was a bit overwhelming, in size, clamor and its sheer physicality. Joy would have felt dwarfed by them all, but for the woman called Marion, who, despite her stature, seemed as impressive as the rest of them.

And then, just as suddenly as it had started, the noise faded away to low murmurs, and all eyes turned toward Campion. How did he gain their attention so easily? Joy wondered, with pride and just a touch of awe. He smiled, and Joy could see how much he was affected by the presence of these people. "Welcome, my sons, but why would you brave such weather?" he asked.

"We were all at Wessex!" someone answered.

"Aye. They've been there for weeks, eating up my stores," the big one, called Dunstan, grumbled. "But we were loath to travel the last miles to Campion until the snow stopped."

Campion laughed with pleasure. "Then I shall not scold you for your trip, but welcome you gladly. You're just in time for the wedding!"

"A wedding! You haven't even met my wife yet!" a tall, rather grim looking fellow groused, acting annoyed. "Who is it? I suppose it's you!" he said, glaring at Stephen as if the brother had long been his nemesis.

Stephen made a low sound of disgust. "It's not me, nor will it ever be me, for I have more sense than the rest of you!" he said.

All the dark heads surrounding them swiveled toward Reynold. "Don't look at me," he said with a grunt.

"Who then?" Dunstan growled.

Reynold tilted his head toward their father.

"Father?" Dunstan stared at his sire with a blank expression of astonishment that made Joy smile.

"Oh, how wonderful!" Marion rushed forward to embrace him and then hugged Joy once more. "Oh, I knew you were someone special," she whispered.

Joy was grateful for the welcome and the support implicit when Marion moved to stand beside her, for she faced seven strapping knights, two rather ferocious looking females and a variety of attendants, holding at least two babies. She swallowed, feeling distinctly uncomfortable under their regard, and she lifted her chin.

"This is Joy, soon to be Lady Campion," Campion said, and the glance he sent her was so filled with pride and love that Joy's anxiety eased. "At first she refused to marry me, but finally I managed to convince her, so please make her welcome, as I don't want to have to harry off after her again to bring her home."

Low laughter filled the hall, and Joy heard a voice call out, "Sounds like he got himself a stubborn wench!"

Although her face flamed, she could not help but smile when three of the massive knights turned a sympathetic expression toward their father. The grim one was heard to mutter, "Aye. Join the rest of us."

Joy laughed aloud when a lovely blond lady beside him elbowed him in the ribs so hard that he grunted. And then the woman stepped forward, and suddenly Joy was surrounded not by dark knights but by beautiful ladies.

"Ignore them," said a slender, ginger-haired woman, directing a fierce frown toward the de Burghs.

"Yes! You are the one who has our sympathy," the blond one said. "I'm Bethia, and I know 'tis not every woman who can handle the men of this family."

"Well, I did not want to give up my independence," Joy said, seeking to explain the reluctance Campion had mentioned. And to her surprise all three of the women nodded in earnest agreement.

"Neither did we," Bethia said.

Joy blinked in confusion. "Then why did you wed?"

All three women glanced at each other before eyeing Joy with what could only be called wicked grins. Then Bethia leaned close, with a meaningful nod toward the men who stood not far away. "'Tis obvious enough," she said.

"As I'm sure you've discovered, these de Burghs can be most persuasive!"

Joy felt herself flush once more as she remembered the manner in which Campion had convinced her to be his bride. Had similar skills in the bedchamber done much to win each of these singular women? Feeling a giddy kind of kinship with them, Joy loosed an answering smile much to their delight. The women immediately dissolved into laughter, making the men turn their heads with varying degrees of suspicion, and Joy realized that she would never be able to look at Campion's sons in quite the same way again.

Considering the pleased expressions of these ladies, the de Burghs were very persuasive indeed.

Author Note

I love Christmas. I love all the baking, the shopping, the wrapping, the whispered secrets. With five children, you can imagine the excitement at our home each Christmas. Traditions, once begun, seem to take on a life of their own.

Because no one at our house, especially Santa, can stay awake until midnight on Christmas Eve, we attend a special children's evening mass, complete with the wonderful Christmas story acted out by four- and five-year-olds. I always cry. I love the feeling evoked by all the beautiful, familiar carols. Afterwards, we have a huge family dinner with turkey and all the trimmings.

On Christmas morning, we go to Grandma Ryan's house for a big breakfast. Christmas afternoon is spent with Grandma Langan, along with several aunts and uncles and assorted cousins. By evening, we're all happy to get home, to sort through all the gifts we've opened and to enjoy the feelings of peace and joy that are generated each year by this glorious holiday.

This Christmas and every Christmas, I wish each one of you peace, joy and, most of all, love.

I dedicate this story

To my family, the perfect ingredients
for a special Christmas.
And to Tom, who adds the dash of spice.

CHRISTMAS AT BITTER CREEK

Ruth Langan

Chapter One

Arizona Territory 1880

He was good at waiting. Hadn't he spent a lifetime perfecting the art?

He sat astride the big roan, watching as the first snowflakes drifted through the canopy of evergreen boughs. At this altitude the air was thin. He breathed it in, filling his lungs. Then he spotted the hoofprint. It wasn't much more than a small depression in the hard-packed soil. But it was what he'd been looking for. He slid from the saddle and studied the print for long seconds. Leading his mount, he walked a few paces, then crouched over a second set of similar prints. He followed them until they disappeared along the rocky path.

He studied the trail ahead. There were a hundred places where a man could hide himself. Until he wanted to be seen.

Drawing his hat low on his forehead, he pulled himself into the saddle and checked his rifle. Very soon now, he'd be called upon once more to use his skill with a gun. It was, he thought with a grimace, the only thing he did well.

"With Christmas approaching, I thought you might all enjoy writing about that first Christmas, and what it means to us today." Laura Conners glanced around at the dozen children who filled the small schoolhouse.

They seemed puzzled. Though she had often spoken about the meaning of Christmas, the children of this tough land had little time to contemplate the significance of anything except the constantly changing weather and how it would affect crops and livestock.

At the thought of the weather, Laura cast a speculative glance through the schoolhouse window and came to a decision. "It appears to be snowing harder. Put away your slates, children. Your parents will be concerned. I'll dismiss you earlier than usual."

Though no one actually cheered, she saw the looks that passed from one student to another. How well she remembered the joy of being given an unexpected break from the dull routine, of being allowed to romp in the snow instead of fretting over the sums on her slate.

As if on cue, coming up the path toward the schoolhouse was Anna Thompson, whose five lively sons seemed to throw her into a constant state of confusion. Anna had confirmed just this morning that there would be another baby on the way next spring. As she had five times before, she had begun knitting a lovely pink blanket.

"Beth, will you help me with the little ones?" Laura asked, leading the way to the cloakroom.

"Yes, Miss Conners."

Working alongside her, a shy dark-haired girl of fourteen buttoned coats and tied scarves. When the younger children were bundled into their warm clothes, her teacher gave her a grateful smile.

"Thank you, Beth."

"You're welcome. I'll help you clean up, Miss Conners."

"Another time. That snow is coming down much too fast. I want you to go straight home before the trails get covered."

"Yes, Miss Conners."

Her teacher heard the note of regret in the girl's voice. Beth Mills was never happier than when she was allowed to stay after school and help with chores. The bright little girl desperately wanted to learn all she could, so that one day she could be a teacher, too. But now that her father had died and her mother had taken a job in the Red Garter, Beth's chances of continuing her education seemed over. Wanda Mills needed her daughter's help. At fourteen, Beth's childhood was almost over.

Laura understood the girl's need to linger at the school. There was little reason for Beth to hurry home to the small cramped room she shared with her mother at Mrs. Cormeyer's rooming house.

Anna Thompson breezed into the school and held out her arms to embrace the sons who bustled about her.

Laura couldn't help chuckling at the sight of the plump overworked woman surrounded by her always busy active boys.

As Beth began to follow the others from the school, Laura hesitated, then called her back. "I baked some apple spice cake last night. Early Christmas presents." She lifted a loaf wrapped in a linen towel. "I thought you and your mother might enjoy this."

The girl's mouth rounded in surprise. "Oh, thank you, Miss Conners." She lowered her head, breathing in the fragrance of cinnamon and apples, avoiding her teacher's eyes. "Mama used to bake when my pa was alive. But she doesn't much care what she eats anymore. Or even if she eats."

"Maybe this will help."

Laura glanced at the sweet child beside her. There was a time when Beth had been part of a happy, loving family. When Bill had died suddenly of a ruptured appendix, Wanda and her young daughter had been devastated. Wanda had simply turned her back on the ranch she and her husband had built in the wilderness, and taking far less for the herd than it was worth, had moved into town. From that moment on, she had spent every waking moment trying to keep herself and her daughter together.

Everyone knew that it was a struggle. There were no secrets here. The town of Bitter Creek was so small, everyone knew everyone else's business almost before it happened.

"I'll see you Monday, Beth."

Laura watched as the girl ran to catch up with the other children. Most of them lived in town, and walked the scant mile to the schoolhouse. A few, whose ranches scattered for miles in either direction, rode horseback or drove small pony carts.

When the schoolhouse was empty, Laura straightened the desks, swept the floor and banked the fire in the small stone fireplace before carefully bracing the door against the north wind.

As she stepped into the cold, she watched the figure of Ned Harrison, mayor of Bitter Creek, trudging toward her.

"Going home early, are you, Laura?"

"Didn't want the parents to worry after their children."

He brushed snow from his whiskers and cleared his throat. "I had hoped to give you a few dollars extra in your pay for Christmas, Laura. But the town just doesn't have enough money right now. And since you don't have any family..." He shrugged his shoulders in an embarrassed gesture as his voice trailed off.

Laura swallowed. She'd been counting on that money to keep the ranch going. But she understood what he meant. Times were hard for everyone. And those with children suffered the most at this time of year.

She forced a cheerful note to her voice that she didn't feel. "It's all right, Ned. I'll be fine."

He smiled and seemed relieved to be finished with this unpleasant duty. "I knew you'd understand, Laura." He touched his hand to his hat and turned away. "You'd better get going. Snow's coming down hard."

Climbing into her wagon, Laura drew a heavy blanket

around her shoulders and flicked the reins. She would not think about the flour that money would have bought. Or the good wool fabric in Ned's mercantile. She would get by. Hadn't she always? Besides, it was almost Christmas. And from her earliest days, she had always believed that Christmas was a special time, a magical time.

By the time she reached home, her dark hair and eyebrows were frosted with snow.

In the barn she turned the horse into a stall and forked hay and water into troughs before milking the cow and gathering the eggs that should have been gathered that morning. But there had been a pump to prime, and wood to chop for the fireplace before she left for the tiny schoolhouse. Her days always began before sunup, and never seemed to end until the logs in the fireplace had long since burned to embers.

With a bucket in one hand and a basket in the other, she ran the hundred yards to the darkened ranch house. The door hung at a lopsided angle on rusted hinges and gave a squeal of protest as she swung it wide.

"I swear, Papa, I'll fix that door tomorrow," she muttered under her breath.

Inside she lit a lantern and set it on the kitchen table. Within minutes she had a fire started in the fireplace. Blowing on her cold hands, she draped a shawl around her shoulders and set about fixing herself a supper of cold meat, bread and preserves.

"I know you wouldn't approve, Papa," she said, glancing at the empty chair across the table. "You always said supper wasn't supper without hot biscuits and gravy." A little smile touched her lips. "But maybe I'll kill the old rooster for Sunday supper. And I'll make bread pudding for dessert."

She knew, even before the words were out of her mouth, that she wouldn't follow through on the threat. There were never enough hours in the day to do all she planned. But it was pleasant just thinking about the way Sunday suppers used to be when she was a girl and Mama and Papa were alive.

When the table was cleared she pulled her chair close to the fire. Dear Lord, it was cold tonight. She thought about staying here a few minutes longer. It was heaven to be warm, full, contented. But with idleness came unbidden thoughts. Thoughts of where her life was going. Thoughts of what might have been.

What had Papa always said? "An idle mind is the devil's workshop." She picked up a broom and swept the porch clean of the snow that had already begun piling up against the door. That finished, she retreated indoors and gathered her mending into her lap as she settled once more into the chair. Squinting in the fading light of the fire, she plied needle and thread. Mama's old gowns had been made over so many times, the fabric was threadbare. Still, she thought, examining the seams of a pale blue calico dress, she might get one more year out of this. There was no money left over for fancy clothes. What little money she made teaching had to go back into the ranch. She glanced around at the snug house. It was all she had. But with Papa's passing away, it took everything she had to keep it going. She had turned it into a somewhat comfortable if shabby retreat. There were several needlepoint pillows on the rockers. There was a colorful rag rug in the center of the floor. And the delicate lace curtains at the windows had once been Mama's wedding dress. Since the gown had begun to rot and fall apart, it seemed a sin not to make use of what was left. Besides, Laura thought with a sudden pain around her heart, she'd never have a chance to wear Mama's wedding gown.

Oh, not that there weren't men around who'd marry her. If she'd have them. Nate Burns was a widower with two small children. Lord knows, those little ones needed a mother. And Nate had let it be known among the townspeople that he considered it his duty to offer his home to the spinster teacher. But Laura knew she'd have to be hog-tied and gagged before she'd consent to marry a man as mean-mouthed as Nate.

There was the banker, Jed McMasters. Some in town figured he'd be the richest man in the territory one day. But the only time she'd ever seen Jed smile was when he was counting money. The rest of the time he looked like he'd just swallowed something vile.

There'd been a man. Once. She pricked her finger with the needle and felt tears fill her eyes. There she was again; thinking thoughts that had no place in her life now.

She sewed until the fire burned low and her eyelids grew heavy. Then, setting aside her mending, she carefully folded her lap robe and picked up the lantern.

With a sigh of exhaustion she crossed to her bedroom. The woman in the looking glass startled her for a moment. Her hair was pulled back in a severe bun and secured with several pins. Despite the pains she took to look like a proper teacher, a few corkscrew curls had pried themselves loose to drift about her cheeks and neck. She touched a finger to the fine lines that had begun to be etched around her eyes. Some days her hazel eyes seemed more green than amber. This night, by the light of the lantern, they were a dull copper. By her own design, the shapeless dress hid all traces of the slender form beneath. Pa had often warned her that the good people of Bitter Creek expected the town's teacher to be neither man nor woman, but rather an authority figure akin to a doctor or preacher.

She had held to her papa's strict upbringing. She had earned the town's respect. She was careful to do or say nothing that could be construed as improper. She lived her life, as Papa had instructed, according to a very rigid code.

"Miss Conners," she said with a trace of sarcasm, studying her reflection. The very name conjured up visions of a crotchety old woman wielding a slate, a Bible and a hickory stick.

She slipped out of her prim gown and petticoats and pulled

on a warm homespun nightgown. Brushing her long hair until it crackled, she stared at the woman in the mirror. She'd heard the whispers of the children outside the schoolhouse. Old Miss Conners. Perhaps the children were right. Though she was not yet thirty, she probably looked to them like a withered old crab apple. She was becoming more and more like her papa. Tough. Strict. Unyielding. But without her constant reminders, she knew that many of the town's children would grow up wild, with little regard for moral principles.

It was this rugged land, she thought, gazing at the snow that curtained her window. The men and women who came here were so busy trying to survive in this wilderness, they had little time left over for the basic rules of civilization. Hadn't she seen it time and again? Hadn't it even happened to people she'd known and…loved?

"You're turning into an old prune, Laura Conners."

With a clatter she dropped her mother's ivory-handled brush and turned away, refusing to look at herself again. It hurt too much.

She blew out the lantern and climbed wearily into bed.

The horse crested the hill, then paused, feeling its rider shift in the saddle.

The moon was a pale thin sliver, almost obliterated by the falling snow.

Slumped low over the horse's neck, Matt Braden gripped his rifle tightly in his right hand. His left arm dangled uselessly at his side. While the horse stamped and snorted, the snow at his feet was stained crimson.

He was growing weaker by the minute. Matt knew that if he hadn't tied himself to the saddle, he would already be lying face down somewhere back there on the trail. But he had to find shelter quickly, before he froze to death.

He saw the light below. Too small for a camp fire. A candle or lantern most likely. Squinting against the falling snowflakes, he saw the light flicker and die.

Had it been his imagination? Or was there a cabin somewhere below?

He gave only the slightest nudge with his knees. But it was enough to signal his horse into a slow walk. Picking through the drifts, the horse moved ahead, sensing the need to carry its burden gingerly. Each movement brought a stab of pain to the rider, who clung to consciousness by a mere thread. When Matt thought he could bear it no longer,the horse came to an abrupt halt. Matt lifted his head. Looming directly in front of him was a wall.

He knew he should check out the cabin before entering. They could be here ahead of him, waiting to finish the job. But there was no way he could slide from the saddle and crawl to a window. He closed his eyes, then blinked them open. For a minute he thought he was home. He knew this cabin. Knew every stick of furniture he would find inside.

There would be the table his father had made out of the bottom and sides of the wagon. And six chairs carved from saplings. In the loft above was a feather mattress, where his father and mother slept. Below, the bunks were lined up against the south wall of the sod shack. Four small bunks, for Matt and his three brothers.

He smiled. What hellions they'd become. Especially after Ma died. They'd grown up wild, free, with no restrictions issued by their grieving father.

Were they inside now, waiting for him?

He shook his head as if to clear it. His mind was playing tricks on him. This wasn't home. There was no home anymore. His father had followed his mother to the grave. And his brothers? They were dead. All three of them. Jase had been shot in a bank robbery. Cal had been gunned down in a saloon in Texas. Dan had met a crazy tenderfoot who wanted to prove to the world that he could draw faster than one of the legends of Arizona Territory. All dead. And all before they had barely tasted life.

Was his lot in life any better? He felt a wave of anger and

despair. Did it matter which side of the law a man chose? When he was dead, he was just as dead. And soon, very soon now, he would join his brothers. But at least he would be free of this pain.

The reins slipped from his fingers. He leaned down until his cheek was resting on the horse's quivering neck. He was so cold he could no longer feel his hands or feet.

He couldn't seem to focus on what to do. And then the fury inside him brought it back to him. Seek shelter. Bind his wounds. Stay alive.

Through a haze of pain he forced his useless hand to seek the knife at his waist. Sweat beaded his forehead as he strained to cut the rope holding him secure. As the knife sliced through the rope, he felt himself falling helplessly. Tumbling into a pit of blackness.

At the sound of something crashing onto her porch, Laura sat straight up in bed. In her years in this wilderness she had faced the fury of nature as well as the fury of man. And though she was never prepared for such battles, she had never backed down.

In the darkness she fumbled for the rusted rifle she always kept on the table beside her bed. The gleaming coals from the fire cast a pale glow over the big front room, lighting it enough to show her the way to the door. Though her hands were trembling, she threw open the door, prepared to face any danger.

The first thing she saw was the riderless horse. Then she saw the man lying at her feet. He was as still as death.

"Dear Lord in heaven!"

She dropped the rifle and touched a hand to the man's throat. A heartbeat. Erratic but strong.

"Here," she said, bending close to his ear. "You'll have to help me if I'm ever going to get you inside."

The man moaned, then struggled to move. Laura draped his arm over her shoulder, then staggered under his weight.

With a tremendous pull, she managed to drag him inside and across the floor to her father's room. With great effort she got him settled in the big bed. Then she hurried back to the porch, where she retrieved her rifle. She quickly slammed the door against the biting cold.

Touching a match to the wick in the lantern, she carried it close and bent over the man. He wore a cowhide jacket and a wide-brimmed hat pulled low over his face. Several days' growth of beard darkened his chin.

From the amount of blood oozing through his faded shirt and staining his jacket, she knew that he was gravely wounded. She poured a generous amount of water into a pan, then set the pan atop the hot coals of the fire. While waiting for the water to boil, she took up her father's sharp hunting knife and began the difficult task of cutting away the man's clothes. When that was done, she leaned back and studied him closely by the light of the lantern.

Despite the beard and the shaggy growth of dark hair that curled over the collar of his shirt and spilled across his forehead, she felt the jolt of recognition.

''Matthew. Matthew Braden!'' His name was expelled in a rush of air.

His lips moved as if he were speaking. But though she leaned close, she could not make out what he was saying. His eyes remained closed.

''Hush now, Matthew, you're safe here,'' she whispered, blinking away the tears that had mysteriously filled her eyes.

But though she spoke the words with fervor, she couldn't dispel the doubt in her heart. He had lost a lot of blood, judging from the looks of his jacket. And he was cold. So cold.

With trembling hands she cut away the last of his jacket and shirt. The sight of his wound caused her to sit back on her heels a moment, feeling light-headed.

It was a bullet wound. Somehow, she had known it would be. Matthew had always lived on the edge of danger.

The skin was jagged and torn; the flesh swollen with infection. Though Laura knew what she had to do, she wasn't certain she had the strength or the nerves for such a task.

She placed the hunting knife in the pan of boiling water, then went off in search of clean linens. Moving the lantern closer, she bent to her task.

With the tip of the knife, she probed the wound until she located the bullet. Though Matt moaned, he made no movement. That fact frightened her. He must indeed be weak to lie so quietly while she inflicted such searing pain. Once the bullet was removed, she cleansed the wound, then dressed it with strips of linen.

With that task done, she removed his heavy boots before drawing the blankets tightly about him.

From the wood piled neatly in the corner of the cabin she selected a log and some kindling. Within minutes she had a fire crackling in the big stone fireplace of her father's old room.

The sound of a horse outside caused her to jump. Her nerves, she realized, were stretched to the breaking point.

After peering out the window to be certain no one else was around, she drew on her shawl and led Matthew's horse to the barn. There she unsaddled the stallion and settled him into a stall with food and water. Shivering, she raced back to the house and stood in front of the fire until the trembling stopped.

At a moan from the bed, she looked up sharply. Though the sound of his pain brought her fresh anguish, there was comfort in it, as well. At least Matthew was still alive.

She took the quilt from her bed and walked to the bedroom where he lay as still as death. Pulling a chair close to the bed, she draped the quilt around her and watched as his blankets rose and fell with each measured breath.

She would stay as close as possible and see him through the night.

Fighting exhaustion, Laura's lids fluttered.

Matthew Braden had come back to Bitter Creek. But had he come back to live? Or to die?

Chapter Two

Laura slept fitfully. Each time she awoke, she leaned close to touch a hand to Matt's forehead. His skin was on fire. Lord, he was so hot.

Without realizing it, she curled her lips into a smile of remembrance. Papa had always called Matt a hothead.

"Damned troublemaker." It took a lot for Will Conners to swear. But Matthew Braden always seemed to bring out the worst in her father. From the time Matt and his brothers first showed up in Bitter Creek, Papa was as nervous as a herd of mustangs stalked by a wildcat.

"A man who lives by the gun will perish by the gun," Papa used to intone regularly. "And believe me, that boy and his brothers are headed for nothing but destruction."

"That isn't fair, Papa. Matthew isn't bad—he's just wild."

Had it been that wild streak that had attracted her to him? She didn't know. She knew only that from the first moment she'd seen Matthew Braden, she'd lost her heart. And her common sense. The more others put him down, the more she seemed driven to defend him.

Papa had recognized it even before she did. He saw the soft look that came into her eyes whenever Matt passed her in town. Matt had a roguish way of touching a hand to his hat and winking. She had a curious way of blushing and studying the toe of her boot. Matt's tone, though gruff, was always respectful in her presence. Papa heard the way her voice caught in her throat whenever the wild youth had spoken to her. And when her father pointed it out to her, he'd made her feel ashamed of the way her heart had betrayed her.

"You watch yourself, girl. You're better than that. I know his kind. Without the proper guidance, they go from bad to worse. One of these days his mischief will get out of hand. Those brothers of his will persuade him to help them steal some cattle or rob a bank. And once the law is after them, their only recourse is a gun. They'll shoot their way out of one scrape after another, until someone comes along with a faster gun."

As much as she hated to admit it, Papa had been right. She'd heard stories of the wild Braden brothers, even after they left Bitter Creek. And though she hadn't heard a thing about Matt for years, it appeared that once again Papa had been right. This time, someone had been faster than Matt.

Agitated, Laura drew the quilt tighter around her shoulders and squeezed her eyes shut to blot out the image of the man who lay near-death.

"Don't die, Matthew," she whispered. "No matter what you've done, I don't want you to die."

Matt lay very still, absorbing the alien feeling of comfort. After a dizzying lifetime of living on the edge, he had always known heaven would be like this. A soft weightless feeling, like floating on a cloud. Warmth. The blessed warmth of a cocoon.

He sighed contentedly and shifted. Instantly pain crashed through him, shattering the mood. He wasn't dead, after all. He was very much alive, and his body was one large mass of pain.

He touched a hand to his shoulder, expecting the sticky

warmth of blood. Instead his fingers encountered clean linen bindings. His eyes flew open.

Where the hell was he? And who had dressed his wounds?

He studied the wooden beams of the ceiling and watched the flickering shadows cast by the fire in the stone fireplace across the room. A cabin. The one he had approached last night. Though he couldn't remember, he'd apparently persuaded the owner to give him aid and comfort. There'd been something familiar about the cabin, but that was probably just his mind playing tricks. He seemed to recall thinking it was his childhood home. But that was impossible. He hadn't had a home in a very long time.

It caused him considerable torment to turn his head even a fraction, but he had to see the rest of this room. His gaze fastened on the figure in the chair beside his bed. A patchwork quilt covered all but the tip of a small upturned nose and a wide forehead covered by a spill of dark curls. As the figure sighed and shifted, he felt as if had just taken a blow to the midsection.

Laura. Sweet Jesus! It couldn't be. With a look of naked hunger he squinted through a haze of pain and devoured the wonderful sight that greeted him.

She was asleep in the rocker, the quilt tucked primly about her. The edge of the quilt had slipped low on her shoulders, exposing an ivory nightdress that clearly revealed the outline of her breasts. The sight caused a rush of heat, which only added to his fever.

How many nights had he dreamed of seeing her like this? For so long now, he had told himself that she couldn't possibly be as beautiful as the girl he remembered. But there she was, all soft and sleepy, curled like a kitten in a rocking chair. And no amount of imagination was as wonderful as this living breathing woman whose chest rose and fell so peacefully.

Before the pain had overtaken him, he had known he was on the trail to Bitter Creek. But in the confusion of the gunfight, his escape and his efforts to stay alive, that thought had been lost to him. He took a shallow breath, fighting the pain that swamped him. No wonder his thoughts had been of home and childhood. Laura Conners had been a special part of his growing to manhood. And all these years, though she had rejected his love, he had carried her in a special place in his heart.

His gaze fell on the pitcher of water that rested on a bed-side table. His throat was as parched as the desert. He was burning with fever. But though he yearned for relief, it was too much effort to speak.

He returned his attention to the woman who slept in the chair, afraid that if he but closed his eyes, the vision would disappear. Though he made a valiant struggle, he could no longer find the strength to stay awake. His lids flickered, then closed.

Thin winter sunlight spilled through a crack in the curtains. Laura came awake slowly, stretching first one leg, then the other. As she did, the quilt slid to the floor. With a sound of annoyance she bent to retrieve it. Her hands paused in midair as she turned in time to see that Matt was fully awake, watching her.

The quilt was forgotten.

"How...are you feeling?"

Without waiting for his reply she automatically reached a hand to his forehead. That was her first mistake. The moment her fingers came in contact with his flesh, she jerked her hand back as if burned.

Aware of her reaction, he gave a weak smile. "I've..." He swallowed and tried again. "I've felt better." Though every word caused him pain, he forced himself to continue. "But at least I'm alive. Thanks to you."

"You gave me quite a scare."

Awkwardly she reached for the quilt, but before she could drape it modestly around her shoulders he croaked, "Could I have some water?"

"Of course." She filled a dipper, then knelt by the side of the bed. Gently lifting his head, she held the dipper to his lips. That was her second mistake. She had forgotten the shock she had always experienced whenever she was too close to this man.

Her hand trembled, causing her to spill some of the water. "I'm sorry."

At her whispered words, he lifted his hand and closed his fingers over hers, holding the dipper steady. Though it cost him a great deal of pain, he decided it was worth it just to be touching her.

She was achingly aware of the big hand holding hers. And though his touch disturbed her, she could not deny the thrill it brought.

When he'd drunk his fill she lowered his head to the pillow and moved away as quickly as she could manage.

Needing to be busy, she bustled about, straightening his blankets, drawing open the curtains. When she spoke again, she prayed her voice would not betray her nervousness. "I could fix you a coddled egg if you think you're up to eating anything."

When he made no response, she turned. The effort to speak, to move his hand, had drained him. He had already returned to his troubled dreams.

Matt lay very still and strained to sort out all the unfamiliar scents and sounds that greeted him. How long had it been since he'd slept in a big feather bed, while the air hung heavy with the mouth-watering fragrance of apples and spices?

He was in a ranch house. Laura's ranch house.

Cattle were lowing in the field. From the barn came the sound of horses blowing and snorting. Outside his window, chickens clucked. In the other room he heard Laura humming.

He needed to see her, to talk to her before her father returned from the fields.

Rolling to his side, he tossed back the blankets and swung his feet to the floor. The room spun in dizzying circles and he waited for the feeling to pass. Focusing on the doorway, he took a step, then another.

She had not yet seen him. Bent over the oven, she removed a pan and quickly set it on the table, then placed a second pan in the oven and closed the lid.

She turned and became absorbed in a task at the table.

Her dark hair was piled on top of her head. Little wisps had pried themselves loose to curl around her forehead and kiss her cheeks. She wore a faded gown of palest pink that outlined every line and curve of her slender body.

She lifted her head and saw him. The look on her face was one of surprise tinged with pleasure.

"Matthew. You shouldn't have tried to get up yet."

"I'm fine." Like hell he was. He was as weak as a kitten and afraid that at any moment he'd fall flat on his face. But it would be worth any price to his pride just to see her like this.

"Here. You'd better sit at the table." She rushed forward, then stopped, embarrassed to offer a hand. When he'd been wounded and bleeding, it had been perfectly normal to undress him and tend his wounds. Now, his state of undress caused a fluttering deep inside her.

He was barefoot and shirtless. She had forgotten how wide his shoulders were, how muscled his arms. The faded pants only emphasized his flat stomach and narrow hips.

"Thanks." If he noticed her hesitation, he quickly dismissed it. Walking slowly, he slumped into the chair she held beside the table. "Something smells wonderful."

"I'm baking apple spice cake for Christmas gifts for some of the women in town."

"Christmas." Matt tried to think when he had last thought about the day that had been so special in his youth. "I had no idea it was even close to Christmas."

"It's just a few days away," she said with a smile. "And

I have plenty of baking planned. One of my students brought me a bushel of apples."

"Students." He looked up. "So you became a teacher."

She nodded, feeling oddly pleased that he remembered her dream. Then, determined to keep the conversation light, she lifted a wrinkled apple. "I want to use them up before they all wither in the fruit cellar. Papa always said waste not, want not." She stared at the loaves cooling by the window. "They aren't much. But Papa always taught me that it isn't the gift that's important—it's the giving. Papa always said that love isn't love until you give it away."

Matt cleared his throat. "How is your father?"

She seemed startled by his question. "I guess there's no way you could have known. Papa died three years ago."

She turned to the stove to fill a cup with coffee.

"Three years." He allowed his gaze to slowly roam the tidy room. "Who's the lucky man you finally settled down with?"

"I live here alone." She placed the cup before him, then began slicing the loaf still warm from the oven.

He sipped his coffee in silence and blamed the sudden warmth on the fever that burned within him.

"How do you manage both the teaching and the ranch chores?"

She glanced at him. A smile touched her lips. "I just live the way Papa taught me. Hard work from dawn to dark every day, and the chores get done." She turned toward a pot that bubbled atop the stove. "I made some soup. I'll fix you a bowl."

Matt nearly laughed. Did she have any idea how much she sounded like her father? The old man had been as tough as rawhide, never veering from his charted course. And he'd had a Biblical quote for practically everything from raising his daughter to curing the ills of the world.

"Takes a lot of muscle to run a ranch. My father couldn't do it, even with the help of four sons."

"Papa used to say that was because you were all too busy raising…" She felt her cheeks flame. Swallowing, she filled his bowl and set it down.

"We did raise a bit too much…dust to please this town, didn't we?"

She smiled at his gentle gibe and watched as he took a taste of broth.

"I see you haven't lost your touch. You still like to cook."

"Papa always complimented me on my fine meals. After Mama died, it seemed important to make up for his loss."

Matt indicated the empty chair. "Will you join me?"

She filled her cup with coffee, then sat down across from him. When she looked at him, she felt herself blushing. It was impossible not to stare at the wide expanse of shoulders, the hair-roughened chest. His body was lean and hard, his arms corded with muscles. It was not a sight she was accustomed to seeing across her table. She stared hard into her cup.

"Tell me about Bitter Creek." He studied the smudge of flour on the tip of her nose and had a sudden urge to kiss it away. His fingers curled into a fist at his side. "Who's the mayor now?"

"Ned Harrison."

"Old Ned." Matt leaned back with a smile. "Does he still run the mercantile?"

Laura smiled back. "Yes. And he still argues with old Mrs. Smithers over the price of every bolt of fabric and spool of thread."

"Those two will go to their graves scrapping with one another." He shifted, trying to find a comfortable way to ease the pain in his chest. "Does old Ned still give out penny candy to the boys who sweep his store?"

Her smile grew. "Is that why you were always helping him?"

"And you thought I did it out of the goodness of my heart."

"I knew old Ned had a fondness for you."

Matt's eyes took on a faraway look. "He was fair with me. He never held me accountable for the sins of all the Braden brothers, the way some folks did." He quickly changed the subject. "What about the Reverend Talbot? Does he still ride all the way out to the Widow Conklin's every Sunday afternoon to read the Good Book with her?"

Laura's eyes grew soft. "Even though she's almost blind, she still cooks him dinner and he reads aloud to her from the Bible." She glanced down at her hands and added softly, "I guess nothing much ever changes in Bitter Creek."

"I expect you're right."

At the sound of a horse's hooves they both looked up. But before Laura could go to the door, Matt had crossed the room and was pressing her against the wall.

She was acutely aware of the warmth of his skin. The sharp odor of disinfectant mingled with the distinctly masculine scent of him.

She hadn't known a wounded man could move that quickly. But the pain it cost him was visible on his face. Sweat beaded his brow. His eyes were narrowed in concentration.

"Who's here?"

"Probably old Judd. He works out at the Ridgely place. He often stops by on Saturday mornings to see if I need anything from town."

"Will he want to come inside?"

She shook her head. "There's no need. I'll just give him my list and he'll be on his way."

Matt felt his strength drain from him. If there had been any danger, he doubted that he could have saved Laura. But he knew one thing. He would have died trying.

He swore loudly, violently. He was suddenly drained of all strength. He despised this feeling of weakness. Leaning against the wall, he felt the room spin.

Laura looked up in time to see the color drain from his face. "What is it? What's wrong?"

"I guess I'm not as strong as I thought." He clutched the wall for support. "I don't mean to impose on you like this. But I'm afraid if I don't lie down right now, I'll be lying on your floor."

She wrapped her arm around his waist. Gripping her shoulder, he leaned weakly against her and allowed himself to be led back to bed.

When he was settled, she lifted a blanket to cover him. Strong fingers closed around her wrist. Surprised by his strength, she merely stared into his dark eyes without a word.

His voice was low, intense. "Where's my horse?"

She licked her lips, suddenly afraid. "In the barn."

"Keep him hidden from view."

"But I—"

His eyes narrowed. The fingers at her wrist tightened perceptibly. "When the old man is gone, bring the saddlebags and rifle in here. Next to the bed."

"But you can't. You're too weak—"

"Just bring them." He paused, seeing the fear leap into her eyes. His tone softened only a little. "I'm sorry, Laura. I didn't mean to bring you trouble."

Laura swallowed. Matthew had been gone from her life for a long time now. She really knew nothing about him. But she knew enough to realize that trouble always seemed to follow him. Hadn't Papa always said…?

Very deliberately she pulled free from his grasp and straightened.

He turned his head and watched as she crossed to her own room. From a peg in the hall she removed her father's old oversize sheepskin jacket and pulled it on.

Matt heard the door slam, and the sound of her boots as she walked across the porch. He strained to hear the words she exchanged with the handyman. A few minutes later he heard her return.

She strode into the room. With a thud the saddlebags landed on the floor beside the bed. She thrust the rifle next to him on the blanket.

"I'll need my bullets," he said, indicating the saddlebags.

She rummaged through them, then handed him a sack of bullets. "Will there be anything else?"

He heard the thread of anger and wished he could think of something to say. But sweet words and kindly gestures had never come easily to him. Besides, the damage had already been done. She had saved his life. And in payment, he had placed her life in grave danger.

Chapter Three

The heavy snowfall forced Laura to go out into the surrounding hills to round up her cattle. For the rest of the winter her small herd would be forced to stay in a fenced area near the barn. She had hoped to build a shelter for them, but there hadn't been enough time before the snow came. Next spring, she promised herself, as she mucked the stalls and filled them with clean straw. Next spring she would build a shelter big enough to hold an entire herd.

She attacked her chores with a vengeance, determined to keep her mind off the man who lay inside the house in Papa's big bed.

She turned her horse into a small enclosure and kept Matt's horse concealed in the barn, then moved on to several outbuildings to feed the chickens and pigs.

While the chickens clucked and scratched at her feet, her mind was awhirl with dark thoughts. After all her years of wondering, after all those nights of regret, Papa had been right about Matthew Braden. Even now, when he ought to be old enough to shed his wild ways, he was living as he always had. He'd been in a gunfight. And the man who'd shot him was still out there, searching for him. Judging by his reaction to old Judd's arrival, he expected retaliation from the gunman at any moment.

The snowfall would have obliterated Matt's tracks. But Bitter Creek was a small place. The man would have no trouble searching the town and discovering that Matt was not there. That would leave the outlying ranches. Sooner or later, the man would be here. And when he came…

She paused in her work and lifted her head to study the surrounding hills. He could be out there right now, watching, waiting.

It was unfair of Matthew to bring his troubles to her very doorstep. Of course, he'd had no choice, she reminded herself. He hadn't deliberately chosen to collapse at her cabin. But now that he had, she could find herself in as much peril as he.

She must stop these unsettling thoughts. Calling upon all her discipline, she swept him from her mind and flung the last of the feed, then made her way to the barn. Inside, she examined the harness and wagon traces. They were wearing clean through. One of these days she wouldn't make it to the schoolhouse and back. She'd hoped to have time to repair them this weekend. But it would take all of her energy to cook and tend to Matthew's wounds.

She gave a sigh. There were only so many chores a body could do in a day. This would have to wait until next weekend.

As she milked the cow and gathered the eggs, she realized that she was drawing out her chores, putting off for as long as possible the time when she would have to return to the house. To Matthew.

In the fading light of early evening she lifted a bucket of milk and a basket of eggs and determinedly made her way to the cabin.

To her great relief, he was asleep.

For long minutes she studied the figure in the bed. The shaggy hair and heavy beard gave him the look of a fierce mountain man. The six-gun by his left hand, the barrel of a rifle peeking from beneath the blankets on his right side, only added to the look of danger. But it had always been his eyes, those dark challenging eyes that had given him an aura of mystery. What went on behind those eyes? Matthew Braden was not a man to give much away. Especially about himself.

She lingered a moment longer, staring at him with a welling of emotion that left her startled. She forced herself to turn away.

The room was cold, as were the other rooms in the house. She added a log to the hot coals and watched as flames raced along the bark. Then she made her way to her own room to build a fire. With that done, she hurried to the main room and stoked the fire until the entire cabin was snug and warm.

She ate quickly, enjoying the soup that had simmered all day on the wood stove and the apple spice cake she had baked the day before. When she had her fill, she picked up her mending and settled herself in front of the fire. Very soon her eyes grew heavy. She had, after all, slept little the previous night. She put aside her mending and made her way to her bedroom.

Pouring warm water into a basin, she bathed away the grime of the day and pulled on her warm nightgown. Taking down her hair, she brushed it until it crackled.

As she extinguished the flame of the lantern, she heard the low moan from the other room. Moving quickly she padded into her father's room and bent over the sleeping man. She touched a hand to his forehead and whispered a prayer of gratitude. His skin was cool to the touch.

Strong fingers closed over her wrist. With no warning, she found herself hauled off her feet and pulled firmly across the massive chest of the figure in the bed.

''Matthew.'' His name came out in a long rush of air, wrenched from between her lips.

''Laura. Sweet Jesus.'' His other hand closed over her shoulder, holding her still when she would have pulled away. He felt like shaking her. An oath sprang to his lips but he swallowed it. "What are you doing sneaking up on me in the dark like that?"

"I wasn't sneaking." She wriggled, trying to free herself from his grasp.

He continued to hold her. Now he no longer wanted to shake her; he just wanted to hold her.

By the flickering flames of the fire, she could see that the surprise in his eyes was gradually changing to a look she couldn't fathom. But it was a look that caused her pulse to race.

"You moaned. I thought you were in pain."

"I am." His words were a low growl against her temple.

He rolled to his side, dragging her with him so that she lay facing him. Her hair swirled in disarray, veiling her eyes. Her nightgown was tangled about her knees.

He'd often imagined her like this, dressed in something pure and white, her hair soft and loose.

He lifted a hand to smooth the hair from her cheek. His eyes narrowed as he sifted the strands through his fingers.

"You're even more beautiful than I remembered."

"Don't Matthew." Her voice was a strained whisper.

"Don't what?"

She heard the gruffness in his tone and felt a growing sense of unease. "Don't do this. It isn't right."

"To tell you that you're beautiful? Oh, Laura. The rules haven't changed that much since I've been gone. Or if they have, I'll just have to break them."

As she opened her mouth to protest, he said fiercely, "You're beautiful. The most beautiful woman I've ever known." He shot her a dangerous smile. "There. I've broken your rules. Now what are you going to do about it?"

He had always been good at breaking the rules. "You know what I mean. You mustn't hold me here like this, in Papa's bed."

"If you object to your father's bed, we can always go to yours."

"Oh, Matthew. Stop twisting everything I say. You can't—"

He lowered his mouth to hers, abruptly cutting off her words.

Ice. At the first touch of his lips, splinters of ice seemed to shatter through her veins, shocking her with their intensity.

Heat. As he lingered over her lips, she felt a sudden rush of liquid fire that raced along her spine, then seemed to radiate outward to her limbs, leaving them heavy. She thought about what she had been going to say. But the words were quickly forgotten. She brought a hand to his shoulder, intending to push him away. But the moment her fingers encountered his warm naked flesh, all thought fled. Her fingers slid over his skin, then curled into his arm, drawing him even closer to her.

Matt lifted his head a moment, touching a finger to her lips. Lips that tasted as cool as a mountain spring. As soft as the muzzle of a newborn foal. Lips that had him so enthralled he could think of nothing else.

He lowered his head again and brushed his lips over hers. It was the merest of touches, but he felt the tremors rock him. And then he was lost. His arms came around her, pinning her to the length of him. His lips closed over hers in a kiss that demanded everything, gave everything.

She was so fragile he feared he would bruise her. And yet even while that thought flitted through his mind, he drew her even closer, until he could feel the thundering of her heartbeat in his own chest.

How long he had waited. But he would wait no more. He would take. He would give. And he would take again, until he was filled with her.

He heard her little moan and felt the excitement build as his hands moved over her, touching, exploring.

His fingers encountered the swell of her breast beneath the soft fabric of her nightdress and he heard her quick little intake of breath. Instantly his touch gentled, and moved to the small of her back, stroking, arousing, until he felt her gradual response.

Laura struggled to control the wild beating of her heart. Never, never had she allowed a man to touch her like this. His touch had her spiraling up like the dust devils that danced across the desert. And then she was falling, falling so fast her heart couldn't seem to catch up with her.

Never before had she known such conflict. She wanted him to stop. And yet she wanted him to go on kissing her, touching her, forever. She knew she had to end this. But not yet. *Oh, Papa!* Not just yet.

"I want you, Laura. God, how I want you," he murmured against her throat.

Though she wanted to protest, to shout her refusal, her words came out in a guttural moan that only seemed to inflame him more.

"Say it, Laura. Say the words we've both needed to hear all these long years. Tell me that you want this, too."

He lifted his head and studied her. Her lips were moist and swollen. Her eyes were closed.

"Look at me, Laura."

Her eyes blinked open.

She saw herself reflected in his eyes. And she saw something more. She saw knowledge. The knowledge of a man who knew the ways of the world, and of men and women. But she knew nothing of such things. And her ignorance frightened her.

And along with knowledge, though she could not put a name to it, she saw naked desire.

With a finger he traced the curve of her eyebrow, the slope of her cheek. Like a kitten she moved against his touch, loving the feel of his rough finger on her skin.

"When I left Bitter Creek all those years ago, I asked you only one thing—that you tell me you loved me." He took a deep breath. "I needed those words to carry me through the long days and the longer nights. But you never did say how you felt.''

''I couldn't, Matthew. Papa forbid it.''

He saw the little frown that furrowed her brow. He touched his lips to the spot with the gentlest of kisses until the frown was erased.

''Your father isn't here now, Laura. It's just you and me. Say the words.''

It would be so easy. Lying here in his arms, with her blood still hot from his kisses, it would be so easy to say she loved him.

Slowly, languidly, she lifted a hand to the dressings at his shoulder. They were warm and sticky where his sudden movements had caused him to begin to bleed once more.

The blood was like a dash of cold water. She pulled her hand back as if burned. What had she been thinking of?

''Let me up, Matthew.'' She prayed he wouldn't notice the little catch in her voice.

His eyes narrowed. ''That isn't what you really want. That's your father speaking. You want what I want.'' He could feel it in the way she trembled at his touch. His own hands were none too steady.

''No.'' She pushed herself from his arms and fought to control the tremors in her limbs. ''I want you to get well enough to leave, before the man who's after you finds out where you are.''

At her words, his hands dropped away in a gesture of defeat. Desire fled. ''I want you to know that I didn't mean to drag you into this.''

She shrugged. ''What's done is done.''

She stood up and smoothed her nightdress. Though her legs were shaking, she forced herself to take several halting steps. She needed to put some distance between them if she was to think clearly.

''You're bleeding again. I'll get fresh dressings.''

As he lay back against the blankets, his hand encountered

the cold steel of the rifle. For a moment his fingers closed over it. Then he pushed it aside and clenched his hand into a fist to stop the shaking.

"This will sting a little." Laura sponged lye soap and warm water over the wound before applying a clean dressing.

She was uncomfortably aware of Matt's eyes watching her while she worked. Not once had he looked away since she'd begun. She heard his low hiss of pain and looked down. Instantly she regretted her lapse. His gaze bored into hers.

"Roll this way a little," she said, wrapping a clean strip of linen about his shoulder.

As he complied with her request, his hand brushed the underside of her breast. Her hands stilled. Then she forced herself to go on until she had tied the final strip of cloth.

By the time she finished, sweat beaded Matt's brow and Laura felt a sting of remorse. It was her touch, after all, that had caused his pain.

"I could get you some coffee or warm broth."

"No." He caught her hand, then abruptly released it. "What I need is a good stiff whiskey."

"I'm sorry. Papa never allowed spirits in the house."

If he hadn't been in such pain he would have laughed. "I guess I figured as much. He didn't approve of guns. He didn't approve of whiskey. And he made it clear that he didn't approve of me."

Before she could protest, he held up a hand. "I'm sorry, Laura. That was unfair. Your father was a good man. A damned good man. And he was right to want to protect you. Especially from a man like me."

A silence stretched between them until he said, "I have some whiskey in my saddlebags. Would you mind if I had some?"

Without a word she picked up the saddlebags from the floor and set them on the bed. With his good arm he rummaged through them until he located a bottle.

She had fully intended to leave the room. But when she saw his clumsy attempts to remove the cork, she relented and surprised him by taking the bottle from his hand.

When she'd uncorked it, she leaned over the bed and cradled his head on her arm. With her other hand she lifted the bottle to his lips.

He drank deeply and felt the warmth snake through his veins. But was it the warmth of the liquor, he wondered, or the warmth of this woman's touch?

"Do you want some more?"

He lay very still. Her touch was so gentle, the scent of her so enticing, he wanted to prolong the moment.

"If you don't mind, Laura, I'd like to wait a minute, then have a little more."

She lowered his head to the pillow and sat gingerly on the edge of the bed. It was terrible to be this close to him. Terrible and wonderful. She felt her heart miss a beat before settling down to its natural rhythm.

"Does it ease the pain?"

"A little."

"I'm glad."

They sat in silence for several minutes before he asked for another drink. Cradling his head in her lap, she lifted the bottle to his lips a second time.

When she corked the bottle, he leaned back against the pillows and closed his eyes. Laura watched him, feeling her heart contract. If only she had it in her power to heal all his wounds.

When he opened his eyes, he saw the concern etched on her brow. Sensing her compassion, he was touched by it.

"You need your sleep, Laura. Why don't you go to bed."

She drew the chair close and sat down. "If you don't mind, I'd like to stay a while."

He stared at the ceiling, feeling the whiskey begin to numb the pain.

She cleared her throat. "You've never told me, Matthew…"

"Told you what?" He waited, his gaze still fixed on the ceiling.

"Did you ever…" She licked her lips and tried again. "Are you…married?"

He turned his head and met her look. "There's no wife. I guess a life like mine, on the trail, never left room for a wife and kids."

She felt a strange sense of relief. For long minutes they sat in silence.

His low voice broke through the stillness. "Tell me how your father died."

"He was thrown from a wagon. Apparently he had whipped the team into a run, trying to beat an approaching storm. When the team returned with an empty wagon, I went out looking for him. I found him along the trail. He was still alive, but unconscious."

"How did you get him home?"

She glanced at the fire for a minute, deep in thought.

"I had to drag him into the wagon, then from the wagon into the house. He lingered for nearly three days. But I couldn't leave him. He was in too much pain."

"Were you alone the entire time?"

She nodded.

Without thinking, Matt reached out and caught her hand. "It must have been terrible for you."

"I was so afraid. I remember breaking down and crying several times, wishing fiercely that someone would come by and offer to go for the doctor. If wishes could come true—" She seemed to catch herself. Her tone sharpened. "But Papa had always said no one is ever alone. There is always One by our side, giving us help when we most need it."

He marveled that this fragile woman could have such inner strength.

''After his death, didn't anyone from the town offer to come out and lend a hand?''

''Oh, yes. They were very kind. The Ridgelys sent old Judd over to tend my cattle until I could handle the chores again. And Ned Harrison sent supplies from his store. The women in the town sent food and baked goods. But everyone is so busy with their own lives, Matthew. They can't keep helping me forever. Besides, I've been alone a long time now. I manage very well alone.''

''You certainly do.'' He loved listening to her voice. It washed over him, soothing him.

She felt him squeeze her hand.

She turned to watch the flickering flames of the fire, feeling oddly contented. It had been a long time since anyone had asked about her father's death. The story had been bottled up inside her for too long.

''Would you like any more whiskey, Matthew?''

She heard the smile in his voice. ''Did you know that you and my mother were the only two who ever called me Matthew? Everyone else has always called me Matt.''

''Do you mind?''

He shook his head. ''I don't mind at all.''

''Then,'' she said, matching his smile, ''would you like any more whiskey…Matthew?''

''No. That did the job. I'm feeling no pain.''

''Then I'll put it away and go to bed.''

As she reached for the bottle, he closed his hand over hers to stop her. There was an immediate rush of heat between them. And though neither wanted to admit it, they were both aware of it.

''Leave it. In case I wake up in the night in pain.''

''Yes. Of course.''

She dropped her hand to her side and turned away. As she crossed the room she heard his voice, low and gruff.

''Sleep tight, Laura.''

''Thank you. And you, Matthew.''

"Laura."

She turned.

By the light of the fire, she could see the laughter in his dark eyes. "If you'd like to check me during the night for fever, be my guest. But I won't be responsible for what might happen."

With heat staining her cheeks, she fled the room.

Chapter Four

Laura lay in the feather bed and drew the blankets up to her chin. Though she had worked since sunrise, sleep eluded her. Her mind was crowded with thoughts. Memories washed over her. So many memories. Many of them were too wonderful to imagine. A few were so painful she had kept them buried all these years.

She turned and stared into the flickering flames of the fire. Once again, in her mind's eye, she was a girl of fifteen.

Every Sunday, Laura had accompanied her father and mother to town. After church, while Papa loaded supplies in the back of the wagon, Mama would visit with the ladies from town and study the latest merchandise in the mercantile. Those few precious hours away from the ranch gave Laura a sense of freedom, which she treasured. Often she studied the pages of the books in Ned Harrison's mercantile, dreaming of exotic places she would never see. Once she had ridden young Billy Harrison's bicycle, until Papa saw her and admonished her for such unladylike behavior. At her age, he scolded, it was improper to hike her skirts above her knees.

"Billy's only ten, Papa. He doesn't care."

"You heard me, Laura. You will not do it again."

"Yes, Papa." She hated growing up; hating being too old

to play with the children, too young to enjoy gossiping with the ladies.

The following Sunday, Laura left the mercantile in search of something to occupy her time. The women were busy examining the new bolts of fabric that had just been delivered. Papa was off to a nearby ranch to see a bull that had been brought all the way from Missouri.

At the end of town stood Purdy's stables. As Laura ambled along the dusty road, she heard voices raised in raucous laughter. Curious, she rounded the side of the stable and paused beside a split-rail fence. Several young men sat atop the fence, laughing and shouting words of encouragement to the rider attempting to stay in the saddle of a bucking horse.

Fascinated, Laura leaned against the rail and watched. Though the rider was only a few years older than she, he handled himself like a man born to the saddle. His shirt was stretched tautly across shoulders that were muscled from years of farm chores. The front of his shirt clung damply, revealing a lean flat stomach. His hat flew into the air. Beneath it the dark hair was plastered to his head and fell across his forehead in an oddly appealing way. As the others whistled and shouted, his eyes danced with excitement. His lips were parted in a grin.

"He's going to throw you, Matt. You know you can't hold on much longer."

"There wasn't a horse born who can throw me," he taunted.

"Whoa, boy. Are you going to feel silly when you land in the dust."

"You'll eat those words, Cal. I'm going to tame this beast."

The horse, its eyes wide, nostrils flaring, leapt high in the air and executed a twisting motion that left Laura dizzy just watching. And though the idea of a man and beast pitted against each other was distasteful to her, she found she could not look away. The scene unfolding before her was too terrible. Terrible and wonderful.

She watched as the rider knotted the reins about his hand until the horse stopped fighting him. At the nudge of the rider's knees, the horse began to prance smartly around the ring.

The rider gave a laugh of pure enjoyment. As he waved to the young men atop the fence, he spied the lone girl. For several seconds their gazes met and held.

Laura found her cheeks growing hot. The young man in the saddle looked so sure of himself, so brave. She was so embarrassed by her reaction to him that she began to turn away.

Out of the corner of her eye she saw the horse begin to race toward her. For a moment she was too stunned to move. Then, as the others shouted and hooted, she backed away from the fence and watched in horrified fascination as the horse came to a sudden halt. The rider sailed through the air, over the fence, landing in the dust at her feet.

While the others jeered, he lay very still. A cry was torn from Laura's lips as she bent to him. *Please Lord,* she prayed as she touched a hand to his shoulder, *don't let him be dead.*

He lay perfectly still. Even when she shook him, he didn't move. Tears sprang to her eyes and she glanced up at the young men who still sat atop the fence.

"How can you sit there when your friend is dead?"

The onlookers' voices faded.

"He's faking it. Come on, Matt," one of them called, breaking the uncomfortable silence. "Get up."

"I tell you he's dead." Laura knelt in the dust, unmindful of the fact that Mama would scold her for soiling her gown. And Papa. If he found out she was at the stables with a group of roughnecks, he would be furious. But at this moment nothing mattered except the daring young man who lay at her feet.

As she tenderly touched a hand to his face, his eyes

opened. The laughter that he had kept under such control now burst free. "Had you fooled, didn't I?"

"Oh." She jumped up and took several steps away from him. Then she bolted.

Instantly he leapt to his feet and ran after her, while behind them the others laughed and shouted.

"I'm sorry," he called, trying to catch up with her. "I didn't mean to scare you."

Struggling for breath, she stopped and faced him. "Why would you do such a foolish dangerous thing?"

"I didn't know how else to meet you."

Her mouth dropped open. "You mean you let that horse throw you just to…"

He nodded his head. "I saw you there, and I was afraid you'd leave before I finished with that old nag. So I just did the only thing I could think of."

"But you could have been killed."

"I've been thrown from plenty of horses." He shrugged off her protest. "A few more bruises won't matter."

For a minute she stared at him, then turned and began to walk as fast as she could toward the mercantile.

He matched his stride to hers. "My name's Matthew Braden. What's yours?"

She kept her mouth firmly closed.

"Not going to tell me, are you? I'll bet it's a pretty name. Because you're just about the prettiest girl I've ever seen."

She felt the heat return to her cheeks.

"Do you live in town?"

She gritted her teeth. He was too bold. She would not dignify his questions with an answer.

"Do you come to town often?" he asked.

She stepped over a boulder and continued walking. Up ahead Laura could see her parents seated in the wagon. Papa was looking at his pocket watch.

"Oh, dear. I'm late." Lifting her skirts she began to run.

As she ran toward the wagon, she could feel his gaze burning into her back. And though she longed to turn for a final glimpse of him, she kept running until she reached the wagon.

"Was that one of the Braden brothers you were talking to, Laura?"

"Yes, Papa." She frowned. She'd forgotten to tell him her name. She saw her father and mother exchange worried glances.

"The Bradens are new in town," her father said softly, "but there are already rumors about them. They're a wild sort. Not much good at ranching, from what I've heard. Without some supervision, they're apt to drift into trouble. You'd be wise to stay away from them."

"Yes, Papa."

Climbing into the back of the wagon, she seated herself on the sacks of flour and watched as the town receded from view. But that night as she went to sleep, she could still see the dark laughing eyes of Matthew Braden.

The following Sunday she told herself firmly that she had no intention of looking for the fool who had thrown himself at her feet. But as soon as their wagon rolled into town, she could think of nothing else. She felt a wild sense of anticipation as she stood beside her parents in the church, singing the words from the faded hymnal. And then she knew. Without turning around, she sensed that Matthew Braden was watching her. And though she continued to stare straight ahead during the long service, she could feel his dark gaze.

When she finally walked out of the church beside her parents, she saw Matthew and his brothers standing beneath the branches of a gnarled old tree. His hair was slicked back from his face. His faded shirt was freshly washed.

When she glanced his way, he winked. She felt her cheeks grow hot and looked away quickly. But later, when Papa and Mama went off to the mercantile, Laura refused to run away when he cautiously approached.

"I found out your name," he said proudly.

"Who told you?"

"Ned Harrison at the mercantile. I give him a hand sometimes, when he needs someone to lift heavy sacks. When I
told him about the girl who looked as clean and shiny as a
Sunday prayer meeting, he said there was only one person I
could mean." A smile lit his eyes. "He said your name is
Laura Conners."

She had never thought much about her name. But Matthew
whispered it as though it were a prayer.

"It suits you," he said, his voice gruff. "A pretty name
for a pretty girl."

"I bet you say that to all the girls in town." Laura kept
her gaze firmly on the pebble she had uncovered with the toe
of her boot.

"I never said it before."

"To anyone?"

"Not to anyone."

They both looked up as Matthew's brothers approached.
"You coming, Matt?" Cal asked.

"I'll be along."

"Don't keep Pa waiting. We got chores."

"I said I'll be along."

When they were once more alone, Matt said, "There's a
new foal at the stables. Want to see it?"

Laura nodded her head.

"Come on then."

They walked side by side, careful not to touch. When they
reached the stables, Laura paused at the doorway, but Matt
walked boldly inside. As her eyes adjusted to the gloom, she
could make out the forms of the mare and her newborn.

Matt approached, his hand outstretched for the mare's in-
spection. When she nickered softly, he caught Laura's hand
and placed it on the foal's velvet muzzle.

"Isn't that just about the prettiest little filly you've ever
seen?"

Laura was too overcome to speak. She continued to stroke

the soft quivering little creature until, on wobbly legs, it made its way back to its mother. In silence Laura and Matt watched as the foal nuzzled its mother, then began to suckle.

When they emerged from the stables, Laura's eyes danced with pleasure. "Oh, Matthew. She was so beautiful. More beautiful even than the calves at our ranch."

"I knew you'd like her." He studied the way Laura looked, and felt as if he'd never shared anything so special before.

At the other end of town Laura could see her father and mother already waiting in the wagon.

"I have to go."

"I'll walk with you."

"No." Laura thought about the things Papa had said about Matthew and his brothers. It was not her intention to do anything wrong. But today had been so special. She didn't want anything to spoil this happy feeling. "You stay here. I'll run back."

"Will I see you next week?"

Laura looked away. "Maybe."

"I know I will."

She glanced at him and saw the laughter in his eyes. "Even if I have to be thrown from a horse again to get your attention," he added.

In the next year, between her fifteenth and sixteenth birthdays, she had come to know the man behind those laughing eyes.

Matthew Braden was like no other person she had ever met. He was a tease who would go to great lengths to make her laugh. She loved his silly jokes, his mocking humor. When she fretted about her mother's fragile health, he could lift her spirits with a single word. And when she worried that Papa might lose the ranch because of debts, he offered to rob a bank for her. Of course, she knew he was only joking. Still, she told him that he must never say such a thing, even in jest.

"Someone might hear you and turn you in to the marshal."

"Believe me, Laura," he muttered, "if the bank gets robbed, the first person the marshal will look for is me. Haven't you heard? The Braden brothers commit all the crimes in the territory."

"Papa says a man's reputation is his most valuable possession."

"Then I guess you know what I'm worth."

"You're worth everything to me."

He caught a strand of her hair and watched as it sifted through his fingers. His eyes were narrowed, thoughtful. "I guess I could just about walk through fire for you, Laura."

"Don't walk through fire, Matthew." She lowered her gaze. "Just walk the straight and narrow."

When Mama died, it was Matthew who had known just what words to say to ease her grief. He had lost his own mother. He understood her pain.

Laura saw a tender side of Matthew, which he kept hidden from the world. Beneath his bravado there was a kind and sensitive man who was willing to take the time to listen to her when she needed to talk about her loss. And when she wept, he offered his quiet strength.

Papa began to depend upon her to take her mother's place. Laura had always been a good cook, but now she assumed the rest of her mother's duties, as well. She sewed and mended, and each week, when she went into town with Papa, he expected her to go to the mercantile and talk with the older women about gardening and cooking. But though Laura assumed the burdens of a woman, Papa resolutely forbade her to speak about courtship. That would come later, Papa said. And not with Matthew Braden. Matthew and his brothers had begun to wear guns and holsters slung low on their hips. There were rumors and whispers about trouble, not only in town, but in surrounding towns. Trouble caused by the

Braden brothers. Matthew Braden's name was not permitted to be spoken in Papa's home.

Laura lay very still, listening to the silence of the house. A glance at the window told her it was not yet dawn. She had been dreaming again. It was the same dream she'd had for years.

It was the summer of her sixteenth year, a hot sultry day. Papa rode up to the hills to find the cattle that had broken away from the herd.

Laura's chores were finished. She sat on the porch, fanning herself. Even that would not relieve the unrelenting heat. Lifting her hair from the back of her neck, she thought about the creek that Papa had dammed up for the cattle.

She checked the pot of stew that simmered on the stove, and covered the freshly baked biscuits with a linen square. Then, latching the door, she ran toward the creek.

She had at least another hour or two of privacy before Papa came down from the hills. Peeling off her dress and chemise, she lathered them with soap, then rinsed them thoroughly and wrung them out before spreading them on some low-hanging branches to dry. Then she began to wash herself. Sitting in the shallows, she moved the cake of soap along her body in slow strokes. Lifting her foot high in the air she ran the soap along her leg, then moved to the other leg. When her body was completely lathered, she waded farther into the cool water.

Oh, how wonderful it felt against her heated skin. She submerged her body completely and came up sputtering. Then she began to lather her hair. Rubbing her scalp until it tingled, she tossed the soap onto the shore, then ducked beneath the water once more until all the suds floated free.

With a laugh she tossed her head. Her hair fanned out around her, sending up a rainbow spray.

It was then that she saw Matthew.

She ducked under the water until it lapped about her

breasts. Her cheeks flamed. Her eyes darkened with fury. "Matthew Braden. How long have you been standing there?"

"Long enough." He had wanted to leave. All his common sense told him that a girl like Laura was entitled to her privacy. She would be embarrassed to have anyone watch her perform such personal tasks. And angry. She would have a right to be angry, he told himself. But despite his best intentions, he had been unable to walk away.

"You'd better get out of here. Papa will be along any minute."

"Your Pa's up in the hills. I passed him some time ago."

"Just leave, Matthew, so I can get dressed and get back to the ranch before Papa comes home."

"I thought I'd join you in the creek."

"Matthew." She saw the way his eyes danced with unconcealed humor. "What are you...?"

When she saw him drop his gun belt and begin to unbutton his shirt, she shouted, "You can't do this."

"Want to stop me, Laura?"

She recognized that look. He was such a tease. But this time, he meant what he said. She decided to try a new tactic.

"Please, Matthew." Her voice purred. "I have to get back to the ranch."

"No one's stopping you. Come on out."

"Matthew." She was no longer smiling. "I have to go. Papa will be angry."

"Then go. But I'm going swimming." As he reached for the fasteners at his waist, she turned around, refusing to look at him.

A minute later she felt a tap on her shoulder. Whirling, she found herself face-to-face with Matthew.

Her voice caught in her throat. "You shouldn't be here."

"We're only swimming, Laura."

"But we have no clothes on."

He gave her a slow dangerous smile. "Really? I hadn't noticed."

"Oh, Matthew." As she started to move past him he dropped a hand on her shoulder. She could feel the tremors clear to her toes.

"Stay a few minutes. Swim with me."

"I can't." She felt awed by the powerful width of his shoulders. She couldn't help but notice the dark mat of hair that covered his chest and disappeared beneath the water. She deliberately turned her head, refusing to look at him.

"I know I'm not as pretty as you." Laughter warmed his tone as he caught her chin and forced her to meet his gaze. "But at least you could look at me."

"I'm afraid to."

"Afraid? Why?"

She sucked in a deep breath. "You're beautiful."

They both seemed stunned by her words. She swallowed, feeling her throat constrict. "I never realized that a man could look so…"

"You're the one who's beautiful." His hand moved along her cheek. "If I had a lifetime to look at you, it still wouldn't be enough, Laura."

Why did his touch have to be so gentle? She wanted to walk away. All her senses were shouting for her to leave, now, before it was too late. But though he did not hold her, she was tied to the spot. She could not find the strength to leave.

"I want to kiss you, Laura."

"No." She was shocked by his suggestion. But even while she recoiled from it, she felt a little thrill of anticipation. What would it be like to touch her lips to his? How would it feel to be held in those powerful arms?

As if reading her mind he bent and touched his lips to hers. It was the sweetest of kisses. A mere brushing of lips on lips. Her eyes were open; so were his. Each of them stood very still, absorbing the shockwaves that collided between them.

He moved his lips to the corner of her mouth, kissing away a tiny drop of water.

''You taste so good, Laura. So clean and sweet.''

She put a hand to his shoulder to steady herself. Was it the current that tugged at her, drawing her closer and closer to his arms? Or was it her need to feel, just once, the strength she knew she would find in him?

''I have to go, Matthew.''

''I know. But I'm not sorry I kissed you, Laura.''

''I'm not sorry, either. Don't look until I'm dressed.''

He laughed. ''I've already seen you.''

''I don't care. I want you to turn around, Matthew.''

''All right.''

She turned, and felt her heart stop. Her father, astride his horse, was watching them from the bank. His eyes were dark with fury.

''Get dressed, girl.'' His voice was hard, tight. She knew it was taking all his willpower to keep from shouting. ''And go home.''

''Papa, it isn't what you—'' She ran a tongue over her lips and tried again. ''We didn't—''

''Not another word, girl. Do as you're told.''

Mortified, Laura waded to the bank and pulled on her damp dress.

As she and her father started away she heard Matthew's low even tones. He did not sound like a man who had just been caught doing something wrong; he talked like a man who knew exactly what he wanted. ''I'd like to talk to you about courting your daughter, Mr. Conners.''

When she hesitated her father pointed a finger. ''Be on your way. This is man-talk, Laura.''

Fighting tears, she ran all the way to the ranch house. When her father returned, he told her that she was never to mention Matthew Braden's name again.

Chapter Five

Matt awoke to sunlight streaming through a gap in the bedroom curtains. A cozy fire crackled in the fireplace and from the kitchen came the wonderful aroma of coffee and freshly baked bread.

He sat up slowly, testing his strength. Though he was still weak and his arm and shoulder throbbed painfully, there was no longer a fire raging where the bullet had been removed, and the fever was down.

Spying a basin of fresh water, he moved stiffly to the dresser and peered in the mirror. He looked more like a grizzly bear than a man. With a string of oaths he reached for the straight razor and set to work. After shaving his beard, he washed, then surveyed himself again. Satisfied, he picked up a clean linen towel and began to dry himself. Turning, he paused with his hand in midair. Laura was standing in the doorway.

Watching him shave with Papa's old straight razor had caused the strangest reaction in Laura. Though it was absurd, she had been riveted to the spot, unable to turn away.

"You look…" She wanted to say handsome. But she was too shy. So she finished lamely, "…fine. You must be feeling better today."

"Today I don't feel like a whole herd of buffalo ran over me," he said with a grin. "Just half a herd."

She smiled at his humor. "I...thought you might want to wear one of Papa's old shirts." She knew she was blushing, which only made her cheeks grow hotter. "Just until I can clean and mend yours."

"Thanks." He crossed the room and took the shirt from her hand.

As he pulled it on, she stared, fascinated at the width of his shoulders.

"It fits fine," he said, tucking it into the waistband of his pants. Her eyes followed his movements.

When he noticed the direction of her gaze, she blushed again and forced herself to look up at his face. He seemed much less fierce without the beard. But every bit as dangerous.

He sat on the edge of the bed and winced as he pulled on first one boot, then the other. While he struggled with the task, Laura noted the beads of water that glistened in his dark hair. She fought a nearly overpowering urge to touch him. How would it feel to be free to run her fingers through his damp hair? To reach a hand to his smooth clean-shaven cheek?

She turned away and headed for the safety of the kitchen. Over her shoulder she called, "Breakfast is ready. If you're feeling up to it."

Matt paused in the doorway and watched while she stirred something on the wood stove. How strange to have a woman cook for him, fuss over him.

She turned from the stove and found him standing in the doorway, watching her with a strange intense look.

He took his place at the table and sipped the strong black coffee while she filled his plate. Then he dug into eggs, fried potatoes and thick slabs of beef. There was a loaf of crusty bread still warm from the oven, as well as slices of apple spice cake.

"It's been a while since I watched a hungry man eat my cooking."

"I don't believe I've ever tasted anything this good," he said, spreading a third slice of warm bread with apple preserves.

Be careful, he cautioned himself sternly. It wouldn't do for a man like him to start enjoying this kind of pampering.

He studied her across the table and she felt her cheeks grow hot.

"I guess there isn't much time to cook when you're out on the trail," she said.

"Or to eat." He finished his coffee and sat back, content. "Or even time to just sit and talk." He glanced at her. "Tell me about Bitter Creek. And the people. And about what you do there."

She stood and began gathering the dishes. While she worked she told him about Jed McMasters, the banker who owned half the town. And about Nate Burns, the hardened widower with two small children.

He studied the way her gown narrowed at her tiny waist, then flared over her hips. Just looking at her made him ache with a hunger that could never be sated.

"Sounds like the town of Bitter Creek is teeming with eligible bachelors."

Laura poured him another cup of coffee and laughed. "I'm thinking of hiring a couple of gunmen to keep them from beating down my door." With a twinkle she added, "Would you care for the job?"

"You might be sorry, Miss Conners. I might be tempted to shoot all of them and keep you for myself. You'd be in big trouble if I was the first in line to get through the door."

Though his humor was light and teasing, she heard the gruffness in his tone and tried to ignore it. But the thought of Matthew's breaking down the door and forcibly taking her had been playing through her mind, especially at night when she lay just a few steps away from the sound of his steady breathing.

She turned the conversation to more mundane topics. She told him about Beth Mills, and how helpful and sweet she was at school. In a soft voice she spoke about Beth's mother, Wanda, and about how confused her life had become since the loss of her husband.

"That woman's playing a dangerous game, working in a place like the Red Garter. She ought to give more thought to her little girl." Matt's tone was harsh. It was odd, but he sounded the way Papa used to.

"I know. The Red Garter is a bad place for a lonely woman like her. But there aren't any other places in Bitter Creek where a woman can work." Laura's voice lowered. "Her only other choice is to marry a man she doesn't love, in order to be taken care of. I respect her for trying to survive on her own, even though at times, it's almost as if Beth is the mother, and poor Wanda the lost child."

"Seems to me you care a lot about that girl and her mother."

"I do." Laura shrugged. "I just want Wanda to find a way to build her life again. And Beth." Laura wasn't aware of the sadness that came into her eyes. "Sometimes she's like my own child. The one I never had. And I share her unhappiness."

When Matt remained silent, she realized how much she had revealed of herself. Feeling a need to fill the silence, she began to tell him about the mischievous Thompson boys, five rogues who kept her on her toes all day.

"They sound a bit like the Braden brothers of old," he said with a grin.

She poured him another cup of coffee and laughed. "Oh, they try my patience. But I know that with the proper guidance, they can grow up to be fine citizens."

"You talk just like a man I once knew." He chuckled

when she shot him a quick look. "Your father said the same thing to me."

She turned away. "I guess I do sound as foolish as my father."

He scraped back his chair and stood so quickly she didn't have time to react. In one quick motion he turned her to face him.

"I didn't say he was foolish." Matt looked down at her, his dark eyes serious. "I never forgot what your father said to me. He was the only one who ever cared what I did with my life."

She heard the intensity of his words every bit as much as she felt the intensity of his touch. She pulled away and took a step back, determined to break contact. When he was too close, when he was touching her, she couldn't seem to control her emotions. And during the long night she had convinced herself that she would keep her distance from this man until he was well enough to ride away.

Very soon, she thought with a pain in the vicinity of her heart, he would ride out of her life, as he had done before. And it would be the best thing for both of them.

Crossing the room, she said, "I guess I'll see to your things. Your shirt and jacket need washing and mending."

He watched her disappear into her father's room. As she emerged, she had his shirt draped over her arm. In her hand was the torn bloody jacket.

"I'll wash these first and try to get all the blood out. When they're dry I'll…" She was holding up the jacket, but it wasn't the blood that she was seeing. It was a badge. A shiny silver badge pinned to the cowhide.

She studied it for long moments, then looked up to see him watching her.

"You never told me. I thought…" She paused and started again. "You're a marshal?"

He nodded. "A territorial marshal."

"You aren't running from the law?"

His voice was low and grim. "I am the law."

"But all the stories of the Braden brothers..."

"Were true. My brothers were always in trouble. And they all died violent deaths. But somewhere along the trail I got to thinking about what your father said. And I knew he was right. Unless I took my life into my own hands, I'd never amount to anything."

She felt a sudden warm glow of pride that her father's words had not been spoken in vain. Those same words had sent away the only man she had ever cared for. But Papa had been right to stand between them. Matthew had needed time to see the error of his ways.

A marshal. A territorial marshal. She hugged the knowledge to her heart.

And then the warmth was swept away by another thought. There was still a wild streak in him, one that caused him to face down cold-blooded killers. He was still a man whose life was spent killing others.

"But Matthew. Why a marshal?"

He shrugged. "Living by the gun was the only thing I knew. And there were people willing to pay me to use my skill."

"Pay you. Is that all you thought about? Getting paid to kill?" Her eyes filled with tears and she quickly blinked them away. "Weren't you listening to Papa?" Her voice was little more than a whisper. "Whether you're on the right side of the law or the wrong side, if you live by the gun you'll eventually perish by it."

He could feel his energy draining. Hadn't he had this same argument with himself a hundred times? He was sick to death of defending his choice. Still, he owed her a reply.

"I've never doubted how I'd die, Laura," he said tiredly. "There are too many gunmen out there just waiting to see if they're better than me, quicker than me, tougher than me. But this is the job I chose." He leaned heavily against the wall, cursing the weakness that plagued him.

Noting his sudden pallor, Laura felt a twinge of regret. "I'm sorry, Matthew. I had no right to attack you for doing your job. Here." She caught his arm and helped him back to the bedroom.

She could sense buried beneath the pain his frustration at his weakness. "I need my wits about me," he said through clenched teeth. "Those men—"

"Men?" She felt her heart lurch. "More than one?"

"Four," he said softly, closing his eyes. "Part of a gang of gunmen who've been robbing and murdering their way across Arizona Territory."

Laura felt a terrible despair wash over her. It was even worse than she had imagined. There was not a single gunman to deal with; there were four. And Papa had been right all along. His words of warning rang in her mind. Woe to any woman who foolishly gives her heart to the wrong kind of man.

As she eased Matt onto the bed, she noticed that his hand automatically closed around his gun before he drifted off into a troubled sleep.

"Where are you going?"

Laura looked up from the dough she was kneading to see Matt lifting her father's old jacket from a peg.

When he pulled it on, he inhaled the soft womanly scent of her that seemed to linger in the folds of the jacket.

"Thought I'd go out to the barn and check on my horse."

"He's fine. You should save your strength. I've seen to it that he has food and water."

"Thanks. But I'd like to check on him, anyway." He frowned. "Are you sure he won't be noticed if old Judd happens by again?"

"Old Judd won't be back again until next Saturday." She laughed. "He was headed to the barn when he was here. I practically threw myself against the door to keep him from going inside."

Matt joined in the laughter. "You never were very good at lying as I recall."

"That was Papa's fault. He raised me to believe that lying was the devil's handiwork."

As he began to walk past her, Matt paused and ran a finger along her jaw. With a thoughtful expression he murmured, "For once in his life your father was wrong."

She looked up at him with a questioning arch of her brow.

"The devil's handiwork was woman."

He moved past her and pulled open the door. She shivered at the blast of frigid air as he slammed it behind him.

Wrapping her arms around herself, she stood by the window and watched as he strode across the snow-covered expanse to the barn.

By the time he returned she had the table set.

He sniffed. "Something smells wonderful."

"Since it's Sunday, I thought I'd make something special for supper."

He removed the jacket and his wide-brimmed hat, then filled a basin with water and washed his hands. When he sat at the table she ladled chicken and dumplings onto his plate. Steam rose from biscuits wrapped in a linen square.

"You sure know how to spoil a man." He bit into a tender flaky biscuit and rolled his eyes heavenward. "I don't know when I've tasted such good cooking."

Laura fussed with her apron, feeling pleased yet awkward. "Papa set great store by Sunday supper. But now that I'm alone, I sometimes forget what day it is. With the preacher off to Kansas, Sunday seems just like all the other days."

He heard the loneliness in her tone. "When will he be back?"

"Any day now." She got up to poke at a log that was smoking in the fireplace, then returned to her place at the table. "The Reverend Talbot promised us he'd be back to Bitter Creek by Christmas."

"He picked a tough time to travel through these mountains."

Laura nodded thoughtfully. "So did you."

"I had no choice." He finished his meal and sipped strong hot coffee.

"Choices." She smiled. "Papa said we spend our whole lives making choices."

For a long moment they both remained silent, thinking about the choices they had made and the consequences of those choices.

To break the uncomfortable silence she asked softly, "How long have you been a marshal, Matthew?"

"It's five years now."

"Was it your choice?"

He drained his coffee and touched a hand to the pouch of tobacco in his pocket. Thinking better of it, he dropped his hand. "You might say the job was just thrust upon me. The sheriff of a small town was shot and killed by a gunfighter, who decided to stick around and terrorize the citizens. They asked for my help to…eliminate the problem."

"You killed him?"

He heard the accusation in her tone and fought down a wave of anger. How could he describe to a sheltered woman like Laura the fear and desperation of the people of that town?

"I gave him a choice. Leave town or face my gun."

"What choice did he make?"

"The wrong one." Matt stood and lifted her father's sheepskin jacket from the peg. Walking to the door he muttered, "Think I'll take a turn in the night air."

As the door closed behind him, Laura sat stiffly in her chair, staring at the empty space across the table. The thought of Matt calmly facing down a dangerous gunman left her stomach churning.

She stood and touched the end of her apron to her brow. She must have been mad to indulge her fantasies about Matthew Braden. Regardless of the badge, he was as dangerous as the gunmen he tracked. And as unpredictable.

When the kitchen was tidy, she peered through the window into the darkness. Where was he? And what would keep him out on a night like this?

As if in answer to her question, she heard a sound on the porch. Opening the door, she found him seated on a railing, watching the gathering storm clouds. In his hand was a thin paper. From his pouch he poured a generous amount of tobacco onto it, then rolled, licked and sealed it. A match flared in the darkness, and he held it to the tip of his cigarette. He inhaled deeply, then emitted a stream of smoke. The sharp bite of tobacco stung the air.

"More snow coming," he said as she stepped outside.

"Aren't you coming in?"

"When I finish this." He held up his cigarette. "I didn't want to violate any of your father's rules."

Laughter warmed her words. "Matthew, come inside before you freeze. And smoke your cigarette in front of the fire."

"You don't mind?"

"I think it might be kind of nice."

Before he followed her inside, he bent and retrieved something from the porch.

"What's that?"

"Your harness. When I went in the barn earlier I noticed it was frayed. Thought I'd mend it."

She flushed as he removed the jacket and eased himself into the big chair in front of the fire.

"I would have gotten around to mending it one of these days."

He shrugged. "I don't mind. Gives me something to do until I get my strength back." He glanced at her as she picked up a basket of mending and sat in the opposite chair.

He smoked the cigarette until he could no longer hold it in his fingers. Laura watched as he tossed the last of it into the fire. She inhaled the fragrance of the burning wood and the tang of tobacco, and thought how long it had been since this old cabin had been filled with something so distinctly masculine.

They worked in companionable silence. Occasionally Laura glanced toward the man who was so intent on his task. How strange to have his presence filling the room. How… comforting.

When Matt finally hung the mended harness on a peg, she looked up to see him rubbing his shoulder.

Tossing aside her mending, she stood and crossed to him, touching a hand to his arm in a gesture of concern. "You've taken on too much. You should have gone to bed right after supper."

"I wasn't tired, Laura. And I was glad for the chore." When she started to draw away, his fingers closed over hers. His voice lowered seductively. "If I'm going to share this cabin with you, I'm going to need a lot of things to keep me busy." His gaze roamed her face before coming to rest on her lips. "Or I might do something we'll both regret."

She felt a rush of heat and knew that the stain on her cheeks would give her away. There was no way she could hide her reaction to his simple touch. And yet, if she was to survive this time with him, she would have to keep fighting. Fighting him. Fighting herself. And fighting her reaction to his simplest touch.

"I'll say good-night now, Matthew."

As she pulled away his grip tightened. Surprised, her glance flew to his face.

His dark eyes narrowed. He could read her fear and indecision. But needs pulsed through him. Needs that fueled a hunger stronger than anything he had ever known.

He reached a hand to her face. With his thumb he stroked her lips.

"Soft. Sweet Jesus, you're so soft, Laura."

She knew he was going to kiss her. And she knew, too,

that if she allowed it, she would be lost. Calling on every bit of willpower she possessed, she took a step back, breaking contact.

His hand dropped to his side.

"Good night, Laura."

She swallowed, but the words wouldn't come. On trembling legs she made her way to her room. And when at last she lay alone in the darkness, she fought down a wave of abject misery.

She had wanted him to kiss her. God help her, she had wanted to throw caution to the wind and kiss him back.

When she finally fell into a troubled sleep, her throat was raw from swallowing back the unshed tears.

Chapter Six

Matt prowled the sitting room, achingly aware of the woman who slept just a wall away. After pacing in circles, he finally paused in front of the fireplace. Sinking into the chair, he studied the glowing coals that offered the only light in the cabin.

He could ignore the pain that radiated from his wounds. He'd spent a lifetime living with pain. But the pain around his heart was harder to bear.

He had thought that all of this had been put to rest many years ago. He had made his peace with the fact that he could never see Laura again. He had convinced himself that in time her image would fade until he would no longer remember what she looked like. She would be like those blurred images he carried in his heart of his father and mother and brothers.

But Laura was different. She haunted him. Whether waking or sleeping, he could see her beloved face in his mind; could hear the sound of her voice, the trill of her laughter whispering over his senses. And all through these years he had carried the image of the shy sweet girl who had captivated him one summer's day and had never released him from the sweetest bonds he'd ever known.

What strange fate had brought him back here? Was this the price he had to pay for his past?

He had left her once because he had loved her. Her father had convinced Matt that a girl like Laura could never fit into his rough life-style. If he truly loved her, her father insisted, he would be man enough to walk away and leave her untouched, unspoiled by his ways.

His hand clenched at his side. The old man had wisely known the one thing that Matt Braden could never turn away from—a challenge. He'd been man enough. Oh, yes. He'd been man enough. But he had regretted his decision every day of his life.

Not that her father had been wrong. Matt knew that his life would have been a cruel fate for a sheltered woman like Laura. She deserved something better.

He glanced around. At the windows the faded curtains shivered against the chill wind that blew through the cracks in the walls. The sagging door barely held to the rusted hinges, which creaked in protest. Outside, the cattle were forced to stand in an unprotected area while the wind howled about them. And daily, Laura was forced to brave the elements in a rickety wagon, miles from her nearest neighbor. It was not the life of ease he had envisioned for her.

It was plain to see she needed a man around the place. This old ranch was coming apart at the seams. But Matt was familiar with that damnable pride of hers. She would work herself into the grave before she would ask for help.

He walked to the window and stared at the darkened shape of the barn. Oh, he'd had a firsthand taste of the Conners pride.

He rolled a cigarette and held a flame to the tip, then inhaled deeply.

As snowflakes danced past the window he thought back to that special Christmas when he'd returned to town after many weeks away. He'd driven a team from Bitter Creek to the railroad, nearly two hundred miles distant. There, he'd spent a month driving spikes with a sledgehammer while freezing in a near blizzard. With his pockets full of his pay he'd headed to the mercantile, happily made his purchase, then ridden out to meet Laura.

She was so cool, so beautiful, he felt robbed of speech. For long minutes he could merely stare at her and marvel that this perfect creature was here waiting for him.

She invited him inside, and he stood, stiff and awkward as her father studied him from across the room.

"I brought you something." He thrust the package into Laura's hands.

"I didn't want anything, Matthew. Except you back home. I prayed every night for your safe return."

He grinned, feeling so proud. "Open it. I know you'll like it."

With the enthusiasm of a little girl she tore the paper and stared at the delicate pink gown with white lace at the collar that had been admired by every woman in Bitter Creek.

She looked up at him with glowing eyes. "Oh, Matthew. How did you know?"

He puffed up his chest, feeling so pleased with himself. If hard work put that glow in Laura's eyes, he would work until he dropped.

"I saw you admiring it in the mercantile."

"But it's so expensive."

"I don't care what it cost. I want the whole town to see you in that gown, Laura."

Her father's stern voice shattered the mood. "I can afford to buy my daughter what she needs."

Laura glanced at her father, then back to Matt.

"Of course you can, Mr. Conners. But I wanted to spend my first pay on something special for Laura."

"It isn't fitting," the older man said, "for a man to buy such things for a woman who isn't his wife."

Matt couldn't prevent the smile that touched his lips. "I'd like to talk to you about that very thing, Mr. Conners."

Laura's eyes widened in sweet surprise.

Her father's words abruptly cut off anything more that

Matt might have said. "We've talked about it before, Braden. My answer is still the same. Now about that dress. The whole town knows that you and my daughter are not man and wife. I will not permit her to keep your gift."

Laura turned to face her father. His lips were a thin tight line of anger. For a moment she merely studied him. Then she glanced up at Matt with a stricken look. "I couldn't possibly accept this from you, Matthew."

"Of course you can. You know you like it. You've been staring at it for months in the mercantile."

"Oh, it is beautiful." She sighed. "More beautiful than any dress I've ever seen."

"Then what's wrong, Laura? Don't you want to be the envy of every woman in town?"

She gave a soft little laugh before touching a hand to his sleeve. Even that simple touch caused him to tremble with need.

"I don't care about making the other women envious, Matthew. I just know that what Papa says is true. Everyone in town would know that I let you buy this for me. And since you aren't my husband, it wouldn't be proper."

"To hell with being proper."

She looked shocked at his rough language. When she glanced across the room, she saw that her father had come to his feet in anger.

Matt frowned. "I'm sorry, Laura. But what's wrong with wanting to see you wearing the prettiest gown in the world?"

"Nothing." She gave a last lingering glance at the dress, then folded the paper over it and handed it back to Matt. "But I can't accept this, Matthew. Papa would never approve."

In his anger, Matt had tossed the parcel on the rough wooden table. "I'm not asking for your father's approval. I bought it because I know how much Christmas means to you. I wanted this to be special for you. I know you'd look beautiful in it. You have a right to pretty things." His tone lowered to a dangerous pitch that she had never heard before. "You have a choice, Laura. You can wear the dress I bought you, or you can just let it gather dust on a shelf. Either way, it's still my Christmas gift to you."

He turned away from her, feeling bitter and frustrated. All the way there he had imagined a grateful Laura falling into his arms and pressing kisses to his hungry lips. Instead, he had left without even touching her. And the words between them had been far from tender.

The next day, he learned that Laura had thought of a third choice. Or maybe her father had. The pink dress once again hung in the mercantile for all the women to dream over. And Ned Harrison returned the money he had spent.

Matt took a last drag of his cigarette and tossed it into the fire. For a moment it glowed, then curled into ashes.

He stuffed his hands into his pockets and headed for his bedroom. That was the last time he had celebrated Christmas. From that day on, he knew that the things he wished for were never to be.

The Conners pride. It was a fearful thing.

He pried off his boots and lay atop the blankets, his hands behind his head. A half smile touched his lips. Just thinking about Laura made him grin. What had she ever seen in him?

It had never ceased to amaze him that a sweet innocent like Laura Conners could be attracted to a rough character like him. She was an only child; adored by her parents. He was the last of a litter of pups who'd been raised without any guidance except that of the fist. Besides trying to please his father, he'd had to contend with Jase, Cal and Dan, three older brothers who never looked back to see if he was following. But he had followed. Followed them into wrangling horses, followed them into working for the railroad, and even followed them into strapping on a gun and learning to use it better than anyone else.

And through it all, Laura had believed in him.

There was a time, when he was young and foolish, that he

had actually believed that her goodness would be enough for the two of them. He'd thought that somehow her integrity would rub off on him, and the gunfights, the brawls, the troubles, wouldn't touch him. Or her. But her father's words had had the desired effect. When Matt had asked permission to court Laura, her father had pointed out Laura's flawless reputation. How long, he'd reasoned, before she would be subjected to the humiliation of seeing her name tarnished beyond repair? If she were to marry a man like Matt Braden, her dreams would be forever shattered. The town would never hire as a teacher the woman whose husband was suspected of committing every crime in the territory. Worse, she and any children she might have would suffer the shame of his imprisonment if he resorted to using the gun at his hip.

"Laura might be heartbroken for a little while if you leave her," her papa said matter-of-factly, "but she'll get over it. But if you take her with you on the trail, the pain could last her a lifetime. If you really love her, Braden, you'll leave her free to chase her own dreams."

Matt frowned now in the darkness. Her father had been a smart man. He'd made Matt see the wisdom of his words. And even now, wanting her with a desperation he would have never believed, he knew he'd made the right choice all those years ago. The trail was no place for a woman like Laura.

He glanced at the snowflakes that swirled outside the window. A storm was moving in. He really ought to get back on the trail before the gunmen came after him. But the thought of leaving Laura so soon was too painful to contemplate. She had taken such good care of him. Whatever he could do in return was little enough thanks.

As he eased out of his clothes he came to a decision. He would stay for another day.

He drew back the blankets and settled himself in the big bed. His hand closed around the barrel of his rifle. His eyes narrowed in the darkness. Laura's pa had been right about one thing. In the dark of the night, a cold gun brought a man no pleasure.

But many a night it had kept him alive.

Chapter Seven

Laura was up and dressed early. When Matt appeared in the doorway looking rumpled and sleepy, she found herself unable to look away. Last night, pain and fatigue had been etched in his face. This morning there was no trace of pain. He looked strong, virile, untouched by the bullet that had brought him to her doorstep.

"Good morning. There's coffee," she said softly, pointing to the blackened pot on the stove. "And I left some biscuits." She finished wrapping a piece of cold chicken and several biscuits in a square of linen. That would be her midday meal at the schoolhouse. "Your jacket and shirt are clean and mended." She pointed to the stack of neatly folded clothes on the chair.

"I'm much obliged. I'll hitch your horse." He lifted the mended harness from the peg on the wall.

"There's no need. I can do that."

"I'll do it." Before she could protest further, he pulled on his cowhide jacket and strode to the barn.

A few minutes later she heard the creaking of the wheels as Matt brought the horse and wagon around to the porch.

She emerged from the cabin with a blanket folded over her arm and a warm shawl draped about her shoulders. It wouldn't do for the town's teacher to be seen wearing her father's old jacket. That was reserved for ranch chores.

Her mane of dark hair had been tamed into a tidy knot. The shapeless gown she wore was buttoned clear to her throat. Yet Matt was achingly aware of the slender, shapely body beneath the gown.

"Looks like it might snow all day." He glanced toward the sky. "Maybe you ought to forget about driving into town."

"I have to go. The children are expecting me."

As she walked up, he put his hand beneath her arm to help her into the wagon. But instead of lifting her, he lowered his head until his lips hovered a fraction above hers.

"That's too bad."

She shivered as his warm breath caressed her lips.

"There are so many things a man and woman can do on a snowy day like this."

"I guess you'll just have to do them alone."

"What I have in mind takes two." His eyes stared deeply into hers. His lips brushed hers as lightly as a snowflake.

"Matthew, I—"

Her words were cut off as his mouth covered hers in a searing kiss.

He'd given her no time to protest. Tremors rocked her. Stunned, she swayed against him. The blanket slipped from her arm and fell unnoticed into the snow at their feet. Her shawl fell away. Neither of them seemed to care.

He brought his arms around her until she was pressed tightly against him. The heat of his body warmed her. The fire in his blood seemed to radiate to hers, until they were both inflamed.

"I should have done this last night," he muttered against her lips.

Before she could form a reply he kissed her again, a kiss so hungry, so demanding, it left her limbs weak, her breathing ragged.

How sweet were her lips. How innocent her touch. She tasted as clean as a mountain stream. The fragrance of evergreen and pine seemed to surround her.

Clean. Untouched. Those were the words that came to mind whenever he thought of Laura.

He fed from her lips again and again, feeling the heat of desire rise within him.

He knew he had to end this or he would take her here, now, in the snow. But reason and logic were pushed aside. His wild pulsing need drove him to linger over her lips for a moment longer.

"Matthew. Matthew."

He heard her cry in the far recesses of his mind, and fought to surface.

He lifted his head.

Her lips were swollen, her eyes soft. Little wisps of her hair had become pried loose from the neat knot at the back of her head.

He placed a hand on each side of her face and stared deeply into her eyes. "It's snowing too hard to travel all that way. I shouldn't let you leave here."

"I have to go. But if it continues to snow, I'll dismiss the students early."

"Then I hope it snows all day."

She lowered her lids, ashamed of the betraying blush that stained her cheeks.

A sudden thought caused her eyes to widen. She stared up at him. She hated herself for asking, but she couldn't stop the words. "Will you be here when I return?"

The moment hung between them, and she felt her heart stop.

"I'll be here."

At his reply she released the breath she had been unconsciously holding.

He held her another moment, then, taking a deep breath, he took a step back and bent to retrieve her blanket and shawl. He caught her hand lightly in his and assisted her up onto the seat of the wagon. When she was settled she picked up the reins. The horse broke into an easy trot.

As the wagon pulled into the snow-filled trail, she stared straight ahead. If it killed her, she was determined not to turn and look at him. But despite her best intentions, she turned at the last moment to find him still standing where she had left him, staring intently after her.

As the horse and wagon dipped below a rise, Laura drew the shawl tightly about her shoulders. Now that she was no longer in Matt's arms, she felt the chill of the winter day seeping through her clothes. The hours spent at the school-house would seem endless.

She was not, she told herself firmly, eager to return home tonight to Matthew. Unknowingly she touched a finger to her lips. His kiss had held the promise of something. Something terrifying. Terrifying and wonderful.

Before Laura could even see her ranch, she spied the smoke coming from the chimney. It was an oddly comforting sight. Since Papa's death, she had been forced to return each night to a cold empty cabin.

When the wagon rolled to a stop, she was surprised to see Matt standing on the porch repairing the sagging door. It no longer hung at a lopsided angle, but straight and sturdy. Matt tested it several times, opening and closing it. Satisfied, he picked up the jacket he'd flung over the porch railing and looked up with a smile.

"I got tired of hearing those hinges squeaking. Figured I might as well make myself useful."

"Thank you."

How handsome he looked without the bushy beard. How tall and muscular. As he pulled on his jacket, she watched in fascination as the muscles of his arms bunched with each movement.

"You sew a fine seam." He ran a hand along the freshly mended cowhide.

"Thank you. I'm glad I was able to mend it."

All the way home she had known she would feel awkward and uneasy in his presence. Especially after that intimate kiss. But despite her initial discomfort, she felt more alive than she had in years. He was still here. He had not left her.

"I guess this old place does need a man's touch." She prayed her voice hadn't trembled.

When he held the door, she walked past him into the cabin. Her mouth rounded in surprise. The table was set for supper. Slices of salt pork sizzled and snapped over the fire. And the cabin was as warm as toast.

"You're making supper, Matthew?"

"You might call it that." He grinned. "It won't be much, I'm afraid. I'm used to eating cold beans and jerky. But I thought, since I'd already collected the eggs and milked the cow, I'd try my hand at making some scrambled eggs."

"For supper?"

He shrugged. "It's all I know how to make."

He watched while she lifted the lid of the blackened pot and inhaled the aroma of freshly made coffee.

She turned to him with a worried little frown. "Oh, my. Mama and Papa believed in a proper time and place for everything. Papa would have never approved of having breakfast at suppertime."

He fought to keep all trace of emotion from his voice. "I know what your mother and father wanted. But what about you, Laura? What is it you want?"

She was startled by his words. It had never occurred to her to question the rules set down by her parents all those years ago. She'd never thought about her own wants.

"Have you never done anything just for the pure fun of it?" Seeing her indecision, he goaded her further. His tone was low, intense. "What does it matter, Laura, if it tastes good and satisfies our hunger?"

What indeed? She could think of no answer. And yet, judging by the way he was looking at her, she wondered whether he was speaking of a need for food or another kind of hunger.

Hesitantly she said, "It might be fun to have breakfast at suppertime."

She accepted the chair Matt held for her and watched in anticipation while he served their plates. She tasted the eggs, then bit into a slice of bread covered with apple preserves.

In her most sugary tone she said, "Why Marshal Braden, sir, I do believe you are the best cook who has ever crossed into Arizona Territory."

"And you, Miss Conners, ought to be ashamed of yourself for lying so sweetly. I thought your father taught you to always tell the truth."

"So he did. But right now, after a day of dealing with all my little darlings, especially the Thompson boys, nothing in the world could taste as good as this."

"Were your students worse than usual?"

She nodded. "With a snowstorm headed this way, and Christmas almost here, the children are a bit of a handful."

While they ate, she regaled him with details of her day. By the time they had finished and were lingering over coffee, they had shared a great deal of laughter.

"I think, for all your complaining about the Thompson boys, you really care about them."

"I didn't think it showed." The corners of her eyes crinkled with unspoken laughter. "They have a way of disrupting things without ever being mean. They're really good boys." She laughed. "But such imps."

They cleared the table together, then drew their chairs close to the fire. While Laura picked up her basket of mending, Matt rolled a cigarette and stretched his feet toward the flames.

Drawing smoke into his lungs, he turned to study the woman beside him. In the flickering light of the fire, her eyes gleamed like precious stones. Her hair was dark and lush.

These few days together had been like a special gift. More precious than gold. Though it had been such a short time, it felt right. As if they had always been together like this.

Dangerous thoughts, he warned himself sternly. There was no room in his life for a woman like Laura.

Her words broke into his dark reverie.

"When you…encountered the gunmen did you know that you were so close to Bitter Creek?"

He stared into the flames. "I was too caught up in the chase to know or care where I was. Then, when I was wounded and unable to go on, I thought this cabin was my boyhood home. I imagined my father and brothers inside waiting for me." He watched a stream of smoke curl toward the ceiling, then said softly, "I felt soft hands and thought my mother had come for me. And when I awoke in that feather bed of your father's, I thought I'd died and gone to heaven."

He glanced at her and gave a bitter laugh. "That was the strangest part of my dream. We all know where I'm going when I die."

"Don't say that, Matthew." In her fervor, Laura pricked her finger with the needle. Tears filled her eyes.

Seeing her distress, Matt took the mending from her and dropped to his knees before her. He lifted her finger to his lips. "Now I've caused you to hurt yourself."

"It's nothing." She tried to pull her hand away, but he held it fast.

"Then why are you crying?"

She felt the tears spill over, and though she despised her weakness, she couldn't stop.

"What is it, Laura?" He was genuinely concerned now. It wasn't like her to weep. "What have I done?"

"Don't talk about your death." She wiped at her eyes but they instantly filled again. "I can't bear to hear you talk about your death."

"I was making a joke." He stood and pulled her into his arms.

"It isn't funny, Matthew." She pushed away and took several steps back, until she was pressed against the cold wall of the cabin. "I can't bear to think about you facing the barrel of someone's gun."

At her angry words he felt a sudden rush of heat. His eyes narrowed. She cared about him. Though she had never said so, she cared. Why else would she cry at such a silly thing?

He walked closer, resting his palms on the wall on either side of her. Then he moved one hand and caught a strand of her hair, twisting it around his finger. In a voice that was barely a whisper he said, "Then I'll never speak of it again."

"Stop it, Matthew."

She shook her head in an attempt to free herself, but he caught her by the shoulder and held her.

"I'm not a child to be teased. I know what a marshal does. I know that you spend your whole life confronting men who care nothing at all about your life. And I know that as soon as you're strong enough, you'll go back out on the trail of those men who shot you and left you for dead."

"All right," he said with no trace of emotion. "The truth, Laura. My wound is healed enough to ride. In the morning, I'll be leaving."

She reacted as if he'd slapped her.

For a moment she couldn't find her voice. The only sound in the room was the hiss and snap of the logs in the fireplace.

She looked up into his dark eyes, then looked away, blinking back tears. She would not cry in front of him again.

Pushing roughly away, she reached for the old sheepskin jacket.

"Where are you going?"

With her back to him she pulled it on and opened the door. A blast of frigid night air rushed against her, bringing with it a spray of fresh snow.

"I'm going to check the stock before turning in."

She crossed the porch and stepped into snow that was already to her knees. If it continued, by morning it could be as high as the porch railing.

She walked to the enclosure where the cattle huddled against the blizzard. Steam rose from their nostrils as they lifted their heads to study her. She checked their feed and saw to it that the gate was firmly closed.

She crossed to the barn and let herself in, grateful for the shelter. She ran a hand along the velvet muzzle of Matt's horse, then sat down on a bale of hay and gave vent to the tears she had been holding inside.

From the first, she had known that Matthew would have to leave when his wounds were healed. And though she had always known that his gun would be there between them, she had steadfastly not permitted herself to dwell on that fact until now.

Her tears ran in little rivers down her cheeks and she wiped them with the back of her hand.

She had foolishly begun to allow herself to believe that he would stay. How childish. What a silly old spinster she had become. Weaving fantasies about herself and Matthew Braden, one of the West's fastest guns. How he must be laughing to himself at her ignorance.

She wept for Matthew, for the life he had chosen. And for herself, the happiness she had glimpsed then lost. And she wept for Papa and Mama, who had tried so hard to mold her into an image of themselves.

At last, there were no tears left. Straightening, Laura let herself out of the barn and started toward the house.

"Forgive me, Papa," she whispered. "But even knowing who and what Matthew Braden is, I shall miss him terribly. And I would give anything if I could persuade him to stay."

Matt leaned a hip against the windowsill and watched as the figure emerged from the barn. Snow gusted and swirled about her, giving her an ethereal appearance.

When the door opened, he remained by the window. Even

from this distance, he could see that her eyes were red and puffy. Snow dusted her dark hair like diamonds. She shook it from her skirts as she removed the jacket and walked to the fireplace.

When she had warmed her hands, she turned toward her room without even glancing at him. It would be too painful, she knew. She needed to salvage what little pride she had.

"I'll say good-night now, Matthew."

"Don't go, Laura."

She paused, but still refused to look at him. "We'll say our goodbyes in the morning. It will be easier then."

"No." He crossed the room and caught her arm.

When she looked up at him, she saw the same look that had caused gunmen from Kansas to Arizona Territory to tremble. His jaw was clenched, his mouth a grim tight line of anger. "It isn't over between us, Laura."

"It has to be."

"No, it doesn't."

"Papa said—"

"Dammit, Laura. I'm not interested in hearing another of your father's famous quotations. This doesn't involve him. This is between you and me."

"There is nothing between us, Matthew. We…cared about each other once. But we can have no future."

"We have tonight, Laura."

His words whispered over her senses, causing the hair at the back of her neck to rise.

"I couldn't." She turned away from him and shook her head, as if to add emphasis to her words. "I just couldn't."

He stood behind her, a hand on each of her shoulders. Drawing her back against the length of him, he brought his lips to her ear. "One night, Laura. If we can't have a lifetime together, at least we'll have this."

When she lowered her head, he turned her into his arms. The hands at her back were strong and firm. She felt them move up and down her spine, igniting fires wherever they touched.

He drew her closer and pressed his lips to her damp lids. She felt the tiny thread of pleasure curl deep inside and begin to spread.

"Is your finger still bleeding?"

"What?" She felt deliciously warm and languid in his arms, and completely incapable of thought.

"Your finger."

"Oh." She glanced down as he caught her hand and lifted it to his lips. He kissed her finger, all the while watching her eyes. Then, before she realized what he was doing, he raised her hand and brought his lips to her wrist.

A tiny pulse fluttered, then raced.

"Your skin is so soft, so fine." He drew her hands up around his neck and pressed his lips to her ear.

She felt her pulse quicken even more as his breath feathered the hair at her temple. And then, without warning, he darted a tongue to her ear and she gave a soft quiet moan of surprise.

She tried to pull away, but he held her firmly against him.

Desire curled in the pit of her stomach. "Matthew. Do you know what you're doing to me?"

He ran his mouth along her jaw, then brought his lips to the sensitive hollow of her throat. "The same thing you've been doing to me, Laura, since I first woke up in your father's bed."

She caught his face between her hands, determined to still his movements. "I can't think when you touch me like this."

"Then don't think, Laura. Feel. Savor." His eyes gleamed in the light of the fire. "I want you. And have from the time I first met you."

"That's your answer for everything, isn't it, Matthew? You see something you want, you take it. But life is never that simple."

That had once been true. His younger days had been wild

and undisciplined. But for years, it seemed, he had walked a narrow straight line, expending all his energies on the safety of strangers. The years of discipline seemed to fall away. At this moment, he felt exactly the way he had in his youth, when he'd done as he pleased. His voice roughened. "Then I'll make it simpler. You want this as much as I do."

At his words she lowered her face, but he lifted her chin and forced her to meet his knowing gaze. "Admit it."

"Oh, Matthew. I'm so afraid." She wrapped her arms about his neck and drew him close. "Hold me. Please hold me." At least through the night, she thought. At least until morning comes, when she would go back to being the town's spinster schoolteacher, and he to chasing outlaws until they were dead. Or he was.

Tentatively she lifted a finger to his face, tracing the outline of his lips, the curve of his brow. She would commit everything about him to memory. And years from now, when she was alone, she would still be able to recall the way he looked this night.

Standing on tiptoe, she offered her lips to him. In a trembling voice she whispered, "Love me, Matthew. At least for tonight, please love me."

How long had he dreamed of this? How long had he yearned to hear her whisper these words?

He reached up and took the pins from her hair. Free, it tumbled in dark silken waves about her cheeks and shoulders. With a sigh he plunged his hands into the tangles, drawing her head back.

His gaze raked her, and the look in his eyes revealed the depth of his desire.

His arms came around her, pinning her to the length of him. He wanted to be gentle. His lips were avid, his kiss taking her higher than she'd ever been. His hunger fueled her own.

His lips roamed her temples, her forehead, the corners of her eyes. She thought she would go mad waiting for his lips to claim hers once more. But slowly, lazily, he kissed her nose before following the slope of her cheek to her lips.

Her mouth moved beneath his, opening for him, as their tongues met and tangled.

He tasted faintly of tobacco, and she knew that scent would forever remind her of him.

His mouth moved lower to follow the column of her throat. With a soft sigh she moved in his arms, loving the feel of his lips on her skin.

His fingers were strong and sure as he reached for the buttons of her gown and undid them, drawing the dress down over her shoulders. As it whispered to the floor, his gaze burned over her.

No man except Matthew had ever before seen her in a chemise and petticoat. But though she trembled before him, afraid and shy, she reached for the buttons of his shirt. Her fingers fumbled until he helped her.

His naked flesh was warm. So warm. She touched a finger to the dressings at his shoulder, then pressed her lips to the spot.

Stunned, he felt his breath catch in his throat at the tenderness of her touch.

With his fingers pressing into the tender flesh of her upper arms, he dragged her roughly against him and brought his lips to her throat. She moaned and arched her neck, inviting his touch. But when his mouth moved lower, to close over her breast, a low moan shuddered from between her lips.

Never, never had she known such feelings. She was hot. So hot she felt as though her flesh were on fire. She needed to be free of the last of her clothes.

As if reading her mind, he untied the ribbons at her shoulders, freeing her chemise. His look burned over her. With a groan he bent his head again to her breast.

His hands caressed her thighs as the petticoat joined the clothing at their feet. Just as quickly he shed the rest of his clothes.

Now they stood, flesh to flesh. And as his mouth covered hers in a burning kiss, his hands caressed her until passion, need, desire became an all-consuming inferno.

Dropping to their knees on the rug, Laura clung to him while his fingertips, his lips, brought her pleasure beyond anything she had ever known.

"My beautiful Laura," he murmured against her lips. "I've carried you in my heart for such a long time."

He dragged her against him, while his hands moved slowly over her, learning all the new intimate places of her body.

Her breathing was growing shallow now. Caught up in all the strange new sensations, she moved in his arms, lost in delights she had never even dreamed of.

Matt stared down at the woman in his arms. Her hair spilled across the rag rug in a cascade of dark silk. Her skin was as pale as ivory. But it was her eyes that held him. Eyes that burned like molten gold. In her eyes he saw himself reflected.

"Touch me, Laura."

For a moment she forgot to breathe. How could she touch him as intimately as he had touched her?

"I've waited a lifetime for you to touch me."

Her heart thundered as she reached a hand to his shoulder. She paused, feeling the corded muscles there. How powerful he was. Strong enough to break her in two. And yet his touch was so tender.

Her fingertips moved over his hair-roughened chest until she encountered several raised scars.

"What are these?"

"A gunfighter's wounds." His voice was low, gruff. "I did too much fighting in my youth."

"Oh, Matthew. If only we could erase the past."

"Don't." He touched a finger to her lips to silence her. "Tonight I don't want to think about the past. Or the future. Just tonight."

She moved her hand lower, across the flat plane of his

stomach, and felt his quivering response. Then her hand moved lower still, until she heard his low moan of pleasure.

Instantly his mouth covered hers in a kiss so hot, so hungry, she felt herself reeling. And then his lips, his fingertips, moved over her body, arousing her until she thought she would explode.

There was no longer any fear or hesitation in her. With her head thrown back, she drew him into her.

As they began to move, he covered her mouth with his. He wanted her first time to be as gentle, as easy as possible. Her hands clutched at him, drawing him even closer. Her strength matched his. Her heartbeat raced, keeping time with his. And as they reached the first crest, Matt forgot to be gentle. He forgot everything except this exquisite woman who was no longer shy but bold. His need for her bordered on insanity. And for tonight, for what little time they had left, she was his. His woman.

A cry broke from her lips as she soared higher than the stars. A million bright lights seemed to explode behind her closed lids. And as they reached the heavens, Matthew murmured incoherent words of love.

At last they lay together, their bodies damp and tangled, still joined as one, neither of them willing to break their fragile bond.

Chapter Eight

Nestled in Matt's arms, Laura felt the last of the shudders subside.

He rolled to one side and drew her close against his chest, pressing his lips to her closed eyelids and tasting salt.

Instantly he pulled away to study her. "I've hurt you."

"No."

He lifted a work-roughened finger to the tears that spilled from her eyes. He swore, low in his throat. "What was I thinking of? All day my thoughts were about you, about how wonderful it could be between us. But I swear, Laura, I never planned to take you like a savage here on the cold floor."

"That doesn't matter. And it isn't why I'm crying." Her lower lip trembled. "It's just that…it was so wonderful…I never dreamed…"

He touched his lips to the corner of her mouth. "It was wonderful for me, too. More wonderful than anything I could have imagined."

They lay in silence for several minutes, listening to the quiet of the night.

"For years," he murmured against her temple, "I've dreamed about you. So many nights, lying beneath the stars, I've thought about you here in this cabin. And I used to imagine what it would be like to face your father's wrath and steal you away to some lonely mountain cabin.''

''What a nice dream.'' She sighed and snuggled closer to him. ''Why didn't you follow your dream?''

He shrugged and kissed the tip of her nose. ''I'd convinced myself that by now you had probably turned into an old hag, your skin burned and wrinkled by the sun, your teeth missing, your hips as wide as that barn out there.''

She giggled at his description. ''Sounds just about right.''

His voice warmed with laughter. ''Yes, I can see that the years have been unkind to you.'' He ran a finger over her flawless complexion. ''Any day now this skin will turn to leather.'' He traced the fullness of her lips, then dipped his finger between them. ''Hmm. These teeth will probably last no more than another month or so.''

Laura laughed harder now. She teasingly bit his finger. Then, with an agility that caught him by surprise, she rolled on top of him. As she straddled him, her hair swirled about, she kissed his cheeks. Then she lowered her mouth to his. ''And what about these hips, Marshal Braden? Are they as broad as a barn yet?''

He placed a hand on each of her hips, then ran his hands lightly up her sides. ''Any day now you'll lose this maiden's figure and rival that cow out in the barn.''

She wriggled over him in a seductive manner and brought her lips to his. ''I can see that I'll just have to look for a lonesome cowboy who could want a fat toothless hag.''

''I believe you've already met him, ma'am.'' How was it possible that his passion could be aroused again so soon? He wanted her. God in heaven how he wanted her.

He thrust his hands into the tangles of her hair and pulled her close for a long hungry kiss. With a little moan she clung to him, pressing her body to the length of him.

With quick movements he rolled them over and stood, lifting her in his arms as easily as if she weighed nothing.

''This floor is too cold and too hard,'' he murmured against her lips.

''And I thought you were a tough lawman.''

Cradling her against his chest, he crossed to her bedroom and placed her gently on the feather bed, then crawled in beside her.

''Now. What were you saying about being tough? Come here, woman,'' he muttered, pulling her roughly into his arms. ''There were some more things I was hoping to teach you.''

He groaned as she pressed her lips to his throat. ''You have my complete attention, Matthew.''

And then they were lost in a world of gentle sighs and soft words. A world where only lovers can go.

Some time during the night, they awoke to the howling of the wind. It whistled down the stone chimney, sending sparks flying. Icy snow and sleet lashed the windowpanes.

Matt climbed from bed and hurried out to the fireplace to add logs to the glowing embers. Instantly flames licked along the dried bark. In no time the room was bathed in the glow of the fire.

He returned to the bedroom and climbed back into bed and drew Laura into the circle of his arms. ''Sounds like our snowstorm has turned into a full-blown blizzard.''

She sighed and snuggled close to him. ''Does that mean you won't be leaving in the morning?''

He seemed distracted by the line of freckles across her shoulder. Bending his lips to the place, he felt her stiffen in his arms.

''Matthew.''

''Hmm?''

''Are you going to answer me?''

''I forgot the question.'' He ran his mouth along her throat, then nipped at her earlobe.

''I asked if—''

"Be quiet, woman. Can't you see I'm busy?" His tongue explored the shape of her ear.

A delicious lethargy seemed to have robbed her of the will to move. She lay, soft and pliant in his arms, while he continued to weave his magic.

"Now." He brought his lips to hers. His hand found her breast. "What was it you wanted to know?"

She opened her lips to him and felt the scrape of his teeth as his mouth teased hers. "I don't remember."

"Mustn't have been important."

He took her with a savageness that had them both shaken. Despite her languor only moments before, she was now charged with energy. She moved with him, matching his strength with a new strength of her own. And when at last they lay sated, their bodies were covered with a sheen.

Content, they slept, still locked in one another's arms.

In the stillness of predawn, Matt lay quietly, studying the woman who slept beside him. She lay on her side facing him, one arm flung upward beneath her head, the other curled against his chest. Her breasts rose and fell in a quiet steady rhythm. Her breath was warm and sweet as it drifted across his cheek.

For the rest of his life he would remember this night. She had given him a most precious gift. The gift of her innocence. Her love.

It had been wrong of him to stay. All through the previous day he'd argued with himself, knowing that he ought to be gone when she returned from the schoolhouse. He owed her that much; to leave her as he'd found her. Innocent. Untouched. But she'd looked so anxious when she'd asked if he'd be there when she returned. And so he'd given his word. And the truth was, he hadn't been strong enough to walk away without one final glimpse of her.

He'd known. He'd known that if he stayed, he'd find a way to seduce her.

She sighed and he studied her, memorizing every line and curve of her lovely face. And then he smiled. Who had actually done the seducing? Could any man resist what she had offered?

He saw her lids flicker and his heart forgot to beat. What if she regretted their night of passion? What if, in the cold light of morning, she felt ashamed of what they'd shared? What, after all, had he offered her, except a few moments of pleasure? He had nothing else to offer. She was opposed to everything he stood for.

"Matthew."

His heart seemed to freeze in his chest.

She touched a finger to the line between his eyebrows.

"Why the frown?"

"Was I frowning?"

She pulled his face down and pressed a kiss to his forehead. "Do you always wake up grumpy? Or have I made you so unhappy?"

"You could never make me unhappy, Laura." His voice was husky with sudden startling desire. "But I was afraid you might wake up with regrets."

"Regrets?" She wrapped her arms about his neck and buried her lips against his throat. "Oh, Matthew. I'll have many regrets in my life. But this night will not be one of them."

He felt the warmth of her words melt the last of the fear that had imprisoned his heart. And when she boldly began exploring his body with her lips, the heat became a fiery blaze.

"Miss Conners. What would your pupils say?"

"Be quiet, Marshal Braden. I'm practicing my newest lesson."

Their laughter stilled in their throats as they moved together. The town of Bitter Creek, the snow, the wind that howled outside the windows, were all forgotten. There was only this room, this bed. And a passion that had been too long denied.

* * *

"I wonder how much it snowed."

"We could get up and look."

Laura moved her head slowly from side to side. "If the snow hasn't drifted to at least the height of the porch railing, I'll have to dress and leave for the schoolhouse."

"Is that the yardstick you use for canceling school?"

She nodded.

"I'll check."

"No, Matthew." She drew him back down on the pillow and dropped light kisses on his temple.

He gave a sigh and twisted a strand of her hair around his finger. If only life could always be this gentle. A warm cabin. A feather bed. And Laura.

"You stay in bed, Matthew. I'll check."

As she started to rise he pulled her down and gave her a long lazy kiss. "We'll both get up."

Drawing a blanket around her for warmth, she padded to the window, with Matt beside her. She drew back the curtain, then stared at the expanse of white. The snow had drifted above the windowsill. The barn and the little cabin were nearly buried in snow.

"Looks like you won't be going to town today," Matt said softly.

She turned to him with a warm smile. "It doesn't look like you could do your job today, either, Marshal Braden."

He gave her a roguish smile that started her heart tumbling. "Looks like we'll just have to spend the whole day locked away in this cabin."

He lifted her in his arms and carried her back to bed.

"What about some breakfast?" she asked against his lips.

"Maybe later. Right now, I'm hungry for something else."

Their lovemaking took on a new sense of freedom and joyousness. They had been given a reprieve. For this one precious day, they would not think about the world beyond their door. They could concentrate only on each other.

* * *

"What was that?"

At the sound of a wild shriek, Laura looked up from the table, where she and Matt were enjoying a leisurely breakfast.

Before she could even react, Matt was across the room, rifle in hand.

"Stay here. Bolt the door behind me."

Without even taking the time to pull on his jacket, he yanked open the door and was gone.

Within minutes Laura had retrieved the rifle from her bedside. Slipping into her father's oversize jacket, she made her way through the snow toward the barn.

A gunshot rang out in the still air, and for a moment she thought her heart would never start beating again.

She broke into a run, nearly losing her footing in the deep drifts.

As she rounded the corner of the barn, she saw Matt on his knees in the enclosure where the cattle were penned.

"Oh, no. Please, God, no!"

She raced to his side, then came to an abrupt halt. Lying in the snow was a huge wildcat. Beside the cat lay a wounded cow.

He saw her ashen features and knew that she had feared the worst. Then he noticed the rifle in her hand and arched an eyebrow. "You, Laura? Actually holding a rifle?"

She gave him a wry smile. "It's of no use to me really. It hasn't worked since Papa died. But I thought it would make me look tougher."

Grinning, he took the rifle from her hands and examined it. "The firing pin is missing. With a little work it can be like new."

"There's no need," she said quickly. "I'd never be able to use it."

"Not even against one of these?" He indicated the wildcat.

She shook her head.

"In that case, these cattle need a shelter from predators."

"I had hoped to get one built before the snow." She shrugged. "Maybe by next year..."

This ranch was too much for one woman, he thought with a trace of anger. "Go back in the house," Matt said roughly. He unsheathed a razor-sharp hunting knife. "I'll put the cow out of its misery."

She nodded. Without a word she turned and fled to the cabin. With trembling hands she returned the rifle to its usual resting place on the table beside her bed.

It was several hours before Matt announced that the cow had been slaughtered, its meat carefully wrapped and stored for future use.

"What of the wildcat? Do you think it has a mate nearby?"

Matt nodded. "I'm sure of it. And when this one doesn't return soon with food, the mate will be lured out of hiding."

"Then I could lose more cattle."

He smiled. "I hope not. I've already set the bait." He pointed to a young bull, tethered just beyond the fence.

"Matthew. I need that bull for breeding more stock next spring. What if the cat gets him before you get the cat?"

His smile grew. "Trust me, Laura."

She gave him a tentative smile. "I guess I have no choice."

Humming a tune, he poured himself a cup of coffee and positioned a chair in front of the window.

Within the hour, a second cat was seen creeping through the snowdrifts toward the tasty offering.

Laura marveled at the stealthy way Matt moved as he crossed the room and let himself out the door without so much as a single sound. From her vantage point at the window she watched as the cat crouched flat, stalking its prey. Suddenly, without warning, the cat leapt high into the air, lunging for the bull. A single shot rang out, echoing in the still mountain air. A moment later the cat lay quietly as a circle of crimson stained the snow beside it.

Matt led the bull back to its enclosure with the rest of the cattle. Then he dragged the body of the cat into the barn.

While she finished her chores around the cabin, Laura thought about the number of cattle she had lost in the past year. She had known about the predators, but this was the first time the wildcats had ventured this close to her home.

"Thank heavens Matthew was here, Papa," she whispered. "No telling how many cattle I would have lost to those two cats."

By the time supper was ready, Matt had still not returned to the cabin. Puzzled, Laura pulled on her father's old jacket and plowed through the deep drifts to the barn.

By the light of a lantern, Laura could see Matt seated on an upturned milk pail, his head bent as he carefully worked over the wildcat's pelt.

"What are you doing, Matthew?"

He looked up, and she saw on his face a look of almost boyish happiness.

"I'm making you something."

"For me? What is it?" She took a step closer.

He held up the two pelts, which he had been carefully scraping. "It doesn't seem fitting for the town's teacher to wear a thin shawl and an old blanket for warmth. There's enough here to make a fine wrap when they're dry."

"Oh, Matthew." She studied the thick white pelts, tinged with shades of yellow, gray and black. "They're almost too beautiful to wear."

"Not nearly as beautiful as the one who'll wear them."

She gave a joyous laugh and caught his hand. "Come on. You've sat out in this cold so long it's addled your brain."

"Ah. Is that why you look so beautiful, Miss Conners?"

"And that's probably why you look so handsome tonight, Marshal Braden."

As they sprinted the distance from the barn to the cabin, their laughter rang on the clear night air.

* * *

The fragrance of baked apples and cinnamon permeated the air of the cabin, along with the aroma of freshly baked bread. Their simple supper took on the festive air of a sumptuous feast.

While Laura tidied up the kitchen table, Matt went back out to the barn with a lantern to work on the hides.

When he returned a few hours later Laura looked up from her mending with a shy smile.

"I wanted to give you something, Laura." He cleared his throat. "Those pelts are my Christmas present. I feel I've taken from you, and I have a need to give, as well."

"Oh, Matthew." She put her work aside and rose to stand in front of him. Wrapping her arms around his neck, she drew him close. "I don't need presents. And you've already given me something special. This whole day has been a gift."

"For me, too." He ran his hands across her shoulder. The words rushed out before he could stop them. "I wish I could stay."

She couldn't hide the excitement in her tone. "Will you?" It was the only gift she wanted.

He looked down into her shining eyes and felt his heart grow heavy. "We both know it's impossible."

She had thought for many years now that she had learned to live with disappointments. After all, she was a simple woman with simple tastes. But these past few days had brought changes that she had never dreamed of. And for just a few minutes longer she wanted to believe that every wish could come true.

"You could just put away your badge and stay here with me."

"And what about my job?"

"You've given enough to the law." When he opened his mouth to protest, she said quickly, "Matthew, I've seen the scars you carry. How many times must you risk your life?"

"And what about the killers who are out there, Laura?"

"Maybe they've moved on. Maybe you'll leave here and

never find them, anyway. Think about it, Matthew. You might risk everything for nothing.''

"And how will I live with myself if those men are out there killing again?''

Her voice trembled with emotion. "Are you saying that it won't end until you kill them or they kill you?''

"Don't do this, Laura.'' His own tone was low. "Don't spoil what little time we have left with this argument. Because neither of us can ever win.''

She turned away, fighting her tears. With her back to him she felt his hands as he caught her roughly by the shoulders and drew her against him. Pressing his lips to her ear he whispered, "These are our last hours together, Laura. I want to spend them loving you, not fighting you.''

With a sob catching in her throat, she turned and lifted her face for his kiss.

He swept her into his arms and carried her to the bed.

Born of desperation, their lovemaking was more passionate than anything they had yet experienced. They came together with the fury of a mountain storm. And long after their desire was spent, they lay tangled together, afraid to release for even a moment their tenuous bond.

Chapter Nine

There wasn't even a hint of a breeze to rifle the snow-laden branches of the evergreens. A dazzling sun glinted on a countryside buried under mounds of snow. The landscape was so white it burned the eyes. At least that was the reason Laura gave for the tears that threatened each time she glanced out the window.

How could this morning be so excruciatingly lovely when her heart was breaking?

Matt was in the barn, saddling his horse and hitching hers to the wagon.

They had said their goodbyes.

Through the long night, Laura had fought her battles with herself and had come to a decision. She had no choice but to let him go without a word. He had a right to his life. She had a right to her beliefs. She also had a need to salvage her pride. And so she would not beg or plead. She would pretend that these days together had been nothing more than a pleasant interlude.

She did not love him, she told herself firmly. She could not afford to love a man who lived by the gun.

She heard the creak of the wagon wheels and saw Matt astride his mount, leading her horse and wagon.

She pulled her shawl around her shoulders and, picking up

the blanket and a linen-clad bundle, stepped out into the frigid air. As she walked from the porch, she carefully avoided looking at him.

He slid from the saddle and walked toward her, intent on helping her into the wagon.

"I wrapped some food for you, Matthew. You'll need it out on the trail."

"Thank you." He placed it in one of his saddlebags, then offered his hand.

"I hope you stay well, Matthew."

"And you, Laura."

As he caught her small hand in his, he felt the first tremors rip through her. "I'm sorry, Laura. You'll never know how sorry I am."

"Don't." She tried to pull away but her strength was no match for his.

He drew her into his arms and pressed his lips to her temple. "I want you to know that I'll never forget you, Laura. And I wish with all my heart that I could stay with you. But I have a job to do."

"I understand." She prayed her voice would not betray her.

Before the words were even out of her mouth, he drew her close and covered her lips with his.

"I love you, Laura. I always have. I always will."

She went very still, allowing his declaration of love to wash over her. But even as she thrilled to the words, she knew they were not enough. She needed to hear that he would give up his guns and his life on the trail.

His lips were warm and firm on hers. She felt his strength, his determination, and clung to it.

Love. He loved her. And though she knew that he wanted desperately to hear the same thing, she could not bring herself to say the words. Papa would be proud of her for her firm resolve. Woe to any woman who loved a man who...

The kiss deepened. And then, abruptly, they both pulled

away. He had his pride. She had hers. They would not prolong this agony. Both of them stood, memorizing the beloved
features of the other.

With stiff awkward movements he helped her into the
wagon. She watched as he pulled himself into the saddle.

Matt touched a hand to his hat, then wheeled his horse and
took off at a gallop.

At the top of a rise he paused and watched as Laura's
wagon rumbled across the snow-covered trail toward town.
When she was out of sight, he gave a last glance at the small
ranch, then moved out at a fast clip.

The days before Christmas were always a time of high
excitement for the children of Bitter Creek. This special day
meant a break in their routine. Ranch chores still had to be
tended to. But there were secrets and whispers, and the rustle
of paper as gifts were lovingly wrapped and hidden beneath
beds or out in the barn. Though even the Thompson boys
were on their best behavior, the children twitched and fidg-
eted at their desks, waiting for school to end.

This year, even their teacher seemed distracted. Behind
their hands the students whispered, wondering about Miss
Conners as she stared out the window and watched as a hawk
made slow deliberate spirals in the sky.

Where was Matthew now? Laura clutched her hands to her
sides and stared at the vast expanse of snow. What if he were
wounded again? Who would be there to tend to his wounds?
Please, Lord, she prayed silently, *keep him safe.*

When she became aware of the silence in the room, she
turned. The children were looking at her in puzzlement.

"You may continue, Joseph."

"I already finished, ma'am."

"Yes. Of course."

Laura crossed the room and sat down at her desk. When
she looked up, the children were still watching her.

"I have a special treat for all of you for Christmas." Even

she was startled by her words. Where had they come from? She never did anything spontaneously. "I am dismissing school early. I hope all of you will have a very pleasant Christmas."

Within minutes the schoolhouse was alive with the sounds of children laughing and chattering as they pulled on their heavy boots and coats and made their way outside. A chorus of voices called out to her as they began the long trek home.

The small building was strangely silent as Laura took a rag and began to wipe down the desks and slates. When that chore was finished she swept the floor and carefully banked the fire.

Her hands were cold as she hitched the horse to the wagon. Pulling herself up to the seat, she flicked the reins. As the horse and wagon plowed across the snow she realized that she had been drawing out the time when she would have to go home. Home. It would be so empty now. There would be no smoke coming from the chimney; no supper simmering on the stove; no one waiting for her.

The first tears surprised her; the second angered her. She admonished herself for her show of weakness. She had been alone for a long time now. Matthew's brief visit had changed nothing. She wiped the tears with the back of her hand and stiffened her spine. She would continue as she had before. She would live as she always had. She would survive. She would endure.

Matt sat astride the big roan and stared down at the tracks in the snow. He'd picked up the trail several hours ago, and there was no longer any doubt in his mind. The outlaws had circled several times, and crossed the river looking for signs of him, but they were definitely headed for Bitter Creek.

Laura. He bit down hard on the oath that sprang to his lips. Turning his horse, he whipped him into a gallop.

The hills were steep, the valleys frosted with snow, which

slowed the horse's efforts. And while his mount picked its way through belly-high drifts, Matt's thoughts were on the scenes of carnage he had witnessed every time these killers had unleashed their violence.

He was sick of the killing. But he could see no end to it as long as men like these threatened the innocent.

Laura added kindling to the log on the grate and watched as the thin flame flickered, then caught and spread along the dry bark. She blew on her hands, then drew the shawl tighter around her shoulders and made her way to the kitchen. As she lifted the kettle to the stove she glanced out the window and saw the horse and rider.

For a moment her heart skipped a beat. Could it be…? In the distance she spotted a second rider, then a third and fourth. Despite the cold, tiny beads of perspiration dotted her forehead.

Four men. Matthew had said there were four of them.

Wiping her hands on her apron, she moved quickly, bracing the front door with a heavy timber, pulling the shutters closed and securing the latch. She gave a little groan as she glanced at the roaring fire. The smoke would alert the strangers that the cabin was occupied.

From a crack in the shutters she watched as they approached. Two of the men urged their mounts toward the front porch. The other two circled toward the back of the cabin.

She heard the sound of booted feet crossing the wooden porch. Lifting Papa's rifle to her shoulder, she faced the door and waited.

Matt crouched in the shadows and thought about the number of times he had been in this situation. He had faced death too many times to count. He did not fear it. He had always known, in some dark place in his mind, that the day would come when another man would be faster, or more accurate. It was one of the risks he was willing to take.

But Laura. She had not been part of the bargain. He hated the fact that it was his carelessness that had placed Laura's life in peril. Seeing the woman he loved shot down before his eyes would be the most terrible price he could pay for his past.

With a little luck, the four men would soon be his prisoners. Without it, he and Laura would both be dead.

For the first time in his life, Matt felt his hand tremble as he reached for his gun.

As the heavy boots crossed the porch, Laura heard a man's voice, low and chilling. The footsteps paused. Then she heard the voice again and realized that it was Matthew's.

For a moment she felt a wave of such relief, she had to lean a hand against the wall to steady herself. It was Matthew. She was safe. Then she froze as she heard a gunshot. And then another. And then a series of them in quick succession.

With no thought to her own safety, Laura dropped the rifle and threw herself at the door. "Matthew!"

Shoving aside the wooden barrier she flung open the door and rushed out onto the porch.

The silence was deafening. The gunman who Laura had seen on the porch now lay still in the snow at her feet. His gun trained on the two outlaws who remained standing, Matthew cautiously approached the fourth who lay sprawled next to the horses.

At Laura's quick intake of breath, he addressed her without taking his eyes off the man. "Go back inside, Laura. Bolt the door and don't open it until I tell you to."

Laura whirled around and raced into the house. Slamming the door behind her, she dropped the timber into place and sagged against the solid wood.

* * *

It seemed like hours before Laura heard footsteps on the porch and Matt called to her to open up. As she swung back the door and he entered she fell into his arms.

She was so relieved to see him unharmed, she had to fight back tears. "You're..." She licked her lips and tried again. "You're not hurt, Matthew?"

"I'm fine, Laura. They won't be bothering you or anyone else for a long time."

"I'm grateful that you came, Matthew."

"So am I." As he stroked her face he saw the pallor on her cheeks and noted the way her hands were clenched tightly at his back.

He wished there was time to hold her, to offer her a few words of comfort. But in his line of work there was no room for such luxuries. "I have to go, Laura."

"What are you going to do?"

"I'm taking these two to federal prison in St. Louis. I'll stop in town and send someone for the others. I have to get moving."

Placing a soft kiss on Laura's brow he turned to go.

Laura followed him out onto the porch and watched as he mounted. The gunmen sat astride their horses, their hands securely in front of them. Matt reached down and untied the reins of their horses from the railing.

"You're safe now, Laura."

Until the next time, she thought as she watched him turn into the road leading the other horses behind him. For the first time she realized how precious a man like Matt was to her quiet community. Greater love hath no man...

The horses' hooves raised a cloud of snowflakes as they rode away.

After the men had departed with the bodies of the two outlaws, Laura wrapped the last loaves of apple spice cake in linen squares and placed them on the windowsill. In the morning she planned to give them to her friends after Christmas services. Christmas. Despite the ache around her heart, she clung to the hope that Christmas had not lost its magic.

The cabin smelled of apples and cinnamon and the darker scent of wood smoke. Snow frosted the windowsills. Laura's hair fell in damp tendrils about her neck and cheeks. She had forced herself to work until she was exhausted. That left no time to think about what had happened earlier. Or to brood about the man who had breezed into her life for a second time only to ride away with her heart.

She heard the sound of a horse's hooves and peered into the night. There was nothing to see but darkness. With her heart pounding she ran into the bedroom and returned with her father's old rifle.

At the sound of footsteps across the porch she tensed.

"Laura. It's Matt. Open the door."

At the familiar voice she threw open the door and drank in the sight of him. His cowhide jacket was covered with snow, as was his hat. He removed the hat, sending a spray of snowflakes into the air. His eyes were dark, intense.

"I thought you'd be halfway to St. Louis by now."

A gust of wind caught her hair. He slammed the door shut and turned to study her.

"I should be." A slow smile touched his lips. "Then I thought about you alone in this cabin. With that rusted old rifle that won't fire. And I knew I couldn't leave again."

Her throat went dry. For a moment she couldn't speak. She swallowed and tried again. "Are you saying you've come back to stay, Matthew?"

"If you'll have me."

"But what about your job…"

"It's over. I decided to turn those men over to the sheriff in Bitter Creek. He'll keep them in jail until a federal judge comes through the territory and they can be tried."

She felt her heart begin to hammer in her chest. "You left me before. Why should I believe you'll stay this time?"

"Laura." He took a step closer and kept his hands at his

sides. He couldn't afford to touch her just yet. "I want you to marry me."

Laura thought about how foolish she had been all those years ago, when she had believed with all her heart that Matthew would return and make her his wife. He had broken her heart instead.

"The last time, you went away without a word."

"I left you before because your father convinced me that I had nothing to offer you. He was right. Life on the trail is no life for a woman like you." He breathed in the rich spicy fragrances that would always remind him of Laura and Christmas. "I still have nothing to offer you. Except this." He held out his hand.

She looked down at the gleaming silver badge, then up into his dark eyes.

"What are you saying, Matthew?"

"My life as a lawman is over. I'd like to try my hand at ranching now. There's a lot that needs fixing around this place."

She swallowed the lump in her throat. "Aren't you afraid you'll miss the adventure?"

"I think," he said, his smile beginning to grow, "that marrying you might just be the greatest adventure of my life."

"Oh, Matthew." She blinked back the tears that threatened. "We've wasted so many years."

"They haven't been wasted. We've learned, we've grown. There's still plenty of time left. Even time to have a family if you're willing."

"A family." Her eyes grew dreamy.

"Say yes, Laura. Tell me what I've always wanted to hear. Tell me you love me."

Oh, Papa, she thought. *Please understand and be happy for me. What did you always say? Love isn't love until you give it away.*

"Yes. Oh, yes." She threw her arms around his neck and

hugged him fiercely. "I do love you, Matthew. I've always loved you." Through her tears she whispered, "Welcome home, Matthew."

Home. He'd waited a lifetime for a place he could call home. And it had been here all along, just waiting for him.

"Merry Christmas, Laura," he whispered against her lips.

And for the first time in years, he found himself believing again, as she always had, in the magic of Christmas.

Modern Romance™
...seduction and
passion guaranteed

Tender Romance™
...love affairs that
last a lifetime

Sensual Romance™
...sassy, sexy and
seductive

Blaze
...sultry days and
steamy nights

Medical Romance™
...medical drama on
the pulse

Historical Romance™
...rich, vivid and
passionate

27 new titles every month.

*With all kinds of Romance for
every kind of mood...*

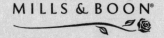

FREE

2 BOOKS
AND A SURPRISE GIFT!

We would like to take this opportunity to thank you for reading this Mills & Boon® book by offering you the chance to take TWO more specially selected titles from the Historical Romance™ series absolutely FREE! We're also making this offer to introduce you to the benefits of the Reader Service™ —

★ FREE home delivery
★ FREE monthly Newsletter
★ FREE gifts and competitions
★ Exclusive Reader Service discount
★ Books available before they're in the shops

Accepting these FREE books and gift places you under no obligation to buy; you may cancel at any time, even after receiving your free shipment. Simply complete your details below and return the entire page to the address below. **You don't even need a stamp!**

YES! Please send me 2 free Historical Romance books and a surprise gift. I understand that unless you hear from me, I will receive 4 superb new titles every month for just £3.49 each, postage and packing free. I am under no obligation to purchase any books and may cancel my subscription at any time. The free books and gift will be mine to keep in any case.

H2ZEC

Ms/Mrs/Miss/Mr ....Initials ....
BLOCK CAPITALS PLEASE

Surname ....

Address ....

....

....Postcode ....

Send this whole page to:
UK: FREEPOST CN81, Croydon, CR9 3WZ
EIRE: PO Box 4546, Kilcock, County Kildare (stamp required)